A Plain & Simple Heart

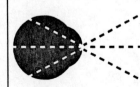

This Large Print Book carries the
Seal of Approval of N.A.V.H.

A Plain & Simple Heart

Lori Copeland
and Virginia Smith

THORNDIKE PRESS
A part of Gale, Cengage Learning

Detroit • New York • San Francisco • New Haven, Conn • Waterville, Maine • London

GALE
CENGAGE Learning

LIBRARY OF CONGRESS CATALOGING-IN-PUBLICATION DATA

Copeland, Lori.
  A plain & simple heart / by Lori Copeland and Virginia Smith.
    pages ; cm. — (Thorndike Press large print Christian historical fiction) (The Amish of Apple Grove series '; #2)
  ISBN-13: 978-1-4104-5002-9 (hardcover)
  ISBN-10: 1-4104-5002-3 (hardcover)
  1. Young women—Fiction 2. Sheriffs—Fiction 3. Amish—Kansas—Fiction. 4. Large type books. I. Smith, Virginia, 1960– II. Title. III. Title: Plain and simple heart.
PS3553.O6336P56 2012b
813'.54—dc23   2012030987

Published in 2012 by arrangement with Books & Such Literary Agency, Inc.

Printed in Mexico
1 2 3 4 5 6 7 16 15 14 13 12

When I was a child, I talked like a child, I thought like a child, I reasoned like a child. When I became a man, I put the ways of childhood behind me. For now we see only a reflection as in a mirror; then we shall see face to face. Now I know in part; then I shall know fully, even as I am fully known.

1 CORINTHIANS 13:11–12

ONE

Apple Grove, Kansas
May 1885

"Rebecca! The laundry will not hang itself. 'An idle brain is the devil's workshop.' "

Rebecca jerked upright, pulled from her daydream by her grandmother's sharp voice. She cast a guilty glance toward the house, where *Maummi* stood in the open doorway, black skirts billowing around her ankles, her arms folded across her crisp white apron. Her stern expression was visible all the way across the yard.

"Sorry, *Maummi.*" The automatic apology came with half-hearted sincerity. It seemed as though she was always apologizing for something lately.

Wet clothing swayed on the half-empty clothesline that stretched between the barn and the well house. Rebecca stooped and selected a black dress from the basket at her feet. She shook the garment with a snap

7

before hanging it on the line beside Papa's trousers, aware that her grandmother had not returned to her chores in the kitchen but stood watching from the doorway. A breeze rustled the leaves of a nearby apple tree and blew the sweet scent of blossoms Rebecca's way. The strings of her *kapp* lifted in the wind and danced around her shoulders as the full wet skirt blew into her face. Quickly, she clipped the dress onto the line before it could blow away. If a clean garment touched the ground, *Maummi* would make her wash it again.

"When you are finished there, come and help me in the kitchen," her grandmother called. "I want you to make *snitz* pie for Emma's table. A treat for the little one."

The reminder of their plans to visit her sister and brother-in-law's farm for the midday meal brightened Rebecca's mood considerably. The day was warm enough that she could romp outdoors with her nephew after the meal. At nearly three years old, little Lucas was a precocious bundle of energy, and Emma, who was expecting another child in a few months, was only too happy to turn him over to Aunt Rebecca for a spell.

One day I'll have children of my own.

Her daydream returned with the thought.

She lifted Papa's shirt from the basket, but in her mind it belonged to a tall, handsome man whose dark eyes lit up when he came in from the fields at the end of the day. She could see him there, just rounding the barn, his gaze searching for hers. He would catch sight of her, and his stride would lengthen as he hurried across grass that waved gently in the Kansas breeze. When he reached her, he would thrust aside the laundry, gather her in his arms, and —

"Rebecca!"

With a jerk, she tossed the shirt across the line. "I'm hurrying, *Maummi*."

She brushed a crease out of the shirt, her hand lingering on the damp fabric. If only her one true love were more than a memory. She could see him so clearly in her mind's eye, sitting tall atop his horse, the brim of his oblong, *Englisch* hat shading his eyes from the glaring sun. Four years had passed since she last saw Jesse, and yet she remembered every detail. Not a single day had gone by that she hadn't thought of him.

A clean apron followed the shirt on the line. Of course, the Jesse in her mind was a little different from the real one. Hers was dressed in Amish trousers, suspenders, and a proper round-brimmed straw hat. Jesse becoming Amish was a matter of expedi-

9

ency because she could only marry an Amish man. Papa had already lost one daughter to the *Englisch,* and he wouldn't stand for the second one to leave the church as well. Once Jesse understood that, he wouldn't mind becoming Amish.

The sweet-smelling breeze whisked away a wistful sigh as Rebecca clipped a pair of *Maummi's* bloomers on the line. Sometimes she worried her dreams were nothing but fancy. What if Jesse had forgotten all about her in the four years since their adventure on the cattle trail, the one where Emma had met her husband, Luke? After all, Rebecca had been little more than a child then, and Jesse a handsome cowboy, a man.

And oh, what a man!

A familiar tickle fluttered in her belly. She had given her heart to that drover, and time had not diminished the strength of her affections. If only he would return to Apple Grove and see that she was now a full-grown woman of seventeen. One look at her, and he would realize God had made them for each other, of that she was certain. He would join the church and they would marry, and he would help Papa on the farm until the day Papa decided to hand the reins over to him.

That's what true love did.

Rebecca turned and gazed at the house, the place where she had been born and lived her entire life. One day it would be hers and Jesse's, and they would fill it with children. They would build a *dawdi haus* for Papa right next door so she could care for him in his old age.

She hung the last apron on the line and picked up the empty basket. The hem of her black dress brushed the grass as she crossed the yard toward the house. Her plans had been laid in painstaking detail over four years of wishing and hoping and straining her eyes toward every *Englisch* stranger on horseback who passed by on the road.

But Jesse did not come. Fact was, no one had heard from him since he returned to Texas a few weeks after Emma's wedding. Even Luke, who had been his best friend, hadn't heard from him in years.

A wave of desolation threatened, but Rebecca brushed it aside. From the first time she laid eyes on him, she had known Jesse was hers. God would not give her a love this strong if He didn't mean for them to be life mates. One day Jesse would come to her. But how much longer would he make her wait?

With the empty basket balanced on her

hip, she skipped up the stairs and into the house.

"What about Daniel Burkholder?" asked Emma. She handed a basket of warm biscuits to Rebecca and nodded toward the laden table, where fragrant ribbons of steam wisped from bowls heaped with food. "Katie Miller told me he fancies you."

Rebecca stood at Emma's kitchen window, admiring the sunlight-drenched green grass in the well-kept yard surrounding her sister's house. Poppy mallows dotted the untended field between the house and the road, their purple blooms swaying in the ever-present breeze. She located the men in the opposite direction, standing near the back fence, their heads turned toward a herd of cattle that grazed in the field beyond. Luke was saying something to Papa, whose round-brimmed straw hat bobbed as he listened. At their feet, Lucas squatted in close inspection of something on the ground.

Wishing she could be outside with the men instead of inside the hot kitchen, she turned her back to the window and arranged her features in a scowl. "He smells constantly of onions. I can't bear him."

"You like onions," *Maummi* said. Her

sharp knife sliced through a plump red tomato on the cutting board.

"To eat, yes, but not to smell. When he brought me home in that tiny buggy of his after church one Sunday, I nearly choked." She set the biscuits on the table and stood back to examine the spread, her hands on her hips. "Emma, you have enough food for a barn raising."

Turning from the high work counter, *Maummi* paused a moment to run a hand lovingly over the giant hutch that dominated the room, and then she focused on the table. " 'The path to a man's heart winds through his stomach,' " she quoted with an approving nod. She fixed her gaze on Rebecca and gave a little sniff. "You would do well to take this to heart, granddaughter."

Rebecca turned away before her grandmother could see her eyes rise to the ceiling. She'd never enjoyed kitchen work the way Emma did. The pie resting on the corner of the second work counter bore evidence of her lack of cooking skill. The top crust bubbled unevenly because she hadn't properly slit the crust to vent the steam, and the rim around the crust had browned nearly black because she forgot to watch it in the oven. However, *Maummi* had stood at her elbow to direct the mixing of every ingredient, so she hoped the taste would make up for its appearance.

"Emma already has Luke's heart. They are married, aren't they?"

"Catching a man's heart is only the beginning." *Maummi* slid thick tomato slices onto a plate with the edge of her knife. "Keeping him happy is where a dull wife fails."

Rebecca chose to ignore the veiled reference to her as dull and instead dropped her gaze toward her sister's bulging belly. "Luke appears to be happy."

A blush colored Emma's cheeks as her hand cupped her stomach in a gesture common to every pregnant woman Rebecca had ever seen. Her time was at least three months off, but already she looked nearly as big as she was when Lucas was born. Even so, she was beautiful as always in her loose-fitting blue gown and with her braided hair wrapped around her head.

Rebecca ran a hand down her own black skirt and battled a surge of envy. When Emma left the church to marry Luke, she had left behind the prescribed Amish black dresses and *kapps.* Though Rebecca tried not to begrudge her sister the ability to wear beautiful colors, she couldn't help wondering what it would be like to don a pretty dress and maybe a matching bonnet like those she saw ladies wear on the infrequent times when Papa allowed her to accompany him into Hays City for supplies.

The thought flooded her with guilt. Bishop Miller would accuse her of vanity.

And he would be right.

"We were talking about you, not me," Emma chided. "So Daniel smells of onions. What of Samuel Schrock?"

"He's too young. He's barely past his sixteenth birthday." Rebecca avoided her sister's gaze by adjusting the placement of a plate at the long table. "Besides, he's taken with Amy Bender. I saw them walking together after church last Sunday."

"There's always Amos Beiler," *Maummi* said as she set the plate of tomatoes on the table.

Rebecca didn't bother to hide her eye-roll this time, nor did she suppress a loud groan, which made *Maummi* cackle.

Emma's brow creased with compassion. "Poor Amos, raising those children on his own. They need a mother, and he needs a wife."

"He isn't raising them on his own. Mrs. Keim tends them while he works the farm, and his sister-in-law is teaching the girls to cook and keep house." Truth be told, the oldest Beiler girl at nine years old was a better cook than Rebecca, but she saw no reason to say so.

"I know, but that's not the same as having a mother." Emma's gaze slid toward *Maummi.* "Or a grandmother."

Their mother had died when Rebecca was a baby. *Maummi* was already living with them, having moved to Apple Grove with Papa and Mama and young Emma to help establish the farm in a new Amish district. Rebecca tried for a moment to imagine what her life would have been like without *Maummi.* The idea wasn't worth considering. With a rush of emotion, she crossed the room to stand beside the older woman, and she smiled as she touched her grandmother's sleeve with a gentle gesture.

"You're right. It's not the same."

Maummi's lips turned up slightly in acknowledgement of the rare display of affection. As a rule, the Amish showed their care for one another through hard work and service, not through physical gestures, but *Maummi* prolonged the contact by lingering a moment before moving away to pick up a bowl of sauerkraut salad from the counter.

"Well, perhaps Amos will find a wife soon." Emma cast an anxious eye over the table. "Everything is ready. I hope Papa will favor my beef-and-noodle casserole."

Emma tried so hard to please Papa, as though food could overcome the pain of having his older daughter leave the Amish way of life. Not that he ever said a word, but Rebecca had seen the hurt in his eyes when he watched his grandson at play, and she knew he deeply regretted the fact that Lucas was being raised in a different faith.

"At least they are Christian," *Maummi* had said more than once.

And they are happy. Anyone can see that in Emma's face when she looks at Luke.

"I'm sure he will love it," Rebecca assured her. "Do you want me to call them in?"

Emma nodded as she bent over the table to lift the cover from the butter dish. "Oh, *Maummi,* I am supposed to pass along a greeting. Mr. McCann stopped by last week."

Rebecca stopped halfway to the door. McCann was the cook on the cattle drive where Emma had met Luke and she had met Jesse.

"Him. He didn't know a spice from a weed until I taught him." *Maummi* waved a hand in feigned dismissal, though Rebecca saw a spark of interest in her hooded eyes. "Happened to be nearby, did he?"

"He was on his way south to join a cattle drive. He'd been cooking for a restaurant over in Abilene, but he said he missed the

17

trail. And the way things are going, with ranchers fencing the open ranges, he said he didn't think there would be too many more cattle drives for a cowboy to take advantage of." Emma removed another lid, this one covering a dish of apple butter. "He stayed for supper and entertained us with tales of life in town and news of some of the old team. Remember Charlie? He married and bought a place in Arizona territory last year. Griff moved down there to help him get set up."

Excitement raced along Rebecca's spine. These men were all friends of Jesse's.

She adopted a casual expression. "Did he mention anyone else? Like . . ." She swallowed, and schooled her voice. "Like Jesse Montgomery, maybe?"

Emma glanced up. "Yes, he did. Luke asked, of course, and Mr. McCann said he'd heard that Jesse had settled over near Lawrence. He wasn't sure what he was doing there." She shook her head. "Luke could hardly believe it. He thought Jesse would never leave the trail as long as there was a trail to drive a herd across."

Lawrence! Rebecca's pulse kicked into a gallop and her head went light. Jesse, her one true love, was in Kansas. On the other side of the state from Apple Grove, true,

18

but Lawrence was a far sight closer than Texas.

A nagging thought tugged at her soaring heart. If he lived in the same state as she, then why hadn't he come to her? He knew where she lived. She set her jaw and tilted her chin. Perhaps he needed a reminder.

"Rebecca?"

Emma's voice drew her from her ruminations. She realized her sister and grandmother were both watching her with curious expressions.

"Are you going to call the men in?"

"Yes. I will."

Rebecca turned toward the door, a plan — devious to be sure — already forming in her mind.

If the cow would not come to the water, she would herd him there.

Two

Lawrence, Kansas

Colin Maddox stepped out of the Lawrence post office and onto Massachusetts Street with the letter he'd been waiting for. It had been all he could do to casually tuck the missive in his vest pocket, but postmistress Betsy Lanham's prying eyes saw far too much, and her tongue wagged like a rattler's tail. If the news was bad, she'd see it in his face, and if the letter said what he hoped it did, he'd have a hard time not shouting. The town would know the letter's contents soon enough and a few brows would lift.

He started across the dusty street, pausing to let a wagon pass by. Across the way an elderly woman exited the general store, a basket swinging from her arm.

"Afternoon, Sheriff." She greeted him with a regal dip of her head.

Colin tipped his hat with a smile. "You're

looking mighty fetching today, Miz Watkins. Is that a new bonnet you're wearing?"

"Why, yes. Yes, it is, Sheriff." A weathered hand rose to hover around the feathers topping a narrow-brimmed hat while her eyelashes fluttered. "Do you like it?"

"I do indeed. Allow me to assist you with that." He took the parcel-filled basket from her and escorted her a few steps to her small wagon. He set the basket in the back and helped her up onto the bench.

"Thank you. It's good to know there are still gentlemen in Lawrence. Not many young men these days are mindful of an old lady." A hard glint sparked in her eyes. "They are taken by the drink and given over to slovenly living."

Colin didn't have the time or the inclination to enter into what was sure to become another heated conversation. The emerging temperance movement had the women in town worked into a lather. If they had their way, there was bound to be a war on liquor, and the men in town didn't cotton to the idea.

"Old lady?" He gave her his most charming smile. "I don't know who you might be referring to, ma'am. The only lady I see here is as spry as a young prairie rabbit."

The glint became a sparkle, and Mrs.

Watkins raised a gloved hand to cover a giggle. "Sheriff Maddox. I do declare, you are a charmer."

He tipped his hat again and took a backward step. "You have a nice afternoon, now. Be careful going home. The town is bustling with business today."

A wagon rolled past, followed by two strangers on horseback. With another girlish giggle, Mrs. Watkins flicked her reins and the wagon rattled off. Colin watched for a moment and then continued on his way, nodding pleasantly at the townspeople he passed. The letter felt like a boulder in his pocket. His future lay inside that envelope.

He reached the jailhouse without further delay, and the noise of the busy street dimmed when he closed the door behind him. With a glance toward the three empty cells, he rounded the desk and lowered himself into his chair. Pulling the letter out of his pocket, he stared at his name in a slanted scrawl across the front.

Sheriff Colin Maddox
Lawrence, Kansas

He turned the envelope over. It was sealed by an uneven blob of wax with no imprint. Unbroken, he noted, though he wouldn't have been surprised to find that the letter had been opened and read. At times Betsy wasn't able to corral her curiosity and had been known to announce pertinent facts when she handed a piece of mail to the owner. She would have done the same with this one if he hadn't made a point of meeting the train and following the mailbag to the post office.

He realized he was stalling. *Open the letter, Maddox. It's no big deal. The letter will either confirm or deny your dream.*

He shook his head to dislodge the thought. The Lord had confirmed his dream a dozen times over. This letter would only establish the timing.

Slipping a finger beneath the paper's edge, he broke the wax seal and unfolded the single sheet of paper.

Sheriff Maddox,
I am pleased to accept the town's offer of employment at the terms specified in your letter. I will arrive on 24 May on the five twenty train from Chicago.

Regards,
Patrick Mulhaney

Colin leaned back in his chair and let the news sink in. Mulhaney had accepted the offer to become the new sheriff of Lawrence. Colin's days in the job were numbered.

He fingered the badge pinned to his leather vest while his gaze circled the empty jailhouse. For more than two years this job had consumed every minute of his life. The small room containing his bed and the few possessions he'd accumulated lay just through the doorway on the other side of the far cell. His deputies all had homes to go to, but something had always stopped him from putting down roots in this town. Something or Someone.

Well, Lord. I guess this seals it. In a few weeks I'll be working solely for You.

In eighteen days, Colin would hand over his badge, pack his bags, and put the town of Lawrence and all of its problems behind him. He would head west until he felt the Lord nudging him to stop.

And then his real life's work could begin.

An uncontrollable grin took possession of his lips. Before he could stop himself, he launched out of the chair, snatched his hat off his head, and tossed it high in the air.

"Waaaaahooooo!"

His joyful cheer rang in the room as his hat fluttered to the floor. Stepping lightly enough that a passerby peeking through the window might accuse him of dancing, he rounded the desk and stooped to pick it up. All he had to do was make it through the next eighteen days without anything major happening. No gunfights. No robberies. No horse thieves to track down.

Lord, I'd sure take it as a favorable sign if You could see Your way to making sure things go smooth from here on out. The people in this town are good folks, by and large. They can behave themselves for a few weeks, with a little help.

Surely eighteen uneventful days wasn't too much to ask, was it?

Rebecca rolled the handcart to a smooth stop and set the handles down softly. Nestled on a pile of straw inside, Lucas had fallen asleep with the suddenness common to young children. An afternoon spent romping with Aunt Rebecca had tired the little boy out.

She glanced toward the chairs they had placed beneath a huge shade tree after the meal, where *Maummi* sat with her chin on her chest. The gentle buzz of her snore bore evidence that Lucas wasn't the only one who could use a nap this lazy afternoon.

Emma heaved herself heavily out of her chair and crossed the grass toward them, her gait bearing signs of the expectant mother waddle.

"I expected this would happen. He was too excited to nap this morning." She bent over to pluck a piece of straw out of the boy's silky hair.

The tenderness of Emma's smile stirred up a longing deep in Rebecca's breast. Someday she would look down on her own child with that same love shining in her eyes. She closed her eyes for a moment, imagining what her and Jesse's son would look like. Dark hair with a touch of curl, like hers. Blue eyes and strong jaw, like his.

She opened her eyes and turned a glance on her sister. "You are so fortunate, Emma."

"Why do you say that?"

Rebecca spread her hands wide to indicate their surroundings: the house, the nearby fields, Lucas. "Your life is perfect."

Emma shook her head. "From the outside it may look so, but life is definitely not perfect. I love our home, and the Lord has blessed us with plenty. We have food and warmth and a beautiful home." Her expression became wistful when her gaze strayed toward the barn, where Papa and Luke had disappeared after the meal to work on a broken piece of farm equipment. "But ours is an isolated life. We have few neighbors. The nearest church is in Hays City, and most of the people there live in town. No one comes calling with a pie or a basket of apples to share over a cup of coffee. Not like at home."

By home, she meant Apple Grove. Rebecca had to admit that the friendliness of neighbors was one thing she loved about the Amish community in which she'd lived her entire life. Though the farms were spread out, there seemed to always be someone to visit, someone to lend a hand when needed.

She peered closely at her sister's face. "Are you not happy, then?"

Emma's eyes lit with joy. "Oh, yes! I would prefer having a family or two nearby, but I wouldn't trade what Luke and I have for anything in the world." Her gaze flew again toward the barn, and a tiny smile played at the corners of her mouth. "Our home is built on love. It is all I ever dreamed of."

Gazing at her sister's face, a sense of longing bloomed in Rebecca. Was anything in life more needed than love? She stooped and plucked a wildflower out of the grass at her feet. "You asked earlier if I fancied anyone. Well, there is someone."

Though she didn't care to look Emma in the face, from the corner of her eye she saw her sister's smile widen.

"I knew it! You're in love. I could tell by the way you found fault with Daniel and Samuel. Who is it? Do I know him?"

"Yes, you know him." The flower's tiny purple petals rested like silk between Rebecca's fingers. "You've met him."

"I have?" The smile wavered. "What is his name?"

She pulled a petal off and let it flutter to the grass. "I'd rather not say."

The flower was snatched out of her hand. Startled, Rebecca looked up into Emma's grinning face.

"Playing coy, are you? Very well, then. At least tell me if this boy returns your affections."

"He's not a boy," Rebecca said. "He's a man. And I . . . I don't know." Her gaze fell away. "I hope he does."

I hope he remembers me at all.

"He has not given any indication of his feelings?"

Reluctantly, Rebecca shook her head.

"Hmm." Emma's eyes narrowed. "Well, if you truly love him —"

"I do," she hurried to say. "With all my heart."

Emma's gaze softened. "Then you must go to him, Rebecca, and find out if he loves you in return."

Rebecca risked an upward glance. "Do you really think so?"

Her sister rested clasped hands on her bulging belly and turned a tender glance toward the little boy sleeping in the handcart. "Never let true love pass, dear sister."

The certainty in Emma's tone strengthened Rebecca's resolve. A smile emerged. Find him and tell him of her love. She was old enough now. He was far older, but age didn't matter.

Her resolve strengthened, Rebecca smiled. "Thank you, Emma. You have helped."

Emma reached out to give her a brief hug. "Isn't that what big sisters are for?"

"It is," Rebecca admitted. "Thank you again."

She just hoped Emma would feel the same when she learned that Jesse Montgomery was the man who held her heart.

THREE

Winding her way carefully between rows of tender green plants toward the place where her father was staking tomatoes, Rebecca called, "Papa, I brought you a glass of cider."

Three days had passed since her decision to find Jesse. She could barely sleep nights for thinking of the adventure awaiting her. Lawrence wasn't that far away, even if it was farther than she'd ever ventured, but love beckoned like a lighthouse in the fog. She performed her daily chores distractedly, torn between two plans. The first involved leaving Apple Grove under the cover of darkness. A daring move, to be sure, but this way she wouldn't have to defend her decision to anyone. She could explain her absence in a note and be well on her way before anyone read it. That's what Nathan Yoder did when he left the church. Only she wouldn't be truly leaving. Just taking a short break.

The second plan was less appealing. She could confess her feelings to Papa and ask for his help. But what if he said no?

If Papa or *Maummi* or even Bishop Miller refused her permission, then she couldn't go to Lawrence without defying them, something she clearly didn't want to do. In a week or two she would return with Jesse, and if she had acted in an openly defiant manner, she would be subject to the bishop's reprimand.

By Tuesday she had known that she had to make a decision. If she waited much longer, she would lose her nerve completely.

Papa straightened from his task and watched her approach, removing the kerchief tucked in the waistband of his trousers to mop his forehead beneath his hat.

"*Danki,* daughter." The cool cider disappeared in one long draught. "Hard work and bright sunshine parch a man's throat." He handed the empty glass back to her and bent again to the plants.

"Papa, may I ask you a question?"

"Asking is free." He focused on his hands and the twine he wound carefully through the branches of a young plant.

She had rehearsed the conversation again and again in her mind, but now that the

31

time had come, she had to force the words. Gathering her courage, she assumed an even tone. "When did you know you were in love with Mama?"

His hands froze at their task. Papa rarely spoke of his deceased wife, whether due to Amish reticence concerning discussions of emotions or because memories of her loss were so painful, Rebecca had never been sure.

The silence that fell between them magnified the bird chatter coming from the branches of a nearby tree. She stood still awaiting his answer, her fingers tight around the empty cider glass. Papa's hands began to move again, and he finished tying the length of twine with a loose knot. He might decline to answer, and if so, she would have to try a different approach.

Finally, he straightened. His gaze did not rest on her face but fixed on the house behind her, the house he and Mama had built together when they moved to Apple Grove. The corners of his mouth moved ever so slightly upward into a mere semblance of a smile that was as distant as his eyes. Then he fixed on her face.

"Always," he said simply.

Warmth flooded her heart. It was the answer she had hoped for, on several levels.

"Then you know what it is like to love truly and deeply?"

"I do, daughter. Why do you ask?" He glanced at the sun. "It is hot and I wish to have this work over."

"I am in love, Papa. Deeply, hopelessly in love."

The almost smile faded, and deep lines creased his forehead. "In love? Who is the young man?"

Rebecca lowered her gaze. "I would rather not say."

That was her right. Many Amish young couples courted and planned marriage in secret, often not telling their families until mere weeks before the wedding.

"You are young for such things."

Ah, that was the response she had expected. In his eyes, she was still a small child. "But wasn't Mama younger than me when you met her?"

Consternation colored his features, and then his expression turned sheepish. "It is a different matter for daughters than for mothers."

"Only for the papas," she told him, a blush warming her cheeks. The discussion was going better than she'd hoped, but it was still awkward. Discussing emotional matters with Papa left her feeling ill at ease.

"He is Amish, this young man?" Papa's glance became searching. "He lives by the *Ordnung, ja?*"

She had anticipated this question too. Of course Papa would ask it, given the fact that his older daughter had married outside the church. No, Jesse was not Amish, but in the true sense of the word, Rebecca was not Amish either because she had not yet attended the classes and been baptized. If her plans progressed as they should, Jesse would return to Apple Grove with her, they would both attend the classes in the fall, and then they would be baptized. Four years had passed, and Jesse had a lot of settling down to do, but by now she was certain he had grown into a fine, upstanding man. One Papa would admire.

Or would he? Would Papa accept this cowhand, or would he insist that she find a husband among the sons of the families in their own Amish community? There were so many unanswered questions, but none deterred her quest.

She said truthfully, "He hasn't completed the classes yet."

"Hmm."

Papa clasped his hands behind his back, his eyes moving as he searched her face. She stood straight and returned his gaze without flinching.

"What would you have me do?" he asked.

Panic flickered inside Rebecca. This moment was even harder than she had anticipated.

Take me to Lawrence to find Jesse and help me convince him to come home to Apple Grove with me.

That was the response she had rehearsed, but now that the time had come, and now that she stood looking into Papa's soft brown eyes, she couldn't force the words from her mouth. If she confessed the depths of her feeling, he might insist that she forget her plans and stay home. Or he might dismiss her emotions as a schoolgirl's fancy, which would be even worse. He saw her as a child. How could he believe that her love was that of a full-grown woman?

She broke eye contact. "Nothing. I am merely curious about you and Mama. You so rarely speak of her."

The frown on his face deepened. "It is not good to speak when pain overtakes the words." He stood still a moment, watching her, and then he gave a nod before returning to his task.

Gripping the empty cider glass in her hand, she turned toward the house. A coward, that's what she was, but still a

35

determined one. Plan one had failed, but she still had the second.

She determined not to consider how Papa and *Maummi* would react when they read the letter she planned to write. Instead, she focused on the warm reception they were sure to give her when she returned to Apple Grove with Jesse.

Then Papa would see her as the woman she had become while he was preoccupied with tomato plants.

FOUR

"Now, Angus, you can't go around destroying people's property." Judge Tankersley leveled a stern look on the defendant. "You're going to have to make restitution."

Sitting on a chair on the front row of the courtroom, Colin studied the man standing in front of the judge's wide desk. A night in a jail cell had done a considerable amount to improve Angus Burrell's attitude. The sheriff rubbed a hand across his jaw, which had taken a wild blow from his prisoner's fist in the course of the arrest. Angus stood steadier on his feet this morning, though the smell of sour whiskey saturating the air was enough to make a man's eyes cross.

The door in the back of the courtroom opened. Colin glanced over his shoulder and suppressed a moan. He knew it. A man couldn't belch in this town without these three there to lecture him. The women entered the courtroom and took seats in the row of empty chairs beside Mrs. Evans. The deep scowls on their faces were set in stone this morning.

Struggling to remain upright, Angus gripped the corners of the judge's desk. "Rest-ee-tooo-shun? What's that mean, Tank?"

The judge peered at the defendant over the top of a pair of spectacles perched on the bridge of his beaklike nose. "That means, Angus, that you're going to have to pay Mrs. Evans for that window you broke in the front of her milliner's shop."

"But I don't have no money, Tank. You know that."

A woman's disapproving voice spoke from behind Colin's head. "You would have plenty of money but for your habit of frequenting that establishment of sin."

Colin rubbed his fingers across his forehead and avoided the judge's suddenly harsh expression.

"Mrs. Diggs, I'll thank you to keep your opinions to yourself in my courtroom," Tank said, his voice stern.

" 'Tis more than mere opinion." Annie Diggs' voice gained volume as she warmed to her subject. " 'Tis a proven fact that whiskey leads to slovenly, disreputable living and violence, which this man proved well enough last night."

Tank leaned across the desk and leveled a glare on her. "Madam, if you cannot silence your tongue for the duration of this court session, I'll have you removed."

Colin slid lower in his chair. He knew who would be asked to strong-arm Annie and her scowling companions from the courtroom.

Angus turned, his movements slow, to face his accusers. His bloodshot glance slid quickly away from Annie to rest on Mrs. Evans. "I'm right sorry about your winder, ma'am. I didn't do it a'purpose. I had maybe one or two more'ns good fer me, and things got a little out of control." He affected an unsteady bow.

One backward glance at the ladies' frowning faces informed Colin the apology failed to meet its mark.

The judge continued, "Angus, how long will it take you to come up with fifteen dollars?"

"Fifteen dollars! Tank, I'll have to sell a coupla m' hogs to pay that. And that's if'n I can find somebody to buy 'em."

"Well, get working on it. When you get the money, give it to Mrs. Evans." His gavel came down with a crack. "Case dismissed."

The ladies indulged in a communal outraged gasp. Chairs scraped across the floor as they rose to their feet as one.

"That's all?" Annie demanded, her eyes snapping fire beneath her tightly wound hair. "Outrageous!"

Tank stood, placed his hands on the surface of his desk, and thrust his bulldog face forward.

Here it comes. He's going to order me to arrest her for contempt.

Colin rose to his feet and turned toward the women. "Now, Annie, hold your peace. Miz Evans will get a shiny new window, and Angus will go home and sleep it off." He spread his arms wide and started herding them forward like chickens. "You ladies go on home now. Court's over."

Apparently Judge Tankersley had decided not to push the matter and was heading toward the side door. Wisely, Angus was beating a hasty retreat on Tank's heels.

Annie drew herself up to her full, not-inconsiderable height, her shoulders stiff beneath her lace collar. "The man broke the law, and he is permitted to go free? An outrage, that's what it is. Or does the judge not realize there are laws against consuming liquor in Kansas?"

The door clicked closed behind him, and Colin relaxed. At least he wouldn't be arresting a pack of women today.

The ladies stood ramrod straight, awaiting an answer. He kept his smile in place by sheer willpower. Things could get tricky. The truth was, liquor had been outlawed in Kansas for four years now, but that was a law few wished to see upheld, especially not the owners of some of the most successful businesses in town.

Especially not when a few of them were numbered among the town's most prominent citizens.

Mayor Bowerstock himself was one of the owners of the Lucky Dollar Saloon, and if the rumors were to be believed, so was Judge Tankersley, though he kept that quiet. And because those two gentlemen were the law in Lawrence, with the consent and turned heads of the town council, men like Angus had little to fear from the justice system.

Which was exactly the reason Colin was counting the days until the new sheriff arrived. It was time to let someone else dance at the end of the council's string.

"Now, Annie, you know I can't speak for the judge." He gently shooed the women toward the doorway. "Why don't you ladies go home and make yourselves a nice cup of tea."

Annie's chin lifted. "Don't be condescending, young man."

"No, ma'am. Wouldn't think of it."

The women allowed themselves to be directed toward the exit. The ruffles that flowed from their bustles shook with every step of their booted feet.

Mrs. Evans turned on the threshold, her sweet old-lady eyes searching his. "Sheriff, is the rumor true? You're not leaving our fair town, are you?"

So, word had finally seeped out. Amazing it had taken three whole days to spread across town.

"Yes, ma'am. That rumor's true enough. The new sheriff will be here in a couple of weeks."

Fifteen days exactly, and every one of them waiting to be marked off on the jail-house calendar.

Annie shoved her head back in the doorway to level a glare at him. "Let us hope the new sheriff will have a stiffer backbone than the current one. We need someone to stand up against the law-breakers in this town."

Colin touched his hand to his hat in a polite gesture. "Yes, ma'am."

That was unlikely, because Mulhaney had been handpicked by the mayor from a list of possible candidates, but the sheriff saw

42

no reason to dash her hopes.

With a ferocious sniff, she marched away.

Mrs. Evans waited until Annie was out of earshot to kindly pat his arm. "I like you, Sheriff. You're between a rock and a hard place, but you're doing a fine job. I'll miss you."

His smile was genuine this time. The petite widow went along with the crowd because she was lonely, but she only followed, never led the rebellion.

"Why, thank you, Miz Evans. I appreciate your kind words."

He stood in front of the courthouse, watching the ladies march down the street, the hems of their heavy skirts raising puffs of dust with every step. The temperance movement was gaining strength among the women of Lawrence, and he saw storm clouds on the horizon. The more of them who joined with Annie Diggs and her outspoken group of ladies, the more like thunder their fair voices sounded.

Clouds raced across the night sky. As the horse plodded down the worn path between open fields, one moved across the moon and plunged Rebecca's surroundings into darkness. The wind blew the chill of night directly into her face. Perched on the bench seat of Papa's buggy, she pulled her cloak more tightly around her shoulders and squinted. Thank goodness Big Ed remembered the way to Emma's house, as well he should. She, *Maummi,* and Papa had visited only three days ago. Her heart stuttered at the thought of her father and grandmother back home in Apple Grove, tucked warmly in their beds. In a few short hours they would wake for the day and find her note.

Would Papa be furious? She'd never seen him even mildly angered, except for the time she'd helped tie four cats' tails together. The childish prank earned her a month of complete silence, an impossible task to be sure. Would he come after her? No, she didn't think so. He would respect her wishes because that was the kind of man he was, but he would be hurt, and though she had assured him in her letter there was no reason to worry, he would.

Her determination wavered.

I've often been accused of youthful fancy. Is going after the man I love yet another foolish act?

She was a woman now, with womanly thoughts. She would never willingly hurt Papa or *Maummi,* but she must explore life while she could. *Rumspringa* came only once before the time of commitment to the

Ordnung began.

When I return with my future husband, they'll understand. And they'll forgive me. Amish forgive their own.

The issue settled in her mind, she flicked the reins to encourage Big Ed into a faster pace.

It wasn't long before Emma's house loomed ahead, a dark structure faintly visible in front of an even darker landscape. The final stop before her adventure truly began.

The windows were black at this time of night. Correction. Early morning. Judging by the position of the obscured moon in the sky, midnight had passed some hours ago. She'd made good time crossing the ten miles from Apple Grove to Emma and Luke's ranch, and thankfully she had encountered no one.

The buggy rolled to a halt near the house. Rebecca hopped down, looped Big Ed's lead over a handy branch, and hurried up the porch steps to the door, the wind battering at her back. She raised her hand but hesitated before her knuckles rapped on the wood. Luke and Emma were sure to put up a fuss about her actions. They would urge her to put her plan out of mind and go home. But she needed their help.

I will convince them that I am a woman now and my mind is set. They have no right to rob me of my rumspringa.

She knocked as hard as she could. The sharp sound echoed inside the house. When, after a moment, she heard no response, she pounded with her fist.

"Emma." The wind tugged at the brim of her bonnet, securely tied beneath her chin. "Emma, please wake up!"

Finally, she heard a noise from the second floor inside. A moment later feet pounded on stairs. Satisfied, Rebecca lowered her hand and waited for the door to open.

When it did, her breath whooshed out of her chest in a rush. Instead of her sister's face, a gun barrel came forward and stopped inches from her nose. Her eyes crossed to focus on it and then rose. On the other side of the rifle she glimpsed her brother-in-law's angry face, though her gaze instantly pivoted back to the metal instrument of death pointed directly at her.

"Whoever you are, you'd better have a good reason for — oh." The barrel lowered and Luke squinted at her. "Rebecca? What in tarnation are you doing here at this time of night?"

"Rebecca?" Her sister's voice sounded from behind him, and in the next minute she hurried into the room wrapping a dressing gown around her round belly. "What's wrong? Is it *Maummi?* Has something happened to Papa?"

For a moment Rebecca couldn't answer. She rested a hand over her thumping heart and forced her stunned lungs to draw in a breath. "They are both fine," she finally managed. "May I please explain?"

Luke stepped aside. "Of course. Come in before you catch a chill."

Rebecca entered the room and stepped to one side while he closed the door. When he had moved to his wife's side, she faced them. Confronted by two expectant gazes, her courage flagged. What if they refused to help?

Then I'll go on anyway. I've come this far on my own.

Straightening her shoulders, she raised her chin and spoke calmly. "I have decided to go to Lawrence and bring Jesse back to Apple Grove."

Two jaws went slack.

"Jesse Montgomery?" Luke's eyebrows crooked toward the center of his forehead. "*The* Jesse who helped drive a herd to Kansas?"

"Shhh!" Emma place a finger over her lips. "You'll wake Lucas."

Rebecca lowered her voice. "The same. He is my one true love, and I will have no one else for my husband."

Luke snorted.

Emma rested her hand on his arm. "Why would you want to bring Jesse to Apple Grove?"

"Because we — or, at least, I fell in love with him, and I'm reasonably sure he loves me too."

"Jesse?" Luke laughed. "Rebecca, you're talking nonsense. Jesse is a friend, but he would be the last man on earth I'd want you to marry. He has a lot of settling down to do."

"Which I'm sure he has done." She lifted her chin. "It's been four years. He must surely have tamed his wild side."

"Jesse?"

Emma gave her husband a look full of unspoken communication. "Luke, why don't you go back to bed? I will handle this."

With obvious reluctance he left the room. Emma stepped forward and took hold of Rebecca's arm.

"Come warm yourself by the kitchen stove. I'll fix a pot of tea."

Rebecca followed her to the table and slid into a chair while the lamp was lit. A warm, yellow glow illuminated the room and cast long shadows from the high-backed chairs onto the walls. When they were seated around the shiny clean surface, Emma entwined her fingers on the table in front of her and said simply, "Tell me."

"I don't know why you find this so surprising. I spoke of my love three days past," Rebecca reminded her. "I've adored Jesse since the moment we met. You yourself told me I must find him and see if he returns my love."

"I said you must find Jesse?"

"You said I must find my love and express my feelings."

"I didn't know you were speaking of Jesse. I thought you were in love with an Amish man."

"She would never tell you to go after Jesse." Luke returned to the kitchen with a blanket wrapped around his shoulders.

Emma frowned. "I thought you went back to bed."

"Not when your sister's talking about going after Jesse." He pulled up a chair and sat down.

"Jesse might be Amish one day." Rebecca set her jaw. "Don't laugh, Luke. Love can work miracles in a man."

"Rebecca, I believe you think you have feelings for Jesse, but they're not real."

49

"How can you say so? Jesse is your friend."

"He is my friend, but I know him. He would disappoint you. Jesse isn't the kind of man to change."

"I refuse to consider the notion. He is a good man."

Emma shook her head. "You did not notice the way he drank too much, fought too much, and led a most unseemly life. This is the man you would favor to be your children's father?"

"Enough time has passed that he has settled his wild side."

"Some men never manage to settle their wild side, Rebecca." Luke reached for a cup. "I'm going to make a pot of coffee. I don't want to injure your tender feelings, but the last time I spoke with him, Jesse didn't return your affections."

"That's because I was only a child when he saw me last," she replied, drawing upon reserves of calm. "I'm not a child any longer."

"No, you're not," Emma agreed. "You're a young woman who is capable of putting childish fancies behind her. There are many good Amish men who would make you a fine husband — and while you traipse across the state looking for Jesse, what of Papa and *Maummi?* Because you are here under the cover of night, I assume you did not tell them of your intentions."

That was a weak point in her plan to be sure, but she felt it was unfair of her sister to call attention to it so early in the conversation. She firmed her lip against a tremble. "I left a note."

"Saying what? That you hope they won't worry about a seventeen-year-old girl traveling across Kansas alone to confront a man who has never given the slightest hint of romantic feelings for her?"

Tears prickled behind her eyes. Emma spoke the truth, but need she say it so harshly?

She tilted her head firmly upward. "I told them I am traveling to Lawrence on *rumspringa* and that I will return."

Her sister drew in a slow breath and leaned back in her chair, her eyes focused on Rebecca's face. "Many do not indulge in *rumspringa*. And most of those who do continue to live at home."

"Just because you didn't take one doesn't mean I can't." Rebecca folded her arms across her chest. "I am not many or even most. I insist on experiencing *rumspringa* my own way. I'm of age, and I may do as I wish."

Her sister's eyes narrowed. "There's a difference between the thing that is permitted and the thing that is wise. As *Maummi* says, 'The beginning of wisdom is the knowledge of folly.' "

The very idea of her sister quoting one of *Maummi*'s proverbs was outrageous. With an effort, Rebecca prevented herself from snapping a reply. "Is it folly to follow one's heart?" She held her sister's gaze. "As you did?"

White teeth appeared and clamped down on a rose-colored lip. Rebecca indulged in a private smile. She'd aimed for Emma's own experience with love and hit her mark.

Luke held up a hand. "Rebecca, we haven't seen hide nor hair of Jesse in almost four years. Who knows where he is by now? Have you considered that he might be married? And he wasn't fond of the Amish." His glance slid sideways toward his wife. "Except for your family."

Rebecca knew Jesse thought the Amish way was strange, but that was then.

"People can change, Luke. Four years ago he wasn't ready to settle down. For all you know, he's ready now."

"For all you know," Emma said, "he might have already settled down and have two or three children!"

Rebecca sat back slowly, letting the words

sink in. She hadn't considered offspring. Jesse was several years older than she. What if he had married? The idea pricked her mind like a burr, painful where it touched.

"If you know he's in Lawrence, write him a letter," Luke set the coffeepot on the stove to perk. "Tell him how you feel and invite him for a visit. He can stay with us and meet Lucas. And he can call on you at home."

"That's a wonderful solution." Emma nodded enthusiastically. "That way Papa and *Maummi* won't worry."

Might a letter work? Rebecca lowered her gaze to her lap and studied her clasped hands. It would be a sensible way of finding out if Jesse had already chosen a wife without embarrassing herself in person. He would reply with the grim news, and she could nurse her wounds in private.

But if he hadn't married — and she couldn't believe that his feelings didn't run as deep for her as hers did for him — then he might discount a letter. It would be much more difficult to ignore a living, breathing woman, especially one declaring eternal love.

"No," she answered, her tone unbending. "I shall go to Lawrence with your help or without it. You married your true love. I shall at least have a chance with mine." She held Emma's gaze without blinking and saw the moment her sister's resolve cracked.

"Oh, Rebecca! You are so willful!"

Rebecca crossed her arms. "As are you."

Sighing, Emma said softly, "Then go. Often one does not learn until they have felt the sting of rejection."

Luke frowned at his wife. "You're not serious."

"She's old enough to do as she wishes, Luke. We can't forbid her to leave." Emma held Rebecca gaze. "She is entitled to *rumspringa* if she chooses. And I believe she will go on her own, with or without us."

How unsettling to be the subject of a husband-and-wife discussion as though she weren't sitting across the same table. Rebecca intruded upon the conversation. "I am going." She held up a hand to forestall Luke's objection. "I've already decided."

Exasperation flooded her sister's face. "Then why did you come? What help do you ask of us?"

"Well, two things. First, the loan of a horse. And second . . ." She lowered her gaze. "To ask that you return Big Ed and Papa's buggy. I . . . uh, borrowed them, and I hate to leave him without a way to take *Maummi* to church on Sunday."

"Borrowed" was so much nicer a word

54

than "stole." And far more accurate too, because she fully intended to return both.

Emma laid a hand on Luke's arm. "May we speak in the other room?"

A private look passed between them, and then Luke helped his wife to stand.

"You're still wearing your outdoor things," Emma said. "Hang them on the peg by the door and make yourself at home." She left the room in front of her husband.

Rebecca shed her cloak, trying to discern the soft voices drifting from the other room. Emma was doing most of the talking, with the occasional low rumble of Luke's voice cutting in. Rebecca removed her bonnet and fiddled with the *kapp* beneath it, tucking in a stray strand of hair here and there. As minutes went by, the muscles in her stomach tightened. She'd meant what she said. She would go to Lawrence with or without the help of her sister and brother-in-law. But the loan of a horse surely would make the trip shorter and easier on the feet.

Finally, they returned. Her gaze flew to Emma's face, and her knotted insides loosened a fraction at the tiny smile she saw there.

Luke spoke. "You may not borrow a horse." His voice was adamant, and Rebecca's heart sank. Then he went on in softer tones. "But if you're determined to follow through with this crazy plan, I will take you to the train station in Hays City in the morning. The railway agent will keep an eye out for you. A train ride to Lawrence will be faster and much safer for a young woman traveling alone. And I'll return the buggy and horse to Jonas for you."

She didn't bother to hide the jubilant smile that broke at his words. Emma also smiled at her husband, though hers held a trace of worry.

"Then it is settled, and I pray God's blessing upon your . . . adventure, however foolish." Emma folded her hands and rested them on her belly. "Now we will get a few hours' sleep. Morning will come before we know it. Luke, will you take care of Big Ed? Rebecca, make yourself comfortable in the spare room."

Rebecca scooted her chair neatly beneath the table, hardly able to contain her excitement. Sleep? How could she, when tomorrow she would board a train — a train! — and by nightfall would arrive in Lawrence.

FIVE

Rebecca stood to one side while Luke spoke to the man behind the window in the train station. Money changed hands, and the railroad agent wrote out a ticket. As her brother-in-law took it, he said something and then turned to point in her direction. She straightened and tried to assume a mature stance as the agent looked her way. He nodded and said something to Luke, who then left the window and crossed the room toward her.

"Here you are." He handed her the ticket, which she tucked carefully into the patchwork fabric bag Emma had loaned her this morning. "The train doesn't leave for another two hours, but there are chairs outside where we can wait."

He started in that direction, but Rebecca stopped him.

"Luke, you need not wait with me. You've done so much to help already, and you have several hours more travel before you can return home."

Despite her expectation of wakefulness, Rebecca had slept deeply for three hours and awakened this morning to Lucas's excited bouncing on the bed beside her. To her dismay, she discovered Emma already dressed and at work in the kitchen on a bountiful breakfast, and Luke outside performing his morning chores. After the meal he'd hitched a spare horse up to the back of Papa's buggy, and they left for Hays City.

"I can't leave you here on your own. Emma would have my hide."

"I do not need a chaperone to sit in a chair," she pointed out. "Besides, in a few hours I will be on my own anyway."

His expression turned uncertain, and she sensed he was willing to be convinced. No doubt he dreaded the upcoming discussion with Papa — nor did she blame him, she realized a little guiltily — and was eager to have the trip underway so he could head for home.

"Go." She gave him a gentle shove toward the door. "If I am old enough to travel to Lawrence alone, then I am old enough to get on the train alone." He opened his mouth as if to argue, but she cut him off.

"And I am old enough, no matter what you think."

"Emma won't like it . . ."

She smiled. "She doesn't have to know. Show me the chairs where I may wait."

He picked up her small travel bag and carried it through the door. Outside they were greeted by bright sunshine and a crowded street. A carriage rolled by with a well-dressed gentleman and a lady in a frilly green dress seated high above the dust generated by the wheels. The man ducked his head at a pair of ladies who paused in their trek across the wide street to let him pass, holding their skirts up to avoid their hems trailing in the dirt.

To Rebecca's right, a wooden bench and two chairs were lined up along the outer wall of the train station's office. Luke set her bag on the bench.

"The agent will come for you when the train arrives." He pointed to the far side of the building, in the opposite direction of town, where the tracks lay across the ground and disappeared into the Kansas prairie beyond.

He paused, and Rebecca thought he might change his mind.

"I will be fine."

His gaze scanned the area, and then he

reached into his vest and pulled out a slender paper-wrapped parcel.

"Emma and I want you to have this." He shoved the parcel into her hands.

They had given her a gift? How sweet of her sister. She started to unwrap the paper, but Luke closed his hand over her fingers to stop her.

"Not here. Not out in the open." He lowered his voice. "It's money. Twenty dollars."

Rebecca gasped. Twenty dollars? Why, that was more than twice what she'd managed to save on her own, and she'd been stashing away her pennies for years. "I can't accept this, Luke. It's too generous."

She tried to push it back into his hands, but he shook his head.

"Things cost more in Lawrence than you think, and we want you to have enough money to stay in a reputable boardinghouse."

"But I have my own money. I have saved."

"Then bring us whatever's left when you return."

One look at his expression, and she knew her protests would be in vain. Reluctantly, she slipped the parcel into her bag.

"I will pay you back whatever I use. I promise."

Nodding, he suddenly seemed eager to be on his way. "If you're sure you'll be okay here . . ."

She laid a hand on his arm. "I am sure. Thank you, Luke. You and Emma have helped me more than I dreamed possible."

"Yeah." He avoided her eyes. "Do me a favor and don't mention it to Jonas, okay?"

A quick image of her father's hurt expression when he discovered her letter this morning sent a shaft of guilt through her.

"I won't," she promised. "But tell him . . ." She bit her lip. "Tell him not to worry. I'll be fine. And I'll be home in a week. Two at the most."

Luke lingered, his gaze scanning the area again. "Are you sure you'll be okay . . ."

"I will," she said.

She dropped onto the bench, folded her hands in her lap, and adopted an attitude of patient waiting. Smiling up at her brother-in-law, she saw the moment of his decision in his eyes.

"Tell Jesse I'd like to see him whenever he can get over this way. I want to introduce him to my son."

"I will," she said. "And you'll see your good friend soon, when he returns with me."

Still looking worried, he tipped his hat and left her. Settling back onto the hard bench,

Rebecca discounted his concerns. Of course Luke would be protective of her. He'd met her when she was a mere thirteen-year-old, and he still thought of her as a child, as did the rest of her family. Which was another reason this *rumspringa* was sorely needed. When she returned, everyone would look at her with fresh eyes. They would see her as a woman in her own right, grown and mature.

A carriage passed, the lady on the bench seat sitting tall, her spine erect, head high, and the horse's lead held firmly in her hands. Rebecca unconsciously straightened her posture to match. Dressed in a smart blue dress with fluffy white lace at the high collar and snugly fitting wrists, the lady didn't deign to look her way. And no wonder. Rebecca glanced down at her own straight black skirt and sturdy shoes. She lifted a hand to touch her plain black bonnet, the laces of her white *kapp* hanging down the sides of her head. Here she was, testing the limits of what the *Englisch* world had to offer by preparing to board a train and leave the confines of tiny Apple Grove dressed like a crow among bluebirds. Once, years ago, she had announced that during her *rumspringa* she would wear a feathered hat and fashionable clothing.

Her eyes strayed to the millinery shop

adjacent to the train station. The establishment had just opened for the day's business. She imagined the wares inside. Fine, store-bought clothing in a wide array of colors and bright ribbons.

Well, why not? The train was still two hours away. Jesse would certainly find her more desirable if she wore a striking dress and fashionable shoes. And now she could afford it, thanks to Luke and Emma's generosity, which she fully intended to pay back.

Anticipation tickled her stomach as she rose from the bench and gathered her satchel in her hand.

Already the excitement of *rumspringa* had begun.

As afternoon stretched into evening, the town atmosphere gathered weight like clouds in the hours before a bad thunderstorm. Colin paced up and down Massachusetts Street, his eye scanning every corner and down every narrow alley between the buildings, scouting for the source of the trouble he felt deep in his joints. Trouble was brewing in Lawrence. Two years on the job had sharpened his instincts, and he could sense conflict even before the culprits were aware of it.

All he had to do was figure out what was happening and plug the hole in the dike before it blew.

Around suppertime the crowds in the wide street lessened as shops closed and folks headed home. From the vantage point of a straight-backed wooden chair in front of the jailhouse, he nodded at Abe Lewis as he placed the "Closed" sign in the window of the general store for an hour or so to go home and have supper with the missus, as he did every night about this time.

The door to Mrs. Evans' shop was already shut and had been for more than an hour. She'd closed the shop early today, Colin noted. The crisscrossed barricade of wooden planks that covered the gaping hole where her front window had been made a worrisome sight.

The only establishment on the street that still boasted a lively presence was the Lucky Dollar Saloon. The wide wooden doors had been thrown open to welcome the man who dared to wet his whistle. Piano music spilled out along with a warm light from the numerous lanterns hanging around the saloon's interior. Even from this distance, the roar of men's voices lifted in laughter floated on the swiftly cooling air.

A familiar noise came from the opposite

direction; the train was coming into town. That would be the Union Pacific on its way to Chicago. Colin pulled his timepiece out of his vest pocket. Five fifty. Ten minutes late.

"Evening, Sheriff." The blacksmith approached from the direction of the smithy. "Pleasant weather we're having, eh?"

"Evening." Colin dipped his head as the big man passed, his tread heavy on the wooden boardwalk. "Right pleasant. Have a good one, Will."

Will continued past the jailhouse, glanced down the street, and then crossed at an angle toward the Lucky Dollar.

Colin shook his head. The fool was just asking for trouble.

He would stay there long enough to knock back a few and flirt with the new girl, Sassy, and then head back to the forge until late in the evening. Will was a good enough fellow, cheerful and hardworking. He liked to sing as he pounded metal on his anvil. Colin watched him push through the swinging doors. If he had a vice, he shared it with a couple of hundred others in Lawrence.

Colin tilted his chair on two legs, the back resting against the jailhouse. Annie Diggs' parting comment yesterday ate at him. She was an intelligent woman and had a way with words, which meant every issue of the *Kansas Liberal,* the newspaper she ran with her husband, might as well be printed with gunpowder. The women in Lawrence devoured it. Most of the men thought it ought to be used for kindling.

Yes, she had a way with words, did Annie. In the two years since he'd pinned on the badge, he'd done some good things in this town. He'd hired and trained five deputies to help him keep the peace. Killings were down. Women were able to walk down the streets without fear of being trampled or worse by rowdy cowboys fresh off the trail who used to make a habit of riding down Massachusetts Street with their guns firing and looking for trouble. The bank hadn't been robbed in more than a year.

That left the matter of the saloons.

The truth was he stood firmly on the side of the ladies. He'd seen alcohol ruin men's lives, and he wanted no part of it. But that was his personal opinion. When they had hired him as sheriff, Judge Tankersley and Mayor Bowerstock and the rest of the town council had been clear about his duties. He was to keep the streets of Lawrence streets peaceful and the residents safe, and leave the saloon owners alone.

He'd done what he could. He'd turned a

blind eye more than once on the ladies' activities, as long as they didn't blatantly disturb the peace. Certainly Patrick Mulhaney wouldn't do that.

The replacement sheriff had been hand-picked by the mayor and Tank after hearing of his reputation in Chicago as a brusque man with an eagle eye who took no quarter from lawbreakers. Their decision, though bad, had been based on further inquiries that revealed Mulhaney once shot the gun right out of a desperado's hand from thirty feet away, even though he'd just downed nearly a bottle of whiskey.

Apparently Mulhaney was known as a man who enjoyed his liquor. Colin wondered how the new sheriff would fare with Annie Diggs and her crew.

Activity at the far end of the street drew his attention. Colin tilted his Stetson forward and watched from beneath the wide brim. A small cluster of women had gathered to stand beneath the awning in front of the Eldridge Hotel. As though she'd materialized from his thoughts, Annie herself stood in the midst of them, a powerful-looking figure who carried herself with confidence and composure. As he watched, a pair of ladies rounded the corner past the bakery and hurried across the street to join her.

What are the good ladies of Lawrence up to tonight?

Colin watched as their number grew from a cluster to what could be termed a group, if not a small mob. So far they seemed to be peaceful, but the sheriff's sense of discomfort swelled like the Kansas River during a wet spring. They weren't breaking any laws. He folded his arms across his chest, his weight still balanced on two chair legs, and watched the sun, an orange ball of fire, sink in the west. When the group started to move, he shifted his gaze to Annie Diggs. Now they were heading his way.

Correction. They were headed toward the Lucky Dollar Saloon.

Fourteen days, Lord. Two weeks without any trouble. That's all I ask.

With a resigned sigh, he let the chair's front legs thump on the wooden planks as they settled into place. He slid his hat back to the top of his head and started to stand when a movement to the left drew his attention. A small stream of people rounded the corner from Berkeley Street. Railroad passengers, probably, looking for a bite to eat or maybe a drink before the train continued east.

A couple, the woman with her hand resting on the arm of a well-dressed gentleman, turned into the Massachusetts Street Diner. Four men passed by and continued in the direction of Annie's group.

They're headed toward the Lucky Dollar.

Dread, like a bad piece of meat, settled heavily in the pit of his stomach. A confrontation was brewing.

A lone figure trailed the men. Female. The young woman wore a frilly dress the color of fresh-churned butter. Atop her head was one of those ridiculous bonnets women wore these days, with an arrangement of bright feathers fanning from the back like a wild turkey's tail. She clutched a bulging patchwork bag in both hands.

And she was limping like a lame mare.

He took a closer look when she passed by on the other side of the street, trailing after the men. She had no injury he could see, but she wore a pair of button-up shoes with heels that threatened to pitch her sideways if she stepped wrong. Ridiculous pointy-toed things the affluent favored. He focused on her youthful features. She was anything but ridiculous looking. With rosy cheeks and round eyes, she was a fine-looking young woman, though her mouth contracted as though she'd been eating persimmons.

She caught sight of the group of women heading toward her and her pace quickened. She'd recognized someone.

He frowned. Another one of those temperance supporters, come to town to meet up with Annie and the others?

That's all I need. Now they're swarming in from out of town.

Resigned to the coming confrontation, he headed across the street.

Every step Rebecca took on the hard-packed dirt street sent pain shooting from her toes to halfway up her legs. The stylish boots had looked so adorably irresistible in the dressmaker's shop, with their high tabbed fronts and buckles. They were nothing an Amish woman would ever wear, which was part of their appeal. That's what *rumspringa* was all about, sampling things of the *Englisch* world. The heels had caused her to stagger a bit at first, but the dressmaker assured her that she would soon grow accustomed to them, and that the narrow toes would stretch to conform to her feet. In a hundred years, perhaps. They had been bearable while seated for the train ride from Hays City to Lawrence, but the moment she'd stood, her toes had cramped in the tight confines of the stiff leather, and the pain grew worse with every step. Rebecca wasn't sure how much longer she could stand the agony.

How did *Englisch* women walk around in these things? And pay good money for them? Was this what God meant when He said, "Pride goeth before destruction, and an haughty spirit before a fall"? Because if she had to endure another hour of this torture, she would fall flat on her foolish face.

Perhaps her feet were malformed and not appropriate for today's fashions. She'd never noticed other women hobbling. The *Englisch* woman had assured her that the shoes, along with the dress that fit Rebecca perfectly, previously belonged to a lady of fashion who met an unfortunate end during childbirth last spring. That's why she'd been able to offer them for such a good price. Rebecca had flinched at the "good price" the dressmaker named. The outfit was a wild extravagance, costing enough money for *Maummi* to make at least a dozen Amish dresses and have enough left over to purchase four pairs of shoes that fit.

Rebecca ran a hand down the soft fabric of her yellow skirt. The garment was truly the finest she'd ever owned or was likely to own again. A sideways glance showed her a dim reflection in the window of the general store. Ruffles trailed from the bustle like a waterfall. The snug waist emphasized a slender frame and accentuated the womanly curves that were effectively hidden behind the black bulk of her Amish dresses. And the hat! Oh, what a lavish purchase that had been. She lifted a hand to brush the feathers that formed a smart display at the top of her head. In this hat and dress, she looked exactly like a stylish *Englisch* woman. Heat rushed into her cheeks at the pleasure her reflection gave her.

Jesse would love it. Bishop Miller would certainly disapprove. Papa would fall down dead.

Another step, and pain shot again from her cramped toes to her heel and up her calf. Movement in the street ahead drew her attention. A group had gathered on the wooden walkway in front of a building. All women. When Rebecca had allowed the conductor to assist her down from the train, she'd been attacked by a sudden fit of nervousness. The dress might look stylish, but she now felt out of place in it. What if the people of Lawrence mistook her for a fashionable woman and expected her to know the mysterious ways of the *Englisch*? The women before her now were all dressed in sensible fabrics, and there was not a hat to be seen.

Rebecca determined to find a sympathetic-looking woman in the group to help her locate an inexpensive boarding-house. Once she was settled, she could begin her search for Jesse and supper for her empty stomach — and of even more importance at the moment, a glass of water. Such a fierce thirst had taken hold of her that she felt she could spit cotton.

Rebecca searched for a caring female face in the crowd.

The four men who had disembarked the train with her headed down the street, and she fell in behind them. When they reached the gathering crowd, they came to a halt so suddenly that she almost ran into them from behind before she limped to a painful halt in the street.

"Pardon us, ladies," one of the men said, "but if you'll step aside, we'll just squeeze past you."

A female voice, rich and masterful, rang out. "Pardon? There is only one who pardons wicked behavior, and if you intend to bestow your patronage on this sinful establishment, then I venture to say you know Him not!"

Rebecca edged sideways to peer around

the backs of the four railway passengers. The speaker was a tall woman, perhaps thirty years old, with smooth skin and hair arranged in a stylish knot on top of her head. The color of her dress was dark enough to satisfy even *Maummi*'s requirements, but the snug waist and buttons at the cuff would never be tolerated in the Amish community, nor would the elaborate lace-and-ribbon collar that hugged high up her neck. Rebecca fingered the lace at her own collar, which was not nearly high enough to brush her chin. The lady stood surrounded by women, her spine erect as she glowered down the length of her nose at the men through light blue eyes that shone with purpose.

"What's this?" The man turned to his companions. "Did she just call us wicked and sinful?"

"I believe she did," one of his companions answered.

"I know what this is." A third man fixed the woman with a narrow-eyed stare. "It's one of those temperance meetings, where the women are against liquor. I heard Kansas was full of 'em."

The lady, obviously the leader, pointed a finger at each of the men in turn.

"We stand in support of the *law,* both of

man and of God. Liquor is the devil's drink, and those who partake stand in danger of being devoured by his fiery flames."

The man in front of Rebecca took a step back. His foot trod upon her stylish boot, and for a moment Rebecca thought those fiery flames had found her. Agony exploded in her toes. Her vision blurred with tears as she staggered sideways to get out of his way.

"Oh! I beg your pardon, miss." The man jerked away and reached to steady her. "I didn't see you back there."

She couldn't find the breath to immediately answer, but she attempted a forgiving smile. When the pain receded somewhat, she found herself returning to the speaker's piercing gaze that now pinpointed her. She swallowed against a parched throat.

"Are you planning to enter this establishment along with these men?" The tone put Rebecca in mind of the time *Maummi* scolded her for fidgeting on the bench during the preaching at church.

She shook her head. "I'm only looking for a drink."

Shock widened the woman's eyes, and several of the other ladies drew indignant gasps. The women stared at her as if they had caught sight of a particularly loathsome spider. Two stepped away.

Confused, Rebecca met their accusing stares. "I'm thirsty —"

Men's laughter erupted, and she became aware of lively music drifting through the swinging doors. She'd heard that kind of music before, in Hays City, from inside a . . .

She drew in a quick breath. A saloon! The women were standing in front of a saloon, and they thought she intended to go inside along with the men from the train.

"Water," she said quickly. "I need a drink of water for my parched throat." She stepped away to disassociate herself from the men.

Suspicion overtook the leader's features. "You don't imbibe strong spirits?"

Rebecca straightened and looked her in the eye. "Never once in all my life."

"She's with us, then, Annie." The woman standing next to the leader strode forward, looped arms with Rebecca, and tugged her back into the midst of the group. Rebecca was pulled along, wincing at the pain the steps inflicted on her feet.

"Look," said an elderly female voice from behind her. "Here comes Sheriff Maddox."

A man approached from across the street, his step firm and his stride long. He wore an *Englisch* hat with an oblong brim that turned up at the sides. His dark hair had

76

been cut short but still showed a hint of curl behind his ears. On his leather vest he wore a metal star, and at his side hung a holstered pistol. A young man, Rebecca realized, with striking dark eyes that swept from the men to the women.

"What seems to be the problem here, folks?" His words were spoken in a pleasant tone and his lips wore the hint of a smile, though caution lay heavy in his gaze.

One of the men spoke up. "Why, no trouble, Sheriff. We just got off the train and were heading into the saloon to wet our whistle." His head dipped toward the group. "Seems these ladies don't want us going inside."

The sheriff's gaze rested on the ringleader, who stood beside Rebecca.

"Annie, didn't I ask you to stay away from the saloon?"

Annie stretched to her full height, which made her nearly a head taller than Rebecca.

"Someone must stand against the devil's schemes to destroy the lives of the men of Lawrence."

Rebecca found her arms caught up, locked at the elbow on one side with Annie and another lady on the other. Women shifted around her and looped arms to form a human chain, three deep, with Rebecca front and center.

At a noise behind her, she turned her head. A large man wearing a stained apron over his shirt had stepped through the saloon's swinging doors. He glowered at the women as he strode around them. Across the street, a couple strolling down the sidewalk stopped to watch and were soon joined by others.

"What's going on out here?" The big man's booming voice matched his menacing stature, and Rebecca found herself avoiding his angry glare.

"I have things under control, Ed." The sheriff tipped his head toward the saloon. "You go on back inside and take care of your customers."

"Yes," Annie said, her voice every bit as weighty as Ed's. "Return to your illegal trade where you may ruin more men's lives."

Rebecca would have shrank back from the fury that erupted in Ed's face, except that she was snared by her elbows and unable to extricate herself. Beside her, Annie's shoulders straightened. How could she stand before such anger without trembling?

"All we want is a drink," one of the railroad passengers said. He glanced at his companions. "We don't want no trouble."

The man beside him offered a nod. "We'll

go elsewhere. I'm certain there are other establishments in town."

The men started to back away.

"Hey!" Ed turned toward the sheriff. "Did you hear that? These women are fixin' to lose me more business. Aren't you going to do something about it?"

The sheriff drew in a calm breath, and Rebecca marveled at his composure. Even an Amish man would be tempted to frown.

"Yes, Ed. I expect I am." He called to the retreating men. "Gentlemen, you don't have to take your business elsewhere. The ladies were just leaving. Weren't you, ladies?"

His glance swept the group and came to a rest on Rebecca. She widened her eyes in what she hoped was an innocent expression. Judging by the way his dark brows knitted into a demand rather than a suggestion, she doubted he'd caught her meaning.

Annie's body became rigid, and she said tightly, "We're . . . not . . . going . . . anywhere."

A silent gasp filled Rebecca. How dare she speak to a lawman in such a manner! Anticipation filled her as she focused on the combatants.

"Ladies," he began, still unruffled, "how many times do I have to tell you that you can't strong-arm a man — or woman —

from entering the Lucky Dollar or any other local establishment?" The sheriff caught sight of someone behind Rebecca. "Miz Evans, what if someone tried to stop customers from coming in your store? Or your husband's barber shop, Miz Kramer? You would expect me to uphold the law for you, wouldn't you?"

A voice behind Rebecca replied uncertainly, "Well, yes. I suppose we would, but this is different."

"No, ma'am. It's not. Now, all of you go on home and we'll end this real peaceable-like."

Annie's head jerked around to deliver a piercing glance. "Not a one of us is operating an illegal business. Nor do we destroy lives in the process of practicing our trades."

Illegal? That was the second time she'd mentioned the saloon being illegal. Rebecca stole a glance at the man named Ed, who apparently owned the saloon. Was he a law-breaker?

The railroad passengers took another few backward steps, apparently eager to escape the conflict that continued to grow. If only she could join them. Confrontations like this never happened in Apple Grove. People there spoke in soft voices to their neighbors, not angry shouts that made her insides twist.

"No, wait." Ed took a step toward the crowd with an outstretched hand. "Don't go. For your trouble, the first drink is on the house."

They stopped their retreat, expressions suddenly eager.

Ed looked at Colin. "Are you gonna do something, Sheriff, or do I have to get the mayor?"

The sheriff closed his eyes, his lips a tight line. When he opened them a moment later, he pushed the hat back on his head, revealing a wide forehead and more thick, dark hair.

He glanced at Annie. "You're making this hard on me." His tone could almost be noted as pleading now. "You don't want to go to jail for disturbing the peace again, do you?"

Jail? The word slapped at Rebecca like a whip. It was time for her to make a polite exit. She tried loosening her arms in an effort to slip out of the chain, but Annie pulled her closer with a firm movement.

A fierce gleam shone in the woman's eyes. "The apostle Paul was jailed for his convictions, and we are no less determined than he."

All around her, women's heads bobbed.

"Jailed for our cause!" someone behind

her cried. Rather than sounding upset, the woman's tone rang with righteous satisfaction.

The sheriff extended a hand. "Now, Annie, be reasonable. Go on home and have a nice supper with your family. Enjoy the pleasant weather."

Annie replied in a fierce tone, not to the sheriff, but to her fellow protesters. "Stand firm, ladies. We are engaged in a battle. But never fear! We have righteousness on our side. We shall win the war!" She burst into song, not in German, as Rebecca was accustomed to hearing, but in English. "Onward, Christian soldiers, marching as to war . . ."

Female voices all around Rebecca joined in. "With the cross of Jesus going on before."

War? Rebecca's mouth went even drier than before. The Amish were peaceful people. She tried again to disentangle her arm, but she was still held fast while the song swelled around her. The crowd across the street grew and moved closer as folks gathered close, their expressions ranging from interested to amused.

A young woman joined the onlookers on the right, her shiny red lips glistening. Her dress was yellow, like Rebecca's, but brighter in hue with an abundance of ruffles and a neckline that dropped down lower than that of any other woman present. Curls of blond hair were piled in an elaborate arrangement on her head and adorned with colorful flowers. With a shock, Rebecca realized she had just come out of the saloon, as had several of the others who stood gawking at the singing women.

She's a fallen woman!

Ed stepped forward and addressed the crowd. "Don't worry, folks. Sheriff Maddox has this under control. Go on back inside. Sassy here will sing you a song, and I'll be right in to pour another round. This one's on the house!"

A cheer went up from the crowd. The blonde caught Rebecca's eye and her smile deepened. The heat in Rebecca's cheeks intensified.

"C'mon, fellas," the girl said. "I have a real special song to sing for you, much better than that old war tune."

She turned and flounced away. Rebecca was horrified to see that much of the crowd followed her. The singing around her increased in volume. If her hands had been free, she would have covered her ears.

Ed turned to face the sheriff, his arms folded across his chest.

"This has gone on long enough, Maddox.

End it."

The sheriff lifted his hat with one hand and ran a hand across his hair. Then he set his hat back on, straight and firm, and with a sideways glance at Ed, stepped forward.

"All right, ladies." He pitched his voice above the sound of their singing. "You're under arrest for disturbing the peace, all of you. Follow me to the jail."

He reached out and wrapped his fingers around Annie's upper arm. Rebecca ducked away.

"I am not fighting in a war," she told him. "I'm merely passing through town."

"Don't lose heart, little sister." Annie's voice held a note of triumph, and she didn't try to pull out of the sheriff's grasp. "Our suffering will be rewarded in the end."

"No, I —" Rebecca tried to shrink back, but she was surrounded by women with faces set in determination.

The sheriff frowned at her. "I said *all* of you. Don't make this any harder than it has to be."

The others fell in beside them as he led Annie across the street.

"How exciting!" said an enthusiastic elderly voice behind her. "We're going to jail."

"I hope we won't be there long," answered

another, this one with a hint of worry in her tone. "George gets irritable if he's left tending the children too long."

Sheriff Maddox's long stride didn't slow, but he turned his head and called over his shoulder. "Do me a favor, would you, Ed? Send a message over to Alvin Diggs and tell him I have his wife down at the jail. Tell him to come get her, and to spread the word to the other husbands."

Panic twisted Rebecca's insides into knots as she was dragged across the street in her painful boots. Her first day on *rumspringa,* and she was going to jail.

Papa would have kittens.

SIX

The three jail cells had two bunks each, positioned on opposite sides of the enclosed spaces. Other than the cells and a wooden desk, the room was dull. Because she was with four women whose combined girth occupied most of the available bunk space, Rebecca stood with her back against the rough brick wall. Bars filled the small window above her head, and the faint sound of distant music drifted through on a light breeze.

Sheriff Maddox sat in a sturdy chair, his boots propped on the desk, whittling. Rebecca didn't know how he could be so calm in the middle of chaos. His prisoners refused to stop singing their battle song.

Rebecca hugged her arms close to her chest and tried not to cry. Her plan had gone terribly awry, and it had only been one day since she set out to find Jesse. What would Emma think when she learned that her sister had been arrested along with a group of unruly women who had declared war on a saloon? Rebecca's feet felt like fire pits. And where had her bag with her black dress and comfortable shoes gone? She stepped to the bars.

"Sheriff?"

When he didn't answer she called again. "Sheriff?"

"He has his ears plugged."

She turned to face the woman who spoke, fighting tears. "How can you stay so calm? We are in jail!"

"Oh, honey, we play this little game at least twice a week."

Well, it wasn't a game to Rebecca, and she didn't enjoy it.

An elderly gray-haired woman rose from a bunk. Wrinkles and creases around her eyes and mouth deepened when she smiled. She approached Rebecca and patted her arm.

"Sit down, child. You look near to swooning."

"I —" Words choked off in her throat, and Rebecca found that she was too exhausted to argue. She allowed herself to be helped to the bunk. The other woman scooted over to make room.

"There." The elderly lady laid a hand on her shoulder and gave her another pat. "I'm

Grace Evans, and these ladies are Eloise Thompson, Pearl Wallace, and Gladys Coulter."

Rebecca managed to squeeze a few words past the misery that clenched her throat nearly closed. "I am Rebecca Switzer."

Other voices called greetings from the other cells.

"A pleasure to meet you, Rebecca."

"Welcome to Lawrence, honey."

"Yes." Annie's disembodied but commanding voice filled the small jailhouse. "Welcome to the cause."

Rebecca winced. Should she tell them that she had no desire to join "the cause," whatever it was? That she simply wanted to find Jesse and go home as quickly as possible?

Standing in front of her, Mrs. Evans searched her face. "I don't believe Rebecca came to Lawrence to join us," she called to those next door. Then she lowered her voice and spoke kindly. "Did you, child?"

"No, ma'am." She shook her head. "I came to Lawrence to find a man."

Pearl and Gladys sat up straighter, and Mrs. Evans' eyebrows arched over watery blue eyes. "Are there no men where you live?"

"No. I mean, yes." She shook her head

with a jerk to clear it. "There are men in Apple Grove, but not the right one. I gave my heart to my one true love years ago, and I am here to tell him."

"A quest of love." Pearl laid her fingers dreamily across her collarbone, while Gladys gave a sentimental sniff.

Mrs. Evans folded her hands and smiled. "What's your young man's name?"

A sudden hope cut through Rebecca's misery. Was it possible that this woman might be able to tell her where to find Jesse?

She straightened on the bunk. "His name is Jesse Montgomery. Do you know him?"

"Montgomery?" Mrs. Evans' forehead puckered in thought, and then she shook her head. "I don't believe so. What work does he do?"

Rebecca nibbled at her lower lip. What did Jesse do? Emma hadn't said. "I do not know. He used to run cattle from Texas to Kansas. That's where we met."

Gladys's lips pursed. "A cowboy." She and Pearl exchanged a disapproving glance.

"A good one," Rebecca said quickly. "We met when my family was robbed while traveling in unknown territory, and he and his friends helped us. His best friend, Luke, and my sister, Emma were married not long after."

"Sisters marrying best friends?" Mrs. Evans clasped her hands beneath her chin, her eyes misting over. A chorus of sentimental sighs sounded from the neighboring cells.

"I love weddings," Pearl confessed.

"There is no wedding planned yet," Rebecca told her. "First I must find him and assure him of my love." She lowered her voice, doubt suddenly looming. "And find out if he loves me in return."

Eloise rose from her bunk. "Does anyone know a man named Jesse Montgomery?"

The answering chorus of "No, I don't believe so" and "Haven't heard that name" served to deepen Rebecca's doubt. Surely if Jesse lived in Lawrence, as Mr. McCann had told Emma and Luke, one of these ladies would know him. Had this entire trip been for nothing?

Then a voice said, "I think I've heard of him."

Rebecca turned quickly toward the speaker, ignoring the sharp pain in her feet. "You have? Where is he?"

"He's not in Lawrence. Used to be, but my Bob mentioned that he was over in Cider Gulch now, across the river. Bob bought a few head of cattle over there last week."

A rancher! Excitement pounded in Rebecca's chest. He had changed and settled down!

"Yes, Jesse is wonderful with cows." She whirled toward Mrs. Evans. "Where is Cider Gulch?"

"It's southeast of here, about two days by coach."

All is not lost. I will hire a coach and —

Her plans jerked to a halt. First she must recover her bag, with the money pouch inside. No, first she must get out of here. She stood and went to the bars of the cell, giving them a frustrated jerk, but the iron didn't bulge.

At that moment the jailhouse's outer door opened, and a group of men appeared. Gladys spoke sharply above the others. "There you are, Fredrick. What took you so long?"

A mild-faced man cast a guilty look toward Gladys, who stood beside Rebecca. "I came as soon as I heard." He nodded to the sheriff and then focused on his wife. "Are you all right?"

The sheriff stood up and removed wads of cotton from his ears.

Gladys drew herself up stiffly. "I'm in jail, Fredrick. Do I look all right?"

Sheriff Maddox reached for a set of keys. "Gentlemen, I'm releasing your wives into your custody."

"What's the meaning of this, Colin?" one of the men asked. "This is the third time this week we've had to come and bail out these women. It's putting a serious dent in my pocket."

"I'm just doing my job, Clyde." He shoved a book to the front of the desk. "Sign here and take it up with the judge. He'll see the women at the courthouse in the morning."

"Do we have to post bail?" A husband glanced toward the cells.

"No bail." Colin slid a pen across this desk toward them and set the inkwell beside it. "I'm releasing the ladies into your custody, and you're to make sure they get to the courthouse at nine sharp. Sign on the dotted line."

Rebecca watched as the men stepped up one by one and scratched out a signature. When the last husband had done so, the sheriff picked up the key ring and rounded the desk. He unlocked the first cell, and Annie Diggs filed out ahead of her cellmates. Rebecca saw in her erect carriage that she had lost none of her composure. When she stopped close to Sheriff Maddox, she stood nearly eye to eye.

She tilted her head back and examined him down the length of her nose. "One day we shall see justice done in this town."

The sheriff returned her stare with a polite smile. "Yes, ma'am. Now run along, Miz Annie. It's past your suppertime."

Her voice took on the commanding tone of leader once again. "Ladies, we shall continue our fight on the morrow." With a swish of heavy skirts, she turned and held a hand out to one of the men. "Let's go, Alvin."

A gentleman stepped forward and offered an arm, and together they marched out of the jailhouse. Shaking his head, the sheriff unlocked the center cell and then at last moved to Rebecca's. When the key twisted in the heavy lock, a weight lifted from her chest. The sight of the door swinging open was as welcome as the first birds of spring after a long winter. She picked up her stylish hat and limped through the doorway.

Pairs formed among the women and their husbands, and two by two they followed Annie and Alvin out into the street. Rebecca would have fallen in with them, but when she approached the exit, the sheriff stepped in front of her.

"Not so fast, miss."

Rebecca tilted her head back to look up at his face. Standing this close, he formed an imposing presence, tall and rugged, his shoulders broad beneath the leather vest. Why, the girth of his arms would make Papa's look like a boy's, and Papa was the strongest man in all of Apple Grove. She took a step backward.

"May I not leave with the others?" She rounded her eyes and assumed the most innocent expression she could, the same one she wore when *Maummi* scolded her for failing to perform a chore as she should have.

He cocked his head. "I didn't see anybody sign for you."

"But . . ." A lump formed in her throat. "I am a visitor. I know no one here."

Skeptical creases appeared between his eyebrows. "You seemed to be right friendly with the rest of those women. A man would almost think you'd come to town to meet up with them on purpose."

He thought she was part of tonight's protest? Rebecca shook her head. "You are mistaken. I am not involved."

He folded his arms across his chest. "I saw you with my own eyes arm in arm with Annie Diggs, who is a known protest leader for all sorts of women's causes."

"I do not protest. I am Amish."

The skepticism on his face deepened. "Amish? You?" His gaze swept from the top of her head down to her toes, and he laughed. "You're not Amish any more than I am."

Outrage rose up inside her. "I am too Amish!" She stamped a foot and then winced as pain exploded in her toes.

The soft sound of a throat politely clearing distracted her. She turned to find Mrs. Evans standing in the far corner, watching the encounter.

"I have no one to sign for me either, Sheriff, as the death of my beloved husband has left me a widow these past twenty years." She swept a wrinkled hand toward the cell they had just vacated. "Must I also spend the night in jail?"

The sheriff ducked his head. "Now, Miz Evans, you know I'm not going to keep you in jail."

Rebecca turned back to face him. Anger and pain loosened her tongue. "I begin to see why the women of this town stand in protest against injustice. 'Tis unfair, releasing her and not me."

His lips became a tight line. "Miz Evans is a respected citizen of this town, a business owner. I think she can be trusted to show up at the courthouse tomorrow on her own. Whereas, Miss Switzer, you are a stranger and a troublemaker."

Never in all her days had anyone called

her a troublemaker. The teacher in her Amish school had called her "spirited" once, which had resulted in a series of proverbs on meekness from *Maummi,* but she was entirely innocent this time. This lawman was purposefully insulting her.

Turn the other cheek.

She could almost hear Papa's calm voice echoing in her head.

But Papa wasn't here, and Rebecca's cheeks already burned with the injustice of the evening and of Maddox's false accusations. She opened her mouth to deliver a scathing reply, but she stopped when a gentle hand lay across her shoulder.

"May I sign for the young lady, Sheriff?" Mrs. Evans' fingers pressed comfortingly. "I believe she can be trusted, and I will take responsibility for ensuring she arrives at the courthouse tomorrow morning on time."

Rebecca's anger evaporated, replaced with a welling of gratitude. She turned tear-filled eyes on the elderly lady and managed a grateful smile.

Sheriff Maddox raked his fingers through his hair, perplexity apparent in his expression. "I don't know that I would advise that, Miz Evans —"

Rebecca's breath caught in her lungs as she waited for his verdict.

The creases cleared from his forehead. "But I'm not eager to keep a woman in my jail overnight. Go on. Just make sure you're in court by nine o'clock. Both of you."

He turned toward his desk in dismissal. Clutching her hat, Rebecca moved as quickly as she could toward the door.

Activity on the street outside had picked up, though suppertime had long since passed. Many of the people appeared to have spilled out of the Lucky Dollar Saloon, though she caught sight of several couples strolling past the storefronts, and light shone in the windows of the general store. Back home in Apple Grove, nobody went out after supper except to do chores. Of course, there was no proper town to stroll around, either.

Mrs. Evans turned to her. "Do you have a place to stay the night, dear?"

Rebecca shook her head. "My intention was to find room and board as soon as I got off the train, but . . ." She waved a hand behind her, in the direction of the jail.

The gray head gave a decisive bob. "You shall stay the night with me, then. Come along."

Another wave of gratitude began to warm the cold knot of uncertainty that had taken hold in Rebecca's stomach. Smiling her thanks, she followed the woman across the street.

Up ahead she spied a familiar-looking bundle in the mouth of an alley. Her bag. With a cry, she hurried over to scoop it up. Pulling the cinched top open, she shoved a hand inside. Two dresses, aprons, under-clothes, *kapps,* her old shoes — *thank You, Lord, for comfortable shoes!* — and . . .

Nothing else.

The chill returned to her insides, and she searched the contents again, her gestures frantic. The paper-wrapped parcel Luke had given her was gone. A sob escaped from her lips.

Mrs. Evans hurried up beside her. "What is it? What is wrong?"

Tears choked her voice. "My money is gone. All of it."

SEVEN

Mrs. Evans led Rebecca to a building on the far end of the street. This area was quiet. There was no glass in the front window as in many they had passed, but the opening had been blocked with boards nailed to the frame.

The widow's lips tightened when she looked at the boards.

"It makes me as mad as a wet hen every time I see it. That new window can't come soon enough to suit me, even if I do have to pay for it myself."

Her stern expression dissuaded Rebecca from inquiring further. Instead, she glanced upward. A sign above the door of the two-story building read in neat letters *Mrs. Evans' Millinery and Mercantile.*

She turned wide eyes on her companion. "You own a shop?"

"Oh, yes." She produced a set of keys from a small pouch at her waist and selected one to fit into the lock. "When my beloved husband lived we ran a mercantile over Missouri way. Well, he ran the store. I kept the books. Lawrence never did have a head for numbers." Her eyes twinkled, and an appealing dimple appeared amid the wrinkles on her cheeks. "After he passed I didn't have the heart to continue, and I didn't know much about running the business anyway. So when the war ended I sold the store and moved west."

"Alone?"

"Oh, yes. There was no one else. We were never blessed with children."

Rebecca looked at the elderly woman with new respect. A short trip such as Rebecca's was one thing, but for a woman to pick up and move into an unknown territory alone was quite another. Rebecca wasn't sure she would be brave enough to attempt such a venture.

Mrs. Evans dismissed her obvious awe with a shrug. "I was younger then and impressed with this town's determination to recover from the terrible ravages of the war. Plus, I liked the name. Moving to Lawrence, Kansas, seemed a fitting tribute to Lawrence, my dear husband. So I settled here and opened up a shop doing something I knew I could handle competently." She pushed the door open and waved toward the dark interior. "Millinery."

Rebecca followed her inside and stood in the doorway while Mrs. Evans bustled across the dark room. A moment later a match was struck, and then warm yellow light flooded the room as a candle's wick glowed to life. Rebecca's jaw went slack as her gaze circled the room. Hat stands decorated every surface, displaying beautiful creations in all shapes and sizes and designs. Against one wall a shelf held bolts of fabric, and next to it, ribbons in every color of the rainbow. Baskets on the floor contained a variety of items, from flowers to silks to feathers. Everywhere she looked, her gaze fell on something new and delightful. The millinery she had visited in Hays City had carried only a fraction of the lovely things she saw here. Breath seeped through her lips in an awestruck, "Oooooohhhh."

Mrs. Evans settled a glass chimney over the candle. "Lock the door, if you will, and bring the key."

Rebecca did as directed, and then she followed her hostess around a long worktable through a doorway into a cluttered storage room. There Mrs. Evans headed up a narrow set of stairs, the candle in her hand shining off dark wood that creaked beneath

Rebecca's feet.

They emerged in a sitting room every bit as charmingly full as the shop below. An upholstered settee was positioned along the far wall, and another wall held two chairs with velvet cushions of deep gold. Even the walls were decorated. Polished frames displayed sketches and paintings with bright colors and even people. While Mrs. Evans went around the room lighting candles, Rebecca dared to step onto the woven rug to inspect a large photograph that seemed to hold a place of honor over an ornate table. It depicted a well-dressed couple, the woman seated, and the man standing behind her with a hand on her shoulder. Though both wore serious expressions, Rebecca glimpsed a hint of sparkle in the woman's eyes. Even though her cheeks were smooth and without wrinkles, Rebecca instantly recognized her.

"That is you."

Mrs. Evans came to stand beside her. "Yes, and that was my husband, God rest his soul." A soft sigh escaped her lips as she gazed upward. "Such a handsome man, my Lawrence."

Rebecca answered politely, though it was hard to see past the stern countenance. "Yes, he was."

She glanced around the room. Their house in Apple Grove contained few adornments. An Amish home reflected a commitment to simplicity and humility, so displays such as this were not indulged. And *Maummi* would certainly have something to say about the photograph because the *Ordnung* strictly forbade graven images of any sort. With an uncomfortable flash of guilt, Rebecca realized she enjoyed the homey atmosphere Mrs. Evans had created with all these frivolous decorations.

"Did you have supper on the train, child?"

At the mention of supper, Rebecca's stomach answered with an embarrassing rumble. Blushing hotly, she covered her waist with her hands. "Please pardon me."

Mrs. Evans laughed. "Don't apologize for what you cannot help. Let's put together a snack."

She led Rebecca back downstairs, where she saw that one corner of the workroom she'd passed through was in use as a kitchen. A stove stood near the front wall, where its heat could warm the entire building in winter. Mrs. Evans set a kettle on the surface and then took a platter from a corner cabinet and set it on a table. She removed an oiled cloth to reveal a wedge of yellow cheese.

"Cut thick slices, dear, while I get the bread."

Rebecca's knife slid through the soft cheese, her mouth watering at the pungent odor released by the blade.

"Mrs. Evans, why did Mrs. Diggs say the saloon is illegal?"

"Because it is. Quite illegal. The Kansas state constitution prohibits the sale of liquor."

The knife paused in the midst of her chore while she turned a surprised look on the elderly lady. "Then why is it open?"

Wrinkled lips pursed as she took another platter from the cabinet. "Because to close it would take money from the pockets of too many influential men."

Rebecca returned to her task, though her knife moved slowly, her attention on her thoughts. "There are saloons in Hays City as well. I saw one this morning."

"Hmm. I expect it's the same all over. That's why the movement is doing such an important work."

"The movement?"

"The Women's Christian Temperance Movement." She picked up another knife and held it poised over a loaf of bread. "Have you not heard of it?"

Rebecca shook her head. Apple Grove was

a small Plain community and isolated from the wider world by choice. No doubt there were many things of which she was ignorant.

The teeth of Mrs. Evans' bread knife made a pleasant sound as it sawed through the crusty loaf. "We stand for decency, Christian living, and social reform." She lifted a glittering gaze that stirred up an answering excitement in Rebecca, though she had no idea what the lady meant by "social reform."

"One day, child, women will have the vote. You wait and see."

Rebecca's excitement dimmed. She'd learned of the practice of voting during her school days, but because Amish communities held themselves separate from the world, it meant little to her.

"And the movement would like to see the saloon close?" she asked.

"We want to see the law enforced. Liquor has been the ruin of many a life." Mrs. Evans bent close to Rebecca and lowered her voice, the twinkle back in her eye. "Though truth be told, my Lawrence was known to take a nip now and then when his rheumatism got the better of him. I don't say that among the ladies." She placed the bread on a smaller plate and whisked the loaf back into the cabinet. "But there were no laws in Missouri like there are in Kansas."

Rebecca arranged the cheese slices on the plate beside the bread and re-covered the wedge. The image of Sheriff Maddox — Colin, she'd heard one of the men call him — rose in her mind's eye. When she stood near him at the jailhouse, she'd been too anxious to do more than notice his looming height. Now she remembered his commanding presence, his muscular build, and the way his hair curled a little behind his ears. A handsome man, to be sure.

A wave of guilt washed away the image. No man was as handsome as her Jesse.

"Why doesn't Sheriff Maddox close the establishments?"

"The poor dear." Mrs. Evans clucked and shook her head. "He does the best he can, though Annie doesn't agree with me on that count. He's in a bad way, what with the town council pulling him one way and the law pulling him the other." Her lips pressed hard on each other again. "And having to deal with that poor excuse for a judge, letting off lawbreakers without proper consequences just so he can prosper from liquor sales. 'The love of money is the root of all evil.' That's what the Good Book says."

The phrase sounded so much like something *Maummi* would say. For a moment Rebecca experienced a stab of homesickness. She blinked against a prickle at the back of her eyes as the kettle began to sing.

Using a towel wrapped around the handle, Mrs. Evans poured steaming water into a teapot she had placed on a tray.

"Bring that plate along, and we'll have a nice tea."

Rebecca picked up the bread and cheese and started after her toward the stairs. Pain sliced through her feet when she took the first step, and she couldn't hold back a hiss.

Mrs. Evans turned. "Is something wrong, child?"

"I purchased new boots this morning." She lifted a foot and thrust it forward so it protruded from the hem of her skirt. The fashionable attire with its shiny buckle didn't look nearly as nice as she'd thought earlier. "The lady in the shop in Hays City said they would stretch, but I do not know if I can wear them long enough for that to happen."

"Stretch? Sit down and let me have a look."

Mrs. Evans set down her tray and turned a straight chair around from its place at the table. Rebecca dropped into the seat thankfully and allowed the woman to unlace the painful shoe. It took a mighty tug for Mrs. Evans to pull it from her foot, and when she did Rebecca couldn't suppress a cry of relief when her cramped toes suddenly found freedom.

Mrs. Evans inspected her foot and then held up the boot. "Child, I'm surprised you're able to walk at all in these. These shoes are far too small for you."

Rebecca stared at the boot. An uncomfortable feeling gathered in her chest. That *Englisch* woman had charged her a high price for boots that didn't fit, and like a simpleton, she'd blithely counted out her money.

Rebecca did not enjoy feeling like a fool.

Colin closed the jailhouse door and stood with his back to its wooden surface, his gaze skimming the street. A few horses were still hitched to the rail outside the Lucky Dollar, waiting for their owners to emerge and ride home. The general store was closed up tight for the night. An orange glow, visible through the open doorway of the smithy, told him Will was working late. In the opposite direction, light shone from most of the windows at the Eldridge Hotel. A trio of gentlemen stood beneath the awning out front. One of them raised a hand to his face, and the fiery tip of a cigar flared in the dark.

Colin stepped off the jailhouse porch and started his nightly stroll down Massachusetts Street. In the two years he'd held this job, he'd discovered the best way to keep peace was to show his face regularly.

Not that his presence had done much good earlier. Drat Annie Diggs and her crusading group of women anyway. It wouldn't surprise him one bit to learn she'd arranged the whole incident to make him look bad one more time before he left town. No doubt the next issue of the *Kansas Liberal* would include a brilliantly worded article describing the confrontation and painting him as a villain for arresting a group of helpless women.

Helpless? Those women were as helpless as a pack of coyotes stalking a chicken coop.

But the new face — that little brunette with creamy smooth skin. He could easily have taken her for an innocent until he saw a glimpse of fire in her expressive eyes. That gal had spunk if he was any judge. Amish? A chuckle rumbled in his chest. A good tale, but not believable. No, she was one of those protesters, recruited by Annie Diggs to swell her numbers.

His step faltered. But why would Annie bring only one lady to join her ranks? One additional female wouldn't make much of a difference to any cause. If there were a bunch, an influx of protesters, they could . . .

He came to a halt in the middle of the street, his thoughts whipping through his mind like winds across the prairie.

What are those ladies planning?

A light came on in an upstairs window. With a start he realized he'd stopped in front of Mrs. Evans' shop, the place where that little gal was holed up for the night. He studied the window. Lamplight glowed around the edges of lacy curtains. A homey sight, but what was going on in that room?

He shook himself. Try though he might, he couldn't picture sweet Mrs. Evans planning and plotting any devious act. Annie Diggs, certainly. Some of the other ladies, maybe. The new girl? Well, sweet smiles and pretty looks might hide a scheming mind.

Whatever it was, he had a bad feeling whatever was brewing wasn't going to hold off for two more weeks until the new sheriff arrived, no matter how much he wished trouble away.

Settling his hat more firmly on his head, he spun on his heel and headed back toward the jailhouse and his bunk in the back room. Tomorrow morning he'd have a word with the judge before court.

And he would keep a close eye on that pretty little newcomer.

EIGHT

The courtroom buzzed with women's voices. Rebecca sat next to Mrs. Evans and tried to look inconspicuous, however unlikely that might be dressed in a prayer *kapp* and plain black Amish clothing amid a sea of brightly colored skirts and fluffy white lace. Perhaps she should have worn her new dress again this morning. She'd considered the idea, but now was glad she'd decided on her customary clothing. The black dress might not be as stylish as those of the other ladies in court this morning, but at least it was familiar. She fingered the seam of her apron. Somehow the feel of *Maummi*'s stitches brought her grandmother closer and gave her courage she didn't possess on her own.

And the relief of well-fitting shoes had done wonders for her mood.

Mrs. Evans had arched an eyebrow when she emerged from the dressing room this morning. "I must say, I thought you might be pulling the sheriff's leg," she'd remarked.

With heat in her face, Rebecca had assured her hostess that she had not touched the sheriff's leg or any other part of him. That had resulted in peals of laughter and an explanation of the strange idiom. Rebecca nodded as though she understood, but she couldn't imagine how such a saying had come about. The ways of the *Englisch* were as mysterious to her as always.

Ladies' voices buzzed around her, discussing the exciting events of the evening past. Yet another mystery, because Rebecca certainly hadn't found the experience of jail exciting.

To her left, on the other side of Mrs. Evans, Annie Diggs sat straight and silent in her chair, her bearing regal and her expression serene. One row behind, Pearl described the conversation she'd had with her husband the night before.

"Then he told me I'd best keep out of trouble and stay home the next time, and I told him I'd go to jail as many times as it takes to —"

The story stopped midsentence when a heavy wooden door to one side of the courtroom opened and three men filed into the room. The first two were strangers. The one in the lead, a gentleman of approximately Papa's age, had a clean-shaven face and neatly oiled graying hair. He went without hesitation to sit behind a desk at the front of the room. The judge, no doubt. The second man was of similar age, though short and stocky enough to be called squat. With a quick step, he crossed to the back of the courtroom, where he settled into a chair in the corner.

Mrs. Evans leaned sideways and whispered in her ear. "That's J.D. Bowerstock, the mayor of Lawrence."

Rebecca nodded absently, her gaze fixed on the third person to pass through the doorway. Colin Maddox. This morning he'd donned a white shirt with a starched collar and string tie beneath his leather vest. She couldn't help notice that his hair had a freshly washed sheen, and she experienced the oddest desire to feel its silky texture. The badge of his office shone on his broad chest. He scanned the gathered crowd of people, and when his gaze fell on Rebecca, his eyes narrowed. With three long-legged strides he crossed the room to stand in front of her.

His whisper rasped through tightened lips. "That's a little extreme, don't you think? Not to mention disrespectful."

Rebecca gazed at him. "What is extreme?"

His eyes shifted to fix on her *kapp,* and his lips twisted into a disapproving line. "Dressing like an Amish person. I don't know what you're trying to pull, but it won't work."

Rebecca was stunned. He didn't believe her. And not only that, but he was openly accusing her of dishonesty. She stiffened her spine and drew breath to deliver a heated reply, but at that moment the *rap-rap-rap* of the judge's gavel rang out in the room, and she snapped her jaw shut.

With a final disapproving look, Colin selected one of the chairs inside the polished wood railing that separated the onlookers from the judge's desk. Hands clasped in her lap, Rebecca lowered her eyes and tried to project a peaceful countenance, as *Maummi* had taught her, while inside she seethed.

"This court will come to order." Judge Tankersley's stern voice echoed in the courtroom, while his glare circled the inhabitants from beneath bushy eyebrows. His gaze came to rest on Colin. "We will hear the accusations against the defendants."

The sheriff rose and held his hat before him. "The official charge is disturbing the peace, your honor. These ladies undertook to divert business from a local establishment at approximately six o'clock last evening, and they refused to disperse when ordered to do so. I had no choice but to arrest them in order to restore peace to the community."

A familiar bald man with muscled arms pushed through the swinging gate in the rail to stand beside the sheriff. "That's right, Tank. They darn near lost me a heap of business, and ended up costing the saloon a round on the house to keep the customers from leaving."

The judge's glower deepened. "How much do you figure that came to, Ed?"

"About six dollars, give or take a shot."

A buzz went up from the ladies around Rebecca. The amount seemed exorbitant, but she knew nothing about the price of "shots."

Colin continued, "Your honor, most of these fine ladies are upstanding residents of Lawrence, and I feel certain this incident is merely a misunderstanding. Perhaps you could see your way clear to dismiss the charges. Again."

"The Dollar ain't going to cover the cost," Ed said. "Make 'em pay up!"

Mrs. Diggs shot out of her chair. "Never!"

The crowd rose hurriedly to stand with her. Rebecca stood shoulder to shoulder with Mrs. Evans on one side and another woman on the other. When everyone else echoed Mrs. Diggs' refusal with utterings of "Ridiculous" and "Us pay for liquor? Impossible!" and "We won't do it," her emotions roiled, swept on the tide of their outrage.

"Outrageous!" she shouted. "We won't do it."

Her voice rang out in the courtroom an instant after everyone else had fallen silent. Mrs. Evans placed a gloved hand on her sleeve, while Mrs. Diggs leaned slightly forward to award her with an approving nod. Colin half turned, one eyebrow cocked, and a flush warmed her face.

"Quiet in the court." The judge's gavel cracked. "Young lady, state your name!"

With something akin to horror, Rebecca realized the judge's question was directed at her. Rational thought evaporated from her mind. "R-R-Rebecca Switzer."

"And just what is your role in this" — his gavel waved in the air in the general direction of the ladies — "demonstration?"

"My role?" Rebecca cast a panicked glance sideways toward Mrs. Evans. "Nothing. I came in on the train only yesterday."

"Her role is the same as the rest of us." Mrs. Diggs' commanding voice filled the courtroom. "We stand on the side of the law and of morality. We stand against evil influences that would destroy men's souls."

"I know what you stand for." The judge's gavel pointed at Rebecca. "I want to hear from her. Approach the bench, Miss Switzer."

Panic snatched the breath from her lungs. For a moment she was so frightened she couldn't move.

Mrs. Evans' fingers tightened on her arm, and she leaned sideways to whisper, "Just tell the truth, child."

One of *Maummi*'s proverbs echoed in her head. *"Truthful lips stand firm, but deceitful words tumble like a dead tree in a storm."*

Aware that every eye in the room was fixed on her, Rebecca stepped out of the row of ladies. From the corner of her eye she saw Colin watching her closely as she passed through the gate in the railing, but she did not look his way. Instead, she approached the judge's desk, her eyes fixed on the floor as was proper for a young lady.

Thank goodness several yards of thick black fabric hid her trembling knees from view.

Colin's fingers gripped the brim of his hat. She might look like a sweet young girl, but pretending a religious conviction you didn't adhere to was downright disrespectful to his way of thinking. He'd known a few Amish men in his time, and he had always been impressed with their firm convictions and tranquility. Her standing there dressed in black with that white *kapp* and laces rubbed him like a burr in his boot.

Unless . . .

Where had she scrounged up a getup like that so quick? Could her claim be true?

Nah. She probably had the clothes with her when she came into town. It was all part of her plan, her act.

Except she didn't look as though she were acting. Would someone who had staged a protest tremble like a kitten in a snowstorm? The hands she clasped in front of her shook visibly, and she gripped them together until her knuckles turned white.

The judge fixed her with a stern look. "Now, young lady, tell me what business you have in Lawrence."

"I . . ." She paused and cleared her throat. "I came to find a man who was reported to live here, though I have since discovered that he does not."

Tank's eyes narrowed. "What do you want with this man?"

From where he sat, Colin saw a red stain

creep up her slender neck. "He is a friend."

A beau? Colin shifted his weight in his chair. Had he spurned her, maybe? Run off with someone else? Or was this another tale to cover up the real reason for her presence in town?

"I see. And I understand you claim to have arrived on the five forty from Hays City last night?" The judged eyed her.

The laces hanging from her head covering swung when she jerked a distrustful look sideways at Colin. He returned it calmly. Why shouldn't he discuss what he knew with the judge? And he'd noted his suspicions about her presence too.

Amish my foot.

She faced forward again. "Yes, that is correct."

"How did you find your way to the Lucky Dollar in time to join a protest that had obviously been planned in advance?"

"I followed other passengers, intending to find water and food and a room for the night. I did not know of plans for a protest."

"Hmm." Tank's stare turned skeptical. "And yet Sheriff Maddox says he saw you arrive and join the protesters without a moment's hesitation."

The look Rebecca turned on him this time held a hint of anger. Colin kept his expression impassive. She was good. Her sincerity certainly made her look as though she was speaking the truth.

Annie's commanding voice filled the courtroom. "Of what is the child accused, your honor?" She made the last two words sound like an insult.

The judge's gaze hardened. "Of nothing yet. All I'm doing so far is trying to get the truth out of this young woman."

Her head snapped forward. "I have spoken the truth, sir."

"And yet you must admit that your story is heavily reliant upon coincidence." He leaned forward over the desk. "I don't put much stock in coincidence."

The narrow shoulders stiffened beneath the heavy black dress. "I have spoken the truth," she repeated, this time in a louder voice. "Dishonesty is not tolerated in an Amish community."

"I'm sure it's not, but how do I know you're really Amish?" The judge's gaze settled on Colin with a conspiratorial wink.

Though she still faced the judge, Rebecca's gaze held Colin's, and he felt himself begin to wither beneath the fire that erupted in her eyes. The same indignant anger he'd witnessed last night had returned.

She did not look away as she spoke.

"There is a saying in my house: Honesty sees honesty. Perhaps he who has no truth in him cannot recognize it in others."

Tittering laughter arose from the women onlookers. Colin remained expressionless. The insult was meant for him, he had no doubt, but the judge apparently thought the barb was directed at him.

Tank grew still behind the desk. "Young woman, what did you say?"

Anyone with a lick of sense could hear the warning in his tone. Colin didn't doubt that Rebecca had sense — normally. But at the moment her face was covered with angry red blotches and the hands that had clutched each other a minute before now clenched and unclenched at her sides. Her chest heaved with fury.

"She's right!" Annie leaped up from her chair, a finger held high in the air. "There is no honesty in this town or in this courtroom. Not when men profit from the destruction of others."

"Mrs. Diggs, I order you to be silent or you'll be removed from the court." The judge's command rose above the female voices who were shouting their agreement. "Yours is not the testimony I am hearing at the moment."

"Speak for us, Rebecca!" someone cried.

Colin straightened. Now it was getting out of hand. If there was a shred of truth in her tale, and he was beginning to suspect there might be, this little gal was messing around in a pasture she knew nothing about, and she was about to disturb a mean ol' bull. Rebecca, still glaring at Colin, opened her mouth to speak. He pressed a finger to his lips in warning.

With a toss of her head that sent her laces flying, she turned away from him and toward the judge.

"I did not come with the intention of joining a protest, but since I arrived I have discovered deception and deceit. It is no wonder Amish men and women hold themselves separate from the world. Those in positions of authority here make money from the illegal trade of liquor. The law is not enforced." She sent another quick glare in Colin's direction. "Truth is held in disregard." She folded her arms across the front of her apron. "It is time for reform."

The ladies erupted in a cheer. Rebecca smiled, clearly pleased with herself.

Oh, brother. That did it.

Colin had never seen Tank so angry, not even when Louis Baldridge's mule got spooked and ran his wagon through the front wall of the bank. While the women cheered, a purple stain colored his face, and his eyes fairly bulged. The gavel crashed down on his desk again and again.

"Young lady, you are in contempt of this court! I find you guilty of disturbing the peace — twice!" He rose from his chair, placed his palms on his desk, and leaned forward. "The fine will be one hundred dollars or ninety days in jail."

The cheers ceased. A collective gasp rose from everyone in the courtroom, Colin's louder than anyone else's. A hundred dollars? Why, nobody could come up with that amount, much less a gal who barely looked sixteen years old.

A shocked silence followed the gasp. Rebecca's mouth had fallen open wider than a jar of pickles at a church supper. Tank abruptly headed toward the exit. At the door he turned and shouted at the assembled women.

"The next time I see any of you in my courtroom, you'll get the same. That goes double for you, Annie Diggs. And you can print that in your paper too. Now go home. Case dismissed!"

His gavel hit the door frame with a fierce blow as he swept through the door and then slammed it behind him.

All the vinegar had gone out of Rebecca

at the pronouncement of her sentence. She turned slowly toward Colin, her eyes glittering with tears.

"I'm going back to jail?"

He struggled to justify the severity of the sentence. True, she'd prodded where she shouldn't, but Colin couldn't help feeling partly to blame. After all, if he hadn't told Tank he suspected her arrival was the signal of a bigger plan to cause trouble in Lawrence, the judge might not have gotten so fired up.

Now he had trouble.

NINE

Rebecca sat in the chair behind the sheriff's desk and tried to staunch the flow of tears with Mrs. Evans' lilac-scented handkerchief while Annie Diggs paced the length of the small jailhouse.

"There, there, dear." Worried lines deepened the creases in the elderly lady's face. "Don't worry. We'll think of something."

"How can I not worry?" Rebecca drew in a shuddering breath. "I don't have one hundred dollars. No one I know has one hundred dollars."

She cast a miserable look at the empty cells. Short of a miracle, one of them would be her home for the next ninety days. And miracles were in short supply for disobedient Amish girls who lost their tempers and loosed their tongues instead of holding them.

If only I had listened to the bishop's sermons more closely. If only I had heeded Maummi's

126

lessons about hot heads and wagging tongues.

"I'm sure the sheriff will convince the judge to change his mind."

No doubt Mrs. Evans intended to sound hopeful, but her words were heavy with doubt.

After the judge had left the room, Colin appeared as dumbstruck as everyone else. He had asked Mrs. Evans to accompany Rebecca to the jail and wait for him while he talked with Judge Tankersley. At least Rebecca had been spared the indignity of being led to jail by a lawman.

Mrs. Diggs paused in her pacing. "We will fight. We have the power of the press behind us, and that is no small thing." Her eyes fairly glowed with determination. "The next issue of the *Liberal* will include a rousing article sure to inspire support for the movement."

Rebecca lowered the handkerchief. A spark of hope flickered to life. "Will the movement free me from jail?"

The woman didn't quite meet her eye. "In time, I have no doubt we shall emerge victorious."

The spark sputtered. "How much time?"

"As quickly as need be." Her hand waved

vaguely in the air. "A week perhaps. Maybe two."

A sob escaped. "But I must find Jesse and return home."

Mrs. Evans' fingers patted Rebecca's back comfortingly. "And so you shall, but in the meantime you shall become a symbol of perseverance, of morality, of justice for our cause. Nothing worthwhile comes without a cost."

Rebecca was beginning to see that. The cost of finding true love had already proven to be higher than she anticipated. Would the price prove worthwhile in the end?

Mrs. Diggs halted in front of the desk, her smile wide with triumph. "My dear, you were magnificent. Not many can maintain their composure and speak with eloquence in the face of such persecution. The movement needs women of your caliber."

Nestled within the flattering words was an invitation. Rebecca wasn't exactly sure what was being asked, but she was certain she had no interest in becoming a symbol of anything, especially if it meant spending two weeks in jail.

"I am none of those things. I am but a Plain girl from Apple Grove."

"That is exactly what we need," Mrs. Diggs insisted. "Wars are waged by generals, but battles are won by soldiers. You, my dear, are a valiant soldier."

"No." Rebecca shook her head. "Amish do not fight. We are peace loving and meek." A flush threatened to flood her face. Her behavior thus far had been anything but meek.

"Perfect." The woman straightened, her smile triumphant. "What did our Lord say? 'Blessed are the meek: for they shall inherit the earth.' Our battle shall be a peaceful one."

The look Mrs. Evans turned on Mrs. Diggs echoed Rebecca's own concern.

"What battle are we talking about?"

"A protest, of course. The idea has just occurred to me. We shall not congregate before a single establishment but march through the streets of Lawrence. Peacefully," she added with a nod at Rebecca.

"But isn't that what we did last night?" Mrs. Evans asked. "And I must say, that didn't turn out exactly as we'd hoped."

"This will be different." Passion burned in Mrs. Diggs' eyes. "This time we have a mission."

Rebecca exchanged a glance with Mrs. Evans. So far she had no idea what was being asked of her. "What is our mission?"

"Why, to set you free, and in doing so to

send a message. We shall raise one hundred dollars, and when we have done so, we shall engage in a victory march. I'll send word to our sisters in the East." Her hands trembled with enthusiasm. "We shall start at one end of town and march down every street, arm in arm, in a peaceful show of solidarity for one of our own who is persecuted. And you, my dear, shall lead us."

She ended with one fist raised high in the air.

Hope rose once again within Rebecca. With a powerful woman like Annie Diggs working on her behalf, perhaps she would see her way clear of this mess after all. But two weeks? Well, that was far better than three months.

One thing still weighed her down. "But what about Jesse?" Fresh tears blurred her vision as she turned her gaze up to Mrs. Evans. "How will I go to him in Cider Gulch if I am in jail?"

"Oh, that." Mrs. Diggs waved a hand. "I neglected to mention that my husband has business in Missouri next week. He has agreed to seek out your beau and deliver your message." She smiled across the desk.

Was this entire trip for naught, then? If she had wanted to send a letter, she could have done that from Apple Grove. "I need to see him. He must hear my message from my own lips."

"Then you shall. Alvin can be extremely persuasive. He will bring your young man to Lawrence." The smile she awarded Rebecca held no hint of uncertainty. "Those of the movement take care of our own."

An image of Jesse loomed in her mind, striding in from the field at eventide, a smile lighting up his face when he caught sight of her waiting by the house. She straightened her shoulders. No price was too great for love.

"What would you have me do?"

Colin stood in the corner of the judge's chamber behind the courtroom, well out of the man's path. Mayor Bowerstock dominated a chair in the far corner.

"Did you see the way that Diggs woman prodded me?" The alarming purple hue of Tankersley's face had settled into a furious red. His voice rose in a feminine mockery. " 'We stand on the side of the law and of morality.' Bah! Blatant defiance of my position in this town, that's what it was."

Colin kept his reply even toned. "She's a trial, no doubt about it."

Bowerstock spoke up. "A trial? She's a menace, that's what she is. If she had her way, women would be running the town, and then where would we be?"

As far as Colin was concerned, there were one or two women in Lawrence who could do a better job than some of the existing members of the town council, but he kept his opinion to himself.

The judge paused to glower toward the mayor. "Did you see the way she led the others? They sat when she sat, stood when she stood, and agreed with every word she said. And the new girl." He raised a finger and stabbed it in Colin's direction. "You were right about her, Maddox. Sweet little female dressed up like a puritan. They brought her in from somewhere to try to make us look like brutes tormenting an innocent."

Colin fingered the brim of his hat. "Well now, maybe I was a bit hasty. She was mighty convincing. She sounded truthful to me."

"Truthful? Did you hear what she said? She called me dishonest!"

"Actually, I think she was calling me dishonest —"

The judge dismissed the exchange. "She was aiming for both of us with the same stone. All three of us, actually." He swept a hand to include the mayor. "We hold positions of authority. We're in this thing to-gether. An insult to one is an insult to all."

Colin cleared his throat. Judge Tankersley had pinpointed the exact reason he'd decided to hang up his badge. If he were going to make a stand with someone, it wouldn't be with these two, and it wouldn't be defending a saloon. "Still, a hundred dollars or ninety days? Don't you think that's a little steep?"

"I do not." Bushy gray eyebrows gathered over stormy eyes. "We have to put a stop to these women now or there'll be no controlling them. It's not just Annie Diggs, either. This group of theirs is everywhere. Ohio. Boston. New York."

"It's true." Bowerstock planted his feet and leaned forward in the chair over his round belly. "Why, if they have their way, every saloon in this country will have to shut its doors."

Over the past two years Colin had kept his opinions to himself and done the work the mayor and the council gave him. After all, as he'd been told many times, his job wasn't to mess around in politics; it was to keep the town clear of outlaws and safe for the townsfolk. Same was true all over Kansas. Some things were best left to politicians. But he'd never had a young woman in his jail before. And right or wrong, he felt responsible for putting her there.

Swallowing back reluctance, he faced the men. "Well, now, liquor sales are against the law. Maybe not in Ohio and New York, but they are in Kansas."

The judge lifted his head slowly, incredulity etched on his features. "Don't tell me you side with these . . . these teetotalers."

Colin raised a hand. "I'm not siding with anybody. I'm just saying they have a point."

"I don't care about their point!" The judge's face once again purpled with the shout. "And I order you not to care about it, either."

Colin's spine became stiff as a rod. "Pardon me?"

Bowerstock's voice took on a wheedling tone. "Now, Maddox, you have two more weeks as sheriff in this town, and after that you can have any opinion you want."

"That's right." The judge's shout echoed harshly in the room. "Until then your job is to keep people from killing each other and carry out the sentences of this court. That's what you're being paid to do, and that's what I expect you to do."

Blood buzzed in Colin's ears. Since being put in charge of keeping the peace in Lawrence, he'd never wanted to punch anyone as badly as he did now. His hat brim crumpled in his tightening grip.

Mustering his resolve, he said calmly, "How about if I leave right now, and the town can keep the rest of its money?"

Bowerstock drew in a sharp breath. The judge's eyes narrowed, and for a moment there was no sound in the room.

Colin returned Tankersley's stare. In the ensuing silence, a list of reasons leaving now was a good idea formed in Colin's mind. He could do that. He could pack his bags, put on his hat, and leave. Half a month's pay wouldn't make or break his plans. His deputies could handle things until Mulhaney arrived. They were good men. Not real aggressive, but decent enough deputies, though not one of the five was ready, or even willing, to step into a sheriff's boots for two weeks.

As the seconds dragged on, Colin felt as though the badge on his vest gained weight. It represented a commitment he'd made, a responsibility he'd agreed to take on. And there was Rebecca, who waited at the jail to begin her sentence, thanks in part to him. Why her presence in his jail should make a difference, he couldn't imagine. But for some unaccountable reason, it did.

Tankersley's features were alive with a visible struggle to regain his composure. He and the mayor exchanged a long glance. When the judge finally spoke, his voice contained a semblance of equanimity.

"Look, Maddox, we may not agree on political matters, but let's not make any hasty decisions. If word spreads that Lawrence is without a sheriff, even for a short time, every outlaw in the territory will be in town by nightfall tomorrow."

"We'll have chaos in the streets," Bowerstock added. "People will get hurt. None of us want that."

With a sense of relief, Colin nodded. "You're right about that."

"All right. Good." The judge lowered his bulk into his chair, clearly relieved.

Now that Tankersley's rage had dissipated, maybe he would listen to a plea. Colin cleared his throat. "About Rebecca Switzer."

Full eyebrows arched over a direct gaze. "The sentence stands."

Colin prided himself on knowing when to make a stand and when to back away.

It was the time to back away.

"Ninety days it is."

There was no way that woman could get together a hundred dollars in five years, let alone ninety days. Which meant she'd spend the entire sentence behind bars.

I won't be here to see the sentence out, though. In less than two weeks she'll be Mulhaney's problem.

Oddly, the thought didn't make him feel better.

TEN

Mrs. Diggs had left by the time the sheriff returned to the jailhouse. When the door opened, hope surged in Rebecca. Maybe he had been able to persuade the judge that last night had been a misunderstanding and her behavior this morning a mistake. She and Mrs. Evans both rose from their chairs, and she stood close to the older woman, drawing strength from her kindly presence.

Colin closed the door, removed his hat, and hung it on a hook on the wall. When he turned, Rebecca caught sight of his expression and her head went light.

"He refused. I'm going to stay in here forever."

"Not forever. Just ninety days. He's a stubborn fool when he sets his mind to a sentence."

She sagged, and Mrs. Evans slipped an arm around her waist. "There, there, you poor child."

Now that her hopes had been dashed, the reality of her situation struck her with force.

"My family —" A sob choked off the word. Papa would be humiliated to discover that his daughter had lost her temper in a most unbecoming manner and been sentenced to jail as a result.

Mrs. Evans led her back to her chair. "I'll personally notify your kin and explain the situation. And I will assure them that I'll oversee your meals and — well, you couldn't be in a finer jail, dear. Colin sounds gruff, and he can be firm, but basically he's a fine young man and real good company."

In the process of lowering herself into the seat, Rebecca stood up again. "No!" She clutched at the widow. "No, they must not know I have become an outlaw."

A low chuckle rumbled from Colin's direction. "Come now, Miss Switzer. You butted heads with a judge. That doesn't make you an outlaw."

She flashed him a frown. "It is hard to see the difference from inside a jail cell."

"Dear, it's only ninety days. Goodness, at my age that's like a night's sleep, and you must tell your family something. If they hear nothing, they will worry to death."

Rebecca felt they wouldn't be concerned to that point, but she must spare them the burden of silence, even though she could do nothing to pardon the shame. *Maummi* would be fit to be tied, Emma's condition was delicate, and Papa . . . she shuddered. She couldn't bear for Papa to know.

"I will write immediately and explain that I will be gone longer than expected."

The letter would have to be very carefully worded to not arouse concern, but as Mrs. Diggs said not long ago, Rebecca was good with words.

Mrs. Evans nodded her agreement to the solution. Then she gave Rebecca a sorrowful look.

"My dear, I'm afraid I must open my shop. Sarah Jardine is coming in for a fitting this morning."

A deepening dread settled over Rebecca. Without the presence of her new friend, she would be truly alone in this dreadful place.

"Of course you must go. Thank you for staying with me as long as you have. I shall be fine." She tried to steady her trembling lips. "Perfectly fine."

The wrinkled face turned sorrowful. "I'll be back as soon as I can."

Mrs. Evans gathered her into a gentle hug. Surprised, Rebecca stood for a moment with her arms hanging awkwardly at her sides. But the warmth of the embrace gave her a sense of comfort that helped to stay the quiet panic that threatened her composure, and she returned the hug.

"Try not to worry, child. Annie won't let you down. This ordeal will be over soon enough."

When she had gone, an uncomfortable silence descended on the jailhouse. A quick glance at Colin told her he looked nearly as miserable as she felt. Why? He wasn't a prisoner. Her suspicions from the courthouse returned. The judge had known what time she arrived in town, and obviously he had been told the circumstances of her joining the ladies in front of the Lucky Dollar Saloon. A guilty look had descended on the sheriff's face during the court session.

She didn't filter the antagonism from her tone. "You told Judge Tankersley I came to town to cause trouble."

He didn't bother to deny it. "From where I was sitting, that's what it looked like."

"*You* are the reason I must go to jail."

"Oh, no." His palms rose in front of him to ward off her accusation. "You did that on your own by accusing the judge of dishonesty in his own courtroom. And all that stuff you said about reform? You might as well have put a noose around your own neck and tossed him the other end of the rope."

Because he was right, Rebecca had no answer, though she wouldn't have lost her temper if the judge hadn't accused her of lying about her Amish roots. And she knew where that idea came from.

Well, if she was going to become a symbol of the movement by being in jail, she might as well get on with it. With a glare at the sheriff, she squared her shoulders and stepped to the center of the room, facing the empty cells.

"Which one is mine?"

The words snapped out of her mouth with more force than she intended. Better that than tears, which might rise again if she let go of the fierce irritation she felt toward Colin.

"Take your pick."

They were identically barren. She selected the one on the far right, because it had a direct view of the front window that let out onto Massachusetts Street. As she marched into it, she grabbed a bar on the door and swung it after her. Better to close herself in than have him do it. The door shut with a metallic clink.

Rebecca stood in the center of the cell and turned in a slow circle, examining her prison. It was about the same size as her bedroom back home, though there were no clothing hooks on the wall, no shelves for her *kapps* and folded aprons, no colorful quilt to give the room a much-needed touch of cheer. A cot-style bunk against each side wall left an open area in the center, and the bare wooden floor was rough and dirty. She suppressed a shudder. How often had the floor been swept? Or the rough wool blanket that lay across the bunk been washed?

She turned to find Colin watching her through the bars.

"Do you mind if I ask you a question?" Curiosity colored his tone and the speculative stare he'd fixed on her.

She didn't trust her voice, so she nodded.

"You were telling the truth, weren't you?" His gaze swept her dress and *kapp.* "You are Amish."

Finally. Her chin shot upward. "I do not . . . pull men's legs."

He folded his arms and studied her. "So the real reason you came to Lawrence is to chase down this Jesse Montgomery?"

His choice of words brought uncomfortable warmth to her cheeks. She was not chasing Jesse down. She was merely making sure their love had an opportunity to fully blossom.

He must have noticed her blush. The grin that widened came dangerously close to being a smirk. "Had a spat, did you? A lover's quarrel?"

"We did not quarrel," she replied with some heat.

"Then why did he run off?"

She didn't intend to discuss Jesse with someone who had proven himself disinclined to believe her, especially not when he stood there watching her with open disdain. With a toss of her head, she turned away and stared at the wall.

"All right. Then answer this. What did Mrs. Evans mean when she said your ordeal would be over soon and 'Annie won't let you down'?"

Having opened her mouth far too often this morning, Rebecca clamped it tightly shut. No doubt he would hear of her part in the peaceful protest soon enough.

Whatever that part might prove to be.

She backed up and lowered herself to the edge of the bunk, determined to maintain silence on the matter.

"Fine," he said. "But it's going to be a long ninety days, Miss Switzer, so you might as well climb off of your high horse and be pleasant."

Sitting down on the bunk, she crossed her arms. Oh, she would be pleasant. She would be so pleasant he would be praying for mercy.

Colin sat at his desk and tried to ignore the young woman in the cell to his right. She was perched on the edge of the bunk, stiff as a sheet in the wind. Every so often he glimpsed movement out of the corner of his eye when she rearranged her folded hands in her lap or, once, when she fingered one of the laces that hung from her white *kapp*. He would have sworn she was staring at him, but when he looked up her gaze was fixed on the wall to the right of the front door, papered with wanted posters. She was a stubborn one. Where had Annie found an Amish woman to fight her war?

He rose from his chair and went to the front window for the third time in the past quarter hour. Massachusetts Street bustled with activity. Riders on horseback could be seen, intent on business or other activity in town. Wagons rolled by, and ladies nodded to each other as they strolled from the shade of one store's awning to another. The two-story buildings lining the town's busiest street cast no shadow with the sun almost directly overhead. Almost lunchtime. Colin would have to run down to the diner and arrange to have meals brought in for his prisoner. Ninety days. He shook his head. Brutal. Why had Tank decided to make a lesson out of this woman?

A noise behind him made him turn. Rebecca had risen and stood near the cell door, her gaze fixed on something across the room. "Sheriff? Who is that?"

Colin followed her gaze to the wall of wanted posters. "Which one?"

"That one." Her arm extended through the bars to point. "The one with the mustache."

Almost every outlaw on the wall had a mustache. He crossed the floor in a couple of steps and tapped one. "This one?"

"No. Two over from him. The one with the pointy chin."

He stepped back, studied the pictures, and located a pointy chin.

"This? That's Cleon Benton. Looks like a sweet-faced little boy, doesn't he?"

She shook her head. "Not really. Tell me about him."

"Cleon?"

She nodded. "Yes. Who is he?"

"He's far from an innocent. He's wanted for killing three men while robbing a bank down in Arizona Territory a few years back. And then he robbed a stagecoach. Shot the driver and four passengers."

"I saw him recently."

"Benton?" He shook his head. "I don't think so. Cleon hasn't been seen in these parts for more than two years. Word has it he's down along the Mexican border. He doesn't show himself often. Too many people would like to collect the bounty for turning him in."

Her gaze fixed on the poster. "Pointy chin. Stocky appearance. A large black mole near his right eye. I saw him on the train yesterday."

A tingle itched beneath Colin's scalp. Benton was a notorious outlaw and mean as a snake. If he was heading for Chicago, he was up to no good. He snatched the poster off the wall and stepped closer to the cell.

"Look again. Are you certain?"

She studied the picture and then nodded confidently. "He's older now and has more whiskers on his face, but that's the man I saw on the train. I'm certain."

Colin's mind raced. The train was headed for Chicago and would have arrived there sometime this morning. He'd notify the authorities, and maybe they would have a good chance of capturing the no-good outlaw.

He turned and grabbed his hat off the

wall. Setting it on his head, he reached for the door handle.

"I'll be back."

"Where are you going?

Irritation flared. He wasn't accustomed to explaining his errands to a prisoner.

"I'm going to notify the Chicago authorities, Miss Switzer. Okay?" Street noise invaded the jailhouse when he opened the door.

Rebecca's voice stopped him. "Okay, but Benton isn't in Chicago."

Skidding to a halt, he turned to face her. Dread sprouted in the pit of his stomach. From the expression on her face, he knew what she was going to say, but he prayed he was wrong.

"You just said he was on the train."

"He was." Her hands clutched the bars of her cell door. "He got off when I did. He's here, in Lawrence."

Eleven

Colin strode to the livery stable, his mind on Benton. He started to pass the diner, but then he remembered dinner was coming up and Miss Switzer had to be fed. One or two of his deputies usually stopped in for a bite to eat about this time.

A woman stood at a tall worktable against the far wall. She glanced up from cutting a thick slice of pie.

"Howdy, Sheriff. Stew's good today. Can I get you a bowl?"

"Sounds good, Alice. Why don't you put it on a tray with a piece of that pie." He scanned the patrons seated at the small tables scattered around the room, and spied the person he sought. "Hal will take it over to the jail as soon as he finishes his dinner. Put it on the town's account."

The man stood, shoved a crust of bread in his mouth, and rounded the table. "I heard we have us a permanent prisoner, Colin."

A man seated at a full table spoke up. "Yeah, and I heard it was a woman."

"The way I heard it," one of his tablemates said, "it was a whole bunch of women, and the sheriff arrested them for singing hymns in the street."

From across the room, someone remarked, "It takes a brave man to round up a whole herd of singing women, don't you know?"

Male laughter joined and grew louder. Colin raised his eyes to the ceiling and shook his head. Their good-natured teasing didn't set well today. "Go ahead. Laugh it up."

To Hal, he said, "Do me a favor, would you? Take that tray over to the jail and stay there until I get back."

The man chuckled. "I heard she's a right pretty gal. My wife won't take kindly to me sitting alone with another woman."

Hal's wife was known for having a jealous streak a mile wide.

"Tell Abigail that Miss Switzer is Amish. That should quiet her down." He turned toward the door. "Is James in the telegraph office?"

Hal nodded. "He was when I walked by

half an hour ago."

Outside, Colin crossed the street and rounded the side of the two-story brick building that housed Randall's Livery, Feed, and Stable. The stables were out back, and for a small weekly fee he boarded his horse there. He caught sight of Billy, the young man who took care of the business for Mr. Randall.

"Howdy, Sheriff," he called. "I'll saddle Gus up for you."

"Thanks, Billy."

When Colin approached his horse's stall, Gus thrust his head eagerly over the gate to accept his hand. Colin obliged by rubbing the velvety muzzle, speaking in a low, soothing voice, his mind busy. What would Benton be doing in Lawrence? Whatever his reason, it meant trouble. If he'd arrived last night, then he must be keeping a low profile, or word would have spread through town like fire through a woodpile. The townspeople had been preoccupied with his clash with the women last night and this morning. The gossips only had so much tongue space to go around.

If Benton had arrived on the train, that meant he didn't have a horse.

Billy returned with his saddle. They led Gus out of the stall and together lifted the load in place.

"Billy, have you had any out-of-town customers recently?"

The young man stooped to grab the girth beneath Gus's barrel.

"No, sir. Business has been a mite slow these days."

Colin frowned. Randall's wasn't the only livery in town. He needed to ask around to see if Benton had inquired about hiring a horse anywhere else.

Easing into the saddle, he nodded. "Much obliged."

The lunch tray balanced on her knees, Rebecca had just taken the last bite of savory stew when the jailhouse door opened and a woman swept in. She stood inside the doorway, alert eyes moving as she scanned the room. By her smooth skin and robust figure, Rebecca judged her to be only a few years older than her own seventeen years. Papa would say she looked like forty miles of bad road, but not unkindly. Deep-set eyes and a hawkish nose would forever deny her of claims to beauty, but her lips were full and her waist trim beneath the lace and ruffles of her dress.

The young woman caught sight of her, and her eyes widened. Seconds stretched as they stared at each other through the cell bars. Rebecca had no idea why the stranger should dislike her, but the woman's lips pressed into a disapproving line.

"Sugar bun!" The deputy who had introduced himself as Hal rose from Colin's chair and walked around the desk. "What are you doing here?"

Her gaze focused on the prisoner. "The boy delivered your message, and I came to see for myself."

The possessive way she snagged his arm answered Rebecca's question. With something akin to wonder, she realized the young woman didn't dislike her. She was jealous of her husband's affections.

Rebecca set her spoon down and moved the tray from her lap to the bunk beside her. With a dab at her mouth with the napkin, she rose and came to stand by the cell door and calmly returned the young woman's frank stare, her expression carefully pleasant.

"Come and meet Rebecca." Hal urged her toward the cell.

The woman sent a sharp glance sideways. "Rebecca?"

"Miss Switzer, sugar bun. You know. The prisoner."

Rebecca winced at the term.

"This here is Abigail Lawson." He offered a tentative grin, and his throat convulsed repeatedly. "My wife."

Rebecca dipped her head in a sedate nod, like *Maummi* at her most composed. "Pleased to meet you, ma'am. Your husband speaks well of you."

A slight exaggeration. Though Hal had mentioned his wife when he delivered Rebecca's lunch, for the most part he had sat tongue-tied behind the desk while she ate. Hal shot her a grateful look.

"You have been discussing me?"

"Oh, no. Not discussing you," Hal assured her. "Just . . . talking."

"Your husband speaks so devotedly of you that it has made me long for the time when I will be reunited with the one I love." Rebecca took Mrs. Evans' handkerchief from the waistband of her apron and dabbed at the corner of her eye.

The woman's icy resolve thawed a fraction. "Oh. You have a husband?"

"Not a husband." Suspicion returned to the gaze fixed on her, and Rebecca went on to explain. "Not yet, but soon. He is the most handsome, the most hardworking, and the most wonderful man in all of Kansas." She didn't hold back, her emotions pouring like fresh spring water. "And I would be with him this moment if it weren't for this dreadful misunderstanding."

The front door opened to admit Mrs. Evans. Draped over one arm was the soft knit blanket that had covered Rebecca's bed last night, and the other arm was looped through the handle of a laden basket.

She smiled. "Abigail, how nice to see you. How are you, dear?" Without waiting for an answer, she addressed the deputy. "Hal, I've brought a few things to make Rebecca more comfortable." She raised the arm with the blanket in his direction, an inquiry on her face.

Hal's brows knitted together. "I don't know, ma'am. The sheriff didn't say nothin' about making her more comfortable. Maybe you ought to wait till he gets back."

"Nonsense." The basket swung when she pointed in Rebecca's direction. "This cell might be fine for brigands and drunkards, but certainly not for a lady. You can't expect the poor child to sleep on a bare bunk. She has certain needs not shared by a man." She turned a smile on Abigail. "Tell him, dear."

She nodded. "That's true enough, Hal. You've only to look at my bureau and yours to see the difference. Why, mine is overflowing, while yours is barely half full."

The tip of Hal's ears turned pink. "But,

honey cake, this is a jail. It ain't no woman's bedroom."

"It is now," Mrs. Evans sent a private wink toward Rebecca. "And as such, it is entirely unacceptable."

"Well . . ." Hal glanced toward Rebecca and then back at Abigail. "I guess maybe a few things would be all right."

"Excellent." Mrs. Evans turned to swing the door open and call outside. "You can bring everything in, boys!"

To Rebecca's delight, the first of a small troop of boys filed into the jailhouse, each with an armload of "necessities."

Sighing, the deputy stepped back when Abigail started to assist.

"Stay outta the way, Hal. This is woman's work."

"Gladly, sweet cakes."

The man stepped to the wall and crossed his arms.

The stale odor of the empty stockyards assaulted Colin when he approached the railroad office. The stocks stood empty, row after row of boxed-in pens stretching past the outskirts of town, the soil dry and uneven inside from thousands of cattle hooves that had tromped through over the years, ever since the railroad came to Lawrence. The coming summer would see a fair number of herds sent this way, though not nearly as many as in years past. The number of cattle driven north for shipment back east had dropped off as ranchers attempted to grab whatever land they could and build fences to establish legal occupancy, thereby dividing the open ranges and cutting off the cowboys' easy access to the north. Between the land rush and the railroad companies expanding their rails in the south, the days of the great cattle drives were drawing to an end. Colin considered that an inescapable sign of progress, but a sad one.

He looped Gus's reins around a post in front of the office and took the stairs two at a time. The man behind the ticket window glanced up when the door opened.

"How do ye, Sheriff?"

"Just fine, Pete. Just fine." Colin approached the window. "Were you working last night when the five forty pulled in?"

"Yes, sir." The little man's lips gathered in disapproval. "Ten minutes late, she was. Pulling a full load and running a little sluggish because of it."

Colin slipped the poster out of his vest, unfolded it, and laid it on the counter facing the railroad agent. "Did you see this man get off?"

Pete picked up a pair of spectacles and set them on the bridge of his nose.

"Cleon Benton," he read. "Wanted for robbery of the Yuma Bank, and cold-blooded killing of three honest men." He looked up, eyes made even wider by his lenses. "He sounds as mean as they come. You think he's in Lawrence?"

"I hope not, but I have a witness who was on that train and says she saw him get off here."

"Would that be the woman you have locked in the calaboose?"

Apparently everybody in town knew about the little Amish girl. Did they all think him a fool for locking her up? "That's her."

"I saw her get off the train. Fine-looking woman. Nice figger. Lame, though. Walked with a limp."

Colin tapped on the poster to redirect the man's wandering attention. "Did you see him?"

Pete picked up the poster and pulled it closer, almost to his nose, and then he held it out at arm's length.

"Why, I swan. I believe I did. There was a man looking something like this that got off. He looked a bit different, though."

Exactly what Rebecca had said. "He has a beard now?"

"Yes. And his hair was longer than this fella." He squinted at the poster again. "Might be the same." He removed his glasses and slid the poster back across the counter. "You'd have to ask the conductor to be sure. He'll be back through town in a week or so."

"Much obliged, Pete." Colin refolded the poster and slipped it back inside his vest as he exited the railway office. A week. If Benton had gotten off that train, the town wouldn't have a week.

Maybe it wasn't Benton. Or if it was, maybe he'd turned over a new leaf. There had been no unusual town activity except from the women, and that was beginning to be a normal nuisance.

His imagination was playing tricks on him. He wanted to get out of here so badly he was conjuring up trouble.

With a snort, Colin swung up into his saddle. Maybe the river would start running north too. And pears would grow on apple trees.

With a gentle tug on the reins, he turned Gus toward Ohio Street. There were several small liveries in town, and he intended to check them all. And the boardinghouses. If Cleon Benton had landed in Lawrence, he'd find him and put a stop to whatever the outlaw had planned.

Thirteen more trouble-free days, Lord. That's all I ask.

A bad feeling balled up in the pit of his stomach as though it was fixing to stay for a while. With a notorious outlaw hiding somewhere in Lawrence, thirteen days seemed like a long time, even for the Lord.

The sun's warm rays were beginning to touch the chimneys on the west side of Massachusetts Street when Colin left Gus at the livery stable. He nodded his thanks to Billy as he handed him the reins and headed for the jailhouse. Activity on the busy street had dropped off, as it always did in late afternoon. He gave an absent greeting to the people he passed, his mind on the conversations that had occupied his afternoon.

Benton had not hired a horse at any of Lawrence's liveries. Based on that fact alone, Colin would have doubted Rebecca's and Pete's accounts. What could a man do without a horse? He might not need it in town, but whatever he had planned would include a fast getaway. Maybe the man on the train only looked like Benton.

But then Colin had stopped at a few boardinghouses over on Louisiana Street.

At the fourth, he'd found the verification he sought.

"Yes, that man rented a room here last night." Mrs. Sawyer, proprietor of the Sawyer House, had nodded in the affirmative when she saw the poster. "He came in on the train all the way from California, he said."

Excitement had prickled along the back of Colin's scalp again. "Is he here?"

"No. He said he only needed a bed for the night and left this morning right after breakfast." Her eyes rounded when she read the words on the poster. "Are you sure this is right, Sheriff? He seemed like such a nice man. Soft spoken and polite. And he paid cash."

Colin shook his head. "He doesn't plan to come back?"

"Didn't mention a word about it. 'Course, you never know."

Benton had woken early, eaten a hearty breakfast, and left. Mrs. Sawyer did not see which way he went.

"You'll send word to me if he shows up tonight?"

"I will, Sheriff. Sure you won't have a piece of mince pie and cold milk?"

"Thank you, ma'am, but it's getting late and I need to be moving on."

161

When he approached the jailhouse later, the door opened. A woman exited, her skirts swishing with every step. Colin recognized Abigail, Hal's wife. He stepped up to hold the door for her and with his free hand tipped his Stetson.

"Hello, Miz Lawson. You look lovely this afternoon."

The look that overtook her features when she recognized him made Colin step backward. If he'd been a bug, she would have squashed him beneath her boot.

"Sheriff Maddox, you should be ashamed!"

Colin could only stare. "Me? Why?"

"Arresting such a charming and vulnerable young woman as Rebecca." She tilted her nose in the air and stared at him. "And then to incarcerate her without even the basic necessities. It's outrageous. I hope you're happy."

With a toss of her head, she flounced off. Colin stood with his hand on the door handle, watching her departure. Basic necessities? What was that supposed to mean?

Shaking off the encounter, he stepped around the door and across the threshold.

And stopped at the sight that met him.

The jailhouse had been transformed.

Correction.

The cell on the far right had been transformed.

Color blared from behind the steel bars. Bright blankets and hand-stitched pillows covered both bunks. A small ornate table rested against the wall beneath the window, with a lacy tablecloth and a tray with a teapot and fancy cups, and a rocking chair was nestled between the foot of the nearest bunk and the cell bars.

And . . . was that silver cutlery he saw reflected in the soft glow of lamplight?

Inside the cell and standing on a chair — his desk chair, he noted with increasing disbelief — stood Deputy Hal Lawson, his arms above his head as he fussed with putting a frill-covered curtain in place across the iron bars. On the floor beside him another deputy, John Callahan, stood with his arms full of fabric, feeding it up to Hal a bit at a time.

Colin took in the scene with growing disbelief. Then his bellow filled the small room.

"What in *tarnation* is going on here?"

TWELVE

Rebecca turned a frown on the sheriff when his shout rang in the room. Amish men never raised their voices. They met each circumstance with a peaceful countenance and voiced their thoughts only when they could maintain a soft-spoken equanimity. She much preferred that to this unseemly display.

Mrs. Evans, who had been overseeing the hanging of the curtains, left her vantage point in the center of the cell and walked toward Colin.

"Don't take on like a wounded moose, Sheriff. We've only brought a few things to make our Rebecca's stay more comfortable."

"A few things?" He pointed at the tea tray. "You have turned my jail into a ladies' boudoir!" He glanced toward his deputy, who had paused in his work. "Hal, what are you doing?"

Hal pointed at the elderly lady, who stood with her hands folded in front of her, projecting an atmosphere of serenity.

"She made me."

Colin's color rose when he looked at Mrs. Evans. "This is a jail, not a boardinghouse."

The second deputy, John, turned a shy smile toward Rebecca before he spoke. "These cells were made for outlaws, Colin, and for men. You can't expect this woman to be treated like a . . . a prisoner."

"She *is* a prisoner."

"I know, but. . . ." The man's voice faded.

"Take this stuff down. She's broken the law and she's not going to get any favors here. Understand?"

Rebecca opened her mouth to speak in her defense, but Mrs. Evans stepped forward.

"I can hardly believe you're taking on so over a few comforts. If I am not mistaken, there was nothing in the judge's directive that said our Rebecca must live in uncivilized surroundings."

She might have been scolding a child. Rebecca hid a smile. Colin's mouth opened a few times before any words came out. When they did, his tone was softer, with more respect.

"But, ma'am, that's a rug." He pointed

165

toward the cell's floor. "Jails don't have rugs."

Rebecca glanced at the beautiful floor covering. When word spread that Mrs. Evans intended to furnish her cell, Mrs. Diggs had sent it over along with a set of soft pillows that were far more luxurious than anything Rebecca had back home in Apple Grove. In fact, she felt a little guilty, even sinful, for the opulence of her new surroundings. Amish lived plainly and simply. There was nothing plain or simple about this cell now. Why, the furnishings were nicer than any she'd ever seen anywhere.

Mrs. Evans replied evenly, "And when Rebecca is gone, the rug will also be gone."

Colin's gaze rose again to Hal, whose arms were high above his head as he fixed the curtain in place. "Will you stop that? Curtains are not a necessity."

Mrs. Evans eyebrows arched high. "They most certainly are. A woman needs her privacy."

"They're done anyway." Hal lowered his arms and got off the chair. He and John stood back and admired their handiwork.

Colin shook his head. Rebecca found herself shamelessly enjoying his discomfiture. She went to the small table Abigail had kindly supplied and touched the side of

Mrs. Evans' teapot to test the temperature. Still warm. With a guileless smile, she lifted the pot and held it toward the sheriff.

"Can I tempt you with a cup of tea?"

From the deepening color of his face, she thought he might explode, but with an obvious struggle, he gained control before replying. "No, I would not like a cup of tea." Not a shout, but the words were spoken in a voice quivering with barely controlled anger.

With a glare for his deputies, he walked into the cell, snatched up his chair, and set it down behind his desk with such force that Rebecca thought the wooden legs might crack. His eyes narrowed.

"Don't you two have something productive to do? Like your jobs, if you want to keep them?"

Hal and John tipped their hats at the ladies. Then they strapped on their gun belts and headed for the door.

"Thank you for helping," Rebecca called after them.

"Yes, ma'am. Yore welcome." Hal closed the door behind the men's retreating backs.

"It's time for me to go as well, dear." Mrs. Evans bent to pick up her empty basket and then straightened. "I'll be back later. Is there anything you need me to bring?"

Rebecca opened her mouth to answer, but Colin interrupted with, "How could she possibly need anything else? It's all in there with her already."

She gave him a dour look and then smiled at Mrs. Evans. "You and the other women have been most kind. Thank you."

A veined hand waved in dismissal. "The women of the movement take care of their own."

When the door closed, Colin rounded on Rebecca. "I thought you said you weren't part of their organization."

"I wasn't." She leaned out of the cell and caught hold of the bars to pull the door shut. "But now I am."

She turned her back on his darkening expression and surveyed her surroundings. The floor covering was as brightly patterned as any quilt and cushioned her step. The coverings on the bunks were soft and cozy, the pillows plump and decorated with lovely needlework. Yes, this was much, much nicer than anything she had at home. Fingers of guilt tapped at the edges of her conscience.

I am on rumspringa.

A smile twitched her lips. What was *rumspringa* without a few luxuries that would be forever out of her reach after she returned home to join the church?

Ignoring Colin, she poured the last cup of tea for herself and settled into Abigail's cushioned rocking chair to enjoy it.

Clouds blocked out the moon when Colin returned from his nightly walk. The scent of rain was in the air. All seemed well in the streets of Lawrence, though he had not ventured much beyond Massachusetts Street. It didn't sit right with him to leave Rebecca alone in her fancified cell for very long, especially with Benton hovering somewhere nearby.

An unsettled feeling gnawed at him. He'd alerted his deputies to keep an eye out for the outlaw, but the day passed with no sightings. It seemed Benton had walked out of the Sawyer House and vanished.

Colin didn't think he could be that fortunate.

He opened the jailhouse door and was met by the warm glow of lamplight. The curtain had been pulled back and latched to one side, giving him a clear view of the cell's interior.

Rebecca sat on the rocking chair, her head lowered over a piece of stitchery. She worked with such focus that she hadn't heard the door, and he paused to study her. The soft light turned her white *kapp* yellow and brought out a chestnut gleam in the thick strand of hair that had come lose from its binding to hang down her shoulder. The smooth skin of her cheek shone like fresh cream. Such a homey sight, even viewed through the bars of a cell, loosened the knots that searching for Benton had tied in his gut.

Her head rose. Spots of pink appeared on the creamy cheeks when she saw him.

Embarrassed to be caught staring at her, Colin turned away to shut the door and hang his hat on its hook.

"Alice seemed pleased at the compliment you paid her fried chicken when I took the tray back to her." He walked to the desk. "She told me to ask if there's anything special you want for supper tomorrow night."

Colin had scoffed at the waitress and informed her that prisoners did not order their meals like paying customers. Her answering glower had set him back on his heels. It seemed that every woman in this town had decided to draw a line between the law and Rebecca, and they had united in her behalf. As far as he could tell, she hadn't done a single thing to encourage the behavior. She'd been in that cell all day. Unless you would call her declaration about

being part of their organization now threatening.

*It's Annie Diggs. And Mrs. Evans causing
the trouble.*

Problem was he had more to worry about
than the women. Namely, Cleon Benton.

"Please tell her I can't think of anything,
but I will be thankful for whatever she
makes."

He glanced up to see a fretful frown on
her face.

"I am unaccustomed to being served. If I
could, I would gladly lend a hand."

"Well, you can't. You're in jail."

"You need not remind me. I know where
I am."

"Do you know what kind of trouble you're
in?" he wondered. She might be taking this
mildly, but did she know exactly how long
ninety days in a tight cell was?

"The Lord will protect me."

"He'd better, because in less than two
weeks I'm not going to be around to help
fight your battles."

She carefully drew thread through her
cloth. "I wasn't aware you were fighting my
battles."

Colin bit his tongue. What was the matter
with him, snapping at a woman like that?
This woman had him feeling sorry for her

171

one minute and mad enough to explode the next. He made a show of unbuckling his gun belt and laying his pistol on the surface of his desk, ready to pick up at a moment's notice.

"Did you find the outlaw with whiskers?" she asked in a conversational tone.

His glance slid to the wall, where the creased wanted poster hung once again. "No. Didn't see a single sign of him."

"Do you believe I saw him?"

"Others saw him too."

"Really? Who?"

"Will, the railroad agent. Miz Sawyer at the boardinghouse."

"Then I wasn't mistaken."

"Maybe a man who resembled Benton got off that train with you."

"Perhaps, or maybe he was merely traveling through and he's left town."

Colin shook his head. "It's possible. Until then, I'm praying —" He snapped his mouth shut. He'd been about to say *I'm praying he holds off whatever he's planning for another thirteen days.*

Rebecca glanced up. "You are praying?" she prompted.

He amended his comment. "I'm praying nobody gets hurt."

The smile that curved her lips transformed

her features. Colin was struck anew with how lovely she was.

"I will pray that too."

She bent to her stitching. Colin studied her for a moment longer, though why he should be surprised at her statement he didn't know. Raised in an Amish family, of course she prayed. Clearing his throat, he asked, "What are you working on?"

"I'm mending a seam." She paused in her work and spread out the fabric bunched in her lap to reveal a lady's dress. "Mrs. Evans suggested that I put my time to good use." She lifted a charming grin toward him. "*Maummi* despairs of my cooking skills, but I am most handy with a needle and thread."

"*Maummi?*"

"My grandmother. She takes care of Papa and me."

The door opened, and Colin turned and crossed the space between him and his gun in two steps. His hand dropped away from the weapon when he spied Mrs. Evans and a small boy.

"Oh, there you are, Sheriff. I was watching for you through my upstairs window, but I didn't see you return."

The lady entered the room and thrust her burden into his hands. Colin found himself holding a washbasin and pitcher. She reached into a pouch that hung from her wrist and extracted a coin.

"There you go, young man. Thank you for helping an old lady."

The curly headed boy pocketed the coin with a grin and handed her a bulging tapestry bag. She shut the door behind him and then brushed past Colin. Voluminous skirts swished as she crossed to his desk, opened a drawer, and extracted the ring holding the keys to the cells.

Colin found his voice. "Ma'am, what are you doing?"

She gave him a surprised look on her way to Rebecca's cell. "I'm settling in for the night." The lock turned with a click, and she entered to place her bag on one of the bunks.

"What? No." He shook his head. "That's where I draw the line. Only prisoners are allowed to stay overnight in the jail."

Without a pause, Mrs. Evans bustled over to him and took the washbasin out of his hands.

"Oh? And where are you going to sleep, Sheriff Maddox?"

"In there, where I always do." He pointed through the open doorway beside the third cell.

Gray eyebrows arched high on the

wrinkled forehead. "Not thirty feet away from a young, single woman? Alone all night without a chaperone? I think not."

Search though he might, Colin could not come up with an acceptable argument. He watched her enter the cell, place the basin on the small table, and then return to swing the door shut behind her. The smile she awarded him through the bars held the smugness of one who knew she'd had the last word. She reached out and hooked the keys around a peg near the cell.

"Pleasant dreams, Sheriff."

With a flick of her wrist, she unlatched the colorful curtain and pulled it closed.

Dear Papa and Maummi,

I am writing to assure you that I arrived safely in Lawrence. I have found a very nice room at a price I can afford, and I am using my time in useful industry doing mending for a milliner.

My circumstances have altered, and I will be gone several weeks longer than expected. Do not worry, for I am fine. As I explained in the letter I left, my absence is only temporary. When my rumspringa ends, my intention is to come home to Apple Grove.

Rebecca

She read the letter out loud one last time while the ink dried. Though nothing would soothe her family's concern for her, the careful wording should serve to placate them for the time being. Guilt nabbed her when her gaze fell on the phrase *a very nice room at a price I can afford.* She glanced at her surroundings. True, every word. Her cell had become quite nice, thanks to Mrs. Evans and the ladies of Lawrence, and because it was free, she could afford it.

The fact that she could afford nothing at all need not be stated.

Mrs. Evans, comfortable in her nightdress and frill-covered sleeping cap, peered at the paper.

"Are you certain you shouldn't tell them of your circumstances, child? If you were my daughter or granddaughter, I would want to know the truth."

The thought of Papa's face heavy with sadness, and *Maummi*'s silent fretting, brought the sting of tears to her eyes. Sniffing, she folded the letter.

"No. It is better this way."

She folded the letter and wrote Papa's name and *Apple Grove, Kansas,* in careful script on the front. When she had applied a few drops of wax to seal it, she handed it to the elderly woman, who secreted it in her bag.

"I will take it to the post office in the morning," she promised.

When the light had been doused and they were both cozy in their bunks beneath the soft coverings, Rebecca lay staring into the darkness. In four days' time, Alvin Diggs would leave to attend to his business in the south. That would take several days, Mrs. Diggs had explained, and then he would return by way of Cider Gulch.

After that I will see my one true love.

The words she had rehearsed, the ones expressing her love and her hopes that they might share a peaceful life together in Apple Grove, repeated in her mind. But when she closed her eyes, the face she had dreamed of for four years refused to materialize. Instead, all she could see was the half-mocking smile of Lawrence's dark-haired sheriff.

THIRTEEN

The door burst open, and Mrs. Diggs' voice preceded her into the jailhouse. "My dear, the news is thrilling!"

She entered waving a piece of paper above her head and then caught sight of the sheriff seated behind his desk. Her mouth snapped shut.

Rebecca looked up from the half-finished ruffled collar in her lap. Her spirits rose at the excitement apparent on Mrs. Diggs' face. Had the ladies raised the entire one hundred dollars? Not a moment too soon! Though her jail cell was comfortable, after four days confined here she had grown thoroughly tired of these walls.

Mrs. Diggs tilted her head back and looked down her nose at Colin. "I had no idea you would be here, Sheriff."

"No? I do work here, though lately my job consists of nothing but babysitting the town women."

Rebecca completed the stitch she had begun. It was true that the ladies of the movement had formed a constant stream into the jail. They were determined to bolster her spirits, and their chatty visits relieved the tedium of long days.

Colin leaned his chair back against the wall and asked, "What's the thrilling news?"

"It's not for you," Annie replied haughtily. "I would like to visit with Rebecca. Privately, if you please."

The chair's front legs slammed against the floor. "Of course you would. Don't they all?"

Scowling, he snatched the keys from the corner of the desk. Rebecca secured her needle in the folds of a ruffle and set her project aside with a private smile. He'd complained yesterday that it was no use storing them out of sight in a drawer when everyone in town knew where they were.

When he'd swung the cell door open, he left the keys dangling from the lock.

"I'll be outside if you need anything."

Rebecca smothered a giggle at the glare he sent her way. With a savage gesture, he jerked his hat off the hook on the wall, set it on his head, and left through the door, closing it behind him.

The moment he was out of sight, Mrs.

Diggs rushed into the cell, waving her piece of paper. "My dear, the news is so thrilling I can barely contain myself!"

Rebecca eyed the paper with growing excitement. "Is it a large donation? Do we have the full amount of my fine yet?"

"No, nothing like that." The paper fluttered in the air again. "Even better!"

Rebecca's shoulders slumped as her enthusiasm flagged. What could be better than raising a hundred dollars so she could be free?

Mrs. Diggs crossed the short space between them and gathered her into a quick embrace. When she pulled back, her face shone with a zeal Rebecca had rarely seen.

"I've had word from back East." Annie lowered her voice to a whisper, lips trembling with the news she could scarcely contain. "Our message has been received, and they are coming!"

Rebecca waited, but no revelation was forthcoming. "Who is coming?"

"Frances Willard and Anna Howard Shaw!" Mrs. Diggs' feet near danced a jig where she stood. "They are coming here, to Lawrence, to march arm-in-arm with us in our demonstration."

The names meant nothing to Rebecca. She maintained a tentative smile in the face of the other woman's glee, though how the arrival of two strangers was more exciting than her release, she could not imagine.

"They are movement leaders," Mrs. Diggs explained. "Their work for the sake of temperance has been tireless. When I wrote to them of your circumstances and our plans, they agreed that this opportunity is one that will make great strides toward our goal."

As far as Rebecca was concerned, unless they came bearing one hundred dollars to free her, their participation was at best mildly encouraging. Still, she tried to assume an appropriately enthusiastic expression.

"Don't you see?" Mrs. Diggs gazed at the missive with something akin to awe. "Their support will further our cause one more step. Why, when the ladies of the movement learn of their impending arrival, they will flock to our side."

Apparently, Rebecca failed to exhibit the joy expected.

"And," Mrs. Diggs continued pointedly, "if ladies flock to our side, they will certainly donate to our cause. *Your* cause, my dear."

This sounded much more hopeful

"How much have we raised?" Rebecca asked.

"Oh, I don't have an exact figure before

me." The woman waved her hand in a vague gesture. "I made a plea at church yesterday, which I expect will result in an influx of donations."

"But how much have we raised so far?" Rebecca pressed.

Mrs. Diggs did not meet her gaze. "Somewhere in the area of fifteen dollars."

The dismal figure hung like a specter in the air between them. Rebecca stepped back and sank into her rocking chair. Apparently, all the ladies who had visited in the past four days had barely managed to scrape together a dollar apiece.

"I shall never get out of jail." Her voice ended on a mournful tone.

"Nonsense." Mrs. Diggs swooped across the floor to engulf her with another brief hug. "Don't lose heart. With support from such giants of the cause as these, we will soon be swept away in a flood of donations."

Never before had Rebecca's thoughts hovered so desperately around money. Why should they, when Papa's labor kept food on the table and a roof over their heads? Now it seemed she could think of little else. To make matters worse, her hands were tied. Confined as she was, there was nothing she could do to save herself.

"I must go," Mrs. Diggs announced.

"They shall arrive on the twenty-fourth, which is only nine days from now. Oh, there is so much to do!" She rushed out of the cell and toward the door.

"Wait!" Rebecca leaped to her feet and started after her. She came to a halt at the boundaries of her cell. "What of your husband's errand in the south?"

The woman didn't turn when she reached the door but answered over her shoulder when she jerked it open. "Patience, my dear. He left this morning. There will be news from your beau soon."

Battling melancholy, Rebecca sank into her chair again and folded her hands in her lap. Dependent as she was on Mrs. Diggs' assistance, she couldn't shake the desolation that settled over her. Five days ago she'd set out from Apple Grove full of enthusiasm. But nothing had turned out as she planned. Surely no Amish girl ever had such a miserable *rumspringa*.

The door opened and Colin returned. She didn't look up from her contemplation of her hands but was aware that he paced in front of his desk.

"Rebecca, I want to talk to you."

She looked up at the note of resolve in his voice.

"Something's going on. I know it. You

know it. Every woman in this town knows it. Will you tell me what it is?" He paused and then added grudgingly, "Please?"

She almost answered his plea. Why not? What good was it doing her to keep news of the movement's planned peaceful demonstration from him? And yet Annie Diggs obviously wanted the protest to remain a secret. Now more than ever, with the promised presence of such powerful leaders.

And regardless of ineffectual efforts thus far, who was working to free Rebecca from her jail sentence and to bring about her reunion with Jesse?

Mrs. Diggs and her faithful followers.

Certainly not Colin Maddox, who put her here in the first place.

She shook her head. "I am sorry, Sheriff. I don't know what you are asking."

An untruth, but one that can't be helped.

A painful lump of tears formed in her throat, and she swallowed against them. First, she failed to control her temper, and now lies fell from her tongue. Perhaps her Amish upbringing wasn't as ingrained as she thought.

Tears blurred her vision, and she turned to the wall so Colin could not see.

"I don't believe you. What's going on here, Rebecca? Are those women planning a big demonstration?"

"I'm sorry, but I have a dreadful head-ache." She unlatched the strip of cloth holding back the curtain and a wall of fabric dropped into place.

Still, his voice penetrated the thin material. "When? Is there any way you can hold them off for a couple of weeks?"

She closed her eyes.

"Two weeks, Rebecca. That's all I ask. You have some say with them. They've taken to you. Make them cool their heels for two more weeks. In return, I'll talk to Tank again. I will try to get him to reduce the sentence."

She heard footfalls as he returned to his desk.

"That's what's bothering me. Benton's not the reason I have this strange feeling that something is about to happen." The chair squeaked.

"Those women are stirring up more trouble. That's what it is."

"Child, I have a job for you." Mrs. Evans made her announcement on Tuesday morning.

Seated behind the sheriff's desk, Deputy Callahan looked up from his perusal of a newspaper.

"Mornin', Miz Evans."

"Good morning, John. How's Bertha?"

"Fine, thanks. She's almost recovered from the birthin', and the boy is a strong one." His chest inflated and a proud grin lit his face.

"Give her my regards," Mrs. Evans said as she let herself into the cell using the key.

Rebecca set her needle down and massaged her fingertips. The constant stitching helped to pass the time, but her fingers were unaccustomed to such abuse. The skin on her thumb and forefinger was beginning to callous. *Maummi* would definitely approve.

Mrs. Evans had a pair of brightly colored dresses draped over her arm. Rebecca stifled a sigh. The amount of mending she had done for her benefactress would meet the needs of an entire Amish community for months. But the elderly woman generously contributed toward Rebecca's fine for every piece. Pennies, but every coin counted. And at least the task gave Rebecca a way to contribute toward her release rather than merely relying on the charity of others.

"Thank you. Put them there." She gestured toward a basket in the corner, which held an apron she suspected Mrs. Evans had rescued from a ragbag simply to give Rebecca a task to occupy her time.

"No, no. Leave those things be. These will come first." The woman's eyes sparkled. "You have a customer."

Rebecca glanced up. "A customer?"

"Yes. She came into my shop this morning with these." Fabric rustled softly when she lifted her arm to indicate the dresses. "She would like them altered." Mrs. Evans lowered her voice and leaned forward. "And she will pay four dollars per garment."

Rebecca drew in a breath. "Four dollars!" The amount would raise the balance in her fund to almost twenty-five dollars.

And then her enthusiasm deflated.

That still leaves more than seventy-five to go.

The amount seemed unreachable. She lifted her hands and stared forlornly at her reddened fingertips. Perhaps she should resign herself to spending the entire three months in jail.

Mrs. Evans' expression became concerned. "What's wrong, dear? Don't you want to do the alterations?"

"Yes." She didn't intend to speak in such a morose tone. "Of course I will do them. I am grateful for the work and for everything that has been done on my behalf."

An understanding look softened the gaze the elderly woman turned on her. "A hundred dollars does seem like an insurmountable obstacle, doesn't it?"

Rebecca nodded. A recent worry returned to nag at her. She swallowed against a gathering lump of tears.

"What if Mr. Diggs returns with my Jesse and I am still here?" Her gaze swept her surroundings. She did not relish the idea of delivering her well-rehearsed marriage proposal in a jail cell.

"I had hoped the fund-raising efforts would have had more effect by now," Mrs. Evans admitted. "But the people of Lawrence are not, by and large, a wealthy lot. If I had not just paid to replace the front window in my shop, I would have more to contribute myself . . ."

The kind face looked so troubled that Rebecca hurried to reassure her with a hand on her arm. "You have done far more than anyone to help a needful stranger. You have become my friend. Without you, I would have no one." The last words came out with a choke. Friend. She thought of Emma. How she wished she could visit with her sister and cry on her shoulder.

"There, there, dear. Don't take on so." A secretive smile played about the wrinkled lips. "I have an idea or two. In the meantime, I think you will enjoy testing the limits of your skills with a needle. Certainly you have never done work like this."

She dropped one dress across a neatly made bunk and held up the other, a lovely royal blue, for Rebecca's inspection. With a noisy intake of breath, Rebecca stared at the garment. It was covered in more frills and lace than she had ever seen. Bows cascaded down the back to end in a splash of ruffles. The neckline dipped low, and heat flooded her face as she visualized how the garment would look on a living woman.

She reached out a hesitant hand to finger the silky fabric and felt almost sinful simply for touching the luxurious cloth.

"Who owns this . . . garment?"

"A young woman who puts more stock in decency than some would think." Mrs. Evans turned at the sound of the door opening. "Ah, here she is now."

When Rebecca caught the first sight of her customer, the burning in her face increased. John leaped to his feet, his mouth gaping, and the chair fell with a crash behind him. The woman who entered the room didn't so much walk as flounce through the doorway.

"There you are, my dear." Mrs. Evans extended a hand toward her. "Come and meet Rebecca."

Though she had only seen her once before, Rebecca knew the newcomer instantly. She was the woman from the saloon. Today her blond curls weren't arranged on top of her head, and her lips weren't covered in bright red paint as they had been the night of the confrontation that landed Rebecca in jail. Her clothing was almost decent, though the starched white blouse did nothing to hide a figure that caused John's jaw to dangle.

Her gaze circled the room as she stepped inside the cell.

"Land sakes! Would ya look at this place?"

"Rebecca," Mrs. Evans said, "this is Sassy. I don't believe you two have met."

The girl turned a cautious look on Rebecca. "Not officially."

Rebecca recovered her manners and bobbed in a brief curtsey, dipping her head. "It's nice to make your acquaintance."

A smile flashed onto Sassy's face and disappeared just as quickly. "I'm sorry for your trouble." She turned in a circle, taking in her surroundings, and then she gave a low whistle. "At least you got some pretty things to brighten up the place. Better'n what I have in my room."

In spite of herself, Rebecca found herself fascinated by her visitor. She'd never been this close to a saloon girl before. Up close she was younger than she'd looked the night of Rebecca's arrival in Lawrence. They were probably close to the same age. Her words took an odd shape as they rolled off her tongue, low and husky and twice as long as normal. The sound was similar to the way Rebecca remembered Jesse speaking.

"Sassy hails from Texas," Mrs. Evans said.

Rebecca brightened. "I have friends who are from Texas."

"Yeah?" Sassy stooped to run a finger over the fine stitches on a pillow. "What part?"

"I don't know. They drive cattle from Texas to Kansas."

"Cowboys?" The girl straightened, a wide grin on her face. "Sounds like my kind of folks. My daddy was a cowhand." Her grin faded. "Leastways, that's what Mama always said. I never met him."

"Girls, I must get back to my shop." Mrs. Evans thrust the silky dress at Rebecca. "Now that you've met, I daresay you can work out whatever needs to be done between you."

After she had gone, an uneasy silence settled between the two girls. Rebecca cast about for a pleasantry, and Sassy seemed equally ill at ease without Mrs. Evans to serve as a buffer. She straightened the pillow she'd been examining and then smoothed a crease out of the soft bed covering. Her glance strayed around the room without meeting Rebecca's eye, and she gave an awkward little cough. Seeing the other girl's nervousness did a great deal to soothe Rebecca's.

"You would like me to alter the dress?" She grasped the garment by the shoulders and held it out before her.

"That's right. Mrs. Evans said you're right handy with a needle, and maybe you could do something with it."

Rebecca gave the dress a little shake, which brought the myriad ruffles and bows to life. She was almost afraid to ask her next question.

"What would you have me do?"

"Well, it's like this. When Mr. Colter hired me — that's Ed, the man who runs the Dollar. Do you know Ed?"

Ed. The large man who had forced the confrontation that ended up with her in jail. Rebecca had not seen him since the disastrous morning in court five days ago.

Sassy didn't wait for an answer. "No, I s'pose you don't. No matter. When Ed hired me for this here job, he said it came with room, board, and a whole wardrobe of clothes. There I was, fresh up from Texas with no more'n a couple of skirts in my bag, and them fairly worn through at the hem. The pay was good, and since I'd spent almost everything my poor mama left me when she passed getting up here, I said yes. But take a look."

She took the dress from Rebecca's hands and held it against her body. With one hand at the shoulders and the other across her narrow waist, Rebecca instantly spotted the problem. Either the dress had been made for a woman of smaller proportions than Sassy, or the original wearer had possessed no shred of morality.

"Ed says I should wear them dresses the way they are and quit my complaining because it'll be good for business. But I promised my mama I'd make a decent life for myself, and this ain't decent."

On that, she and Rebecca were in complete agreement. She gathered the sweeping skirt in her hands and eyed the length.

"It might be possible to add a collar," she suggested.

Sassy's eyes brightened. "Yeah. Something like that. Only . . ." Her gaze swept Rebecca's black dress, and an apologetic smile flashed on and off. "Not quite so plain as yours. I can't see Ed standin' for that, and I can't afford to lose this job yet."

Rebecca gazed at the dress's narrow waist, the decorative stitching around the low neck, the cascading ruffles. It would take a far more skillful needle than hers to turn this garish garment into a dress plain enough for an Amish woman. But perhaps she could give it a semblance of decency.

What would *Maummi* say if she heard her granddaughter was doing needlework for a saloon girl? Rebecca had no doubt that her grandmother disapproved of saloons as much as Mrs. Diggs and the other women of the movement. But Mrs. Evans had brought Sassy here. And at four dollars per dress, could she turn her away?

"What do you do at the saloon?"

"I sing. Someday I'm going to New York City, where I aim to be a famous actress."

"Actress?" Rebecca had only a vague idea of the word, and she couldn't even remember where she had heard it.

"My mama told me before she passed that I'd better do something with my voice and my looks, 'cause I sure didn't have nothin' else goin' for me, and I decided right then and there that as soon as I could, I'd head for New York City." She lowered her voice and her eyes glowed. "After that, I might even go to England."

Why anyone would want to go to England,

Rebecca couldn't imagine. It sounded so far away. But how could she not admire a girl with such a lofty goal? At the moment the only aspirations she had involved raising another seventy-five dollars and reuniting with Jesse so she could return to her Plain life in Apple Grove.

She gestured toward the dress. "You had best put it on."

Sassy turned her head with a pointed stare. Rebecca followed her gaze and realized that the deputy stood staring at them.

"Could we have some privacy, darlin'?" Sassy tossed her head, a pretty dimple appearing on her cheek when she reached for the top button on her blouse. "Unless you think your wife wouldn't mind your sticking around for this part."

Though Rebecca's cheeks flamed at the girl's boldness, she couldn't stop grinning over the speed with which the deputy vacated the jailhouse.

When Colin turned the corner and saw John standing outside in front of the jail, his teeth clamped together with an irritated snap. Annie or Mrs. Evans or one of the others had kicked him out, as they did with increasing regularity. The situation had gotten out of hand and it had to stop. He stretched his stride and covered the ground at a near run.

"I thought I told you to keep an eye on things in there."

"But there's women's stuff going on. It wouldn't be right for a man to be in the room." John lowered his voice and confided, "Besides, Bertha would skin me alive if she heard I saw Miss Sassy in her skivvies."

Colin paused. "Sassy? What's she doing here?"

"Miss Rebecca's fixing up a dress for her."

"She's doing what?"

"You heard me. She's in there trying it on right now."

A loud grating filled Colin's ears, and it took a moment to realize it was his teeth grinding together.

"That's it," he snapped, reaching for the door. "I'm putting a stop to this right now."

"Now, don't go getting all riled up, Colin. They ain't botherin' a thing."

"I'm not putting up with turning this jail into a woman's dress shop, John. Are you with me or not?"

Colin put a hand over his eyes, jerked the door open, and stepped inside, John following close on his heels.

"Ladies? We're coming in!"

"That's fine with us," Rebecca replied calmly.

Dropping his hand, the sheriff spotted Rebecca kneeling on the floor before a blue-clad figure, her head bent as she fingered the hem of a wide skirt, the laces of her prayer *kapp* dangling. Wearing the dress, Sassy stood erect on a chair, her back to the door, a thick mass of blond curls hanging down her back.

She grinned over her shoulder. "How do, Sheriff."

"Now, look, ladies. I don't know what's going on here, but —" Sassy turned on the chair to face him. Heat crept up his neck to create an uncomfortable moisture beneath his collar.

"Nothing's going on, 'cept we've been getting to know each other." Sassy put her hands on her hips and gave her hair a toss. "You ought to be ashamed, Sheriff, locking a sweet girl like this in the stockade. Why, did you know her mama passed, just like mine?"

Whatever demands he'd planned to make died. He tore his gaze away from the sight of Sassy in the indecent dress. When he half turned to stare at the wall he caught sight of John's bulging eyes. Awarding him a stern glare, he knocked the back of the deputy's hat over his eyes as Rebecca rose from her kneeling position and casually picked up a shawl. She draped the garment across Sassy's shoulders and closed it in the front. Then she straightened to face him, hands folded serenely in front of her. When Colin glanced back into the cell, he caught the hint of a smile on her lips, and a flush rose up to his face.

"I am hired to alter this dress," she informed him in the calm tone he had come to recognize as Rebecca when she knew she'd confounded him. "I thought adding a collar might be attractive."

He swallowed.

"Don't you think that's a good idea?"

"Collar? Yes. Fine."

"That's what I'll do. Add a small but attractive collar. Thank you ever so much for your help."

Colin turned on his boot heel and John started to argue. "But I thought you said —"

Colin silenced his deputy with a look. "They're adding a collar, John. Let's go over to the diner and get a cup of coffee."

"Women," John was heard to utter before the door closed.

FOURTEEN

Amos Beiler hefted his end of the long board and placed it above the previous one. With strong hands he pounded the pegs in place. The sound of hammers cracking against wood rose into the clear Kansas sky. When they finished, he grabbed the board and gave it a tug. It held firm, and he exchanged a smile with Jonas Switzer, who occupied the place next to him.

Jonas braced himself on the crossbeam to peer down the length of the pitched roof. *"Die scheier schee, ja?"*

"Ja," Amos agreed. A fine barn they were building for John Hostetler.

Satisfaction settled over Amos as his glance roved the half-finished barn and down to the ground, where women bustled around long tables in the yard. Here, among his friends, with his hands busy and his mind focused on the task at hand, he felt at peace. He could set aside for a while the dull ache of loneliness that was his constant companion when he worked his fields in solitude.

A slight figure exited the house carrying a laden platter of warmly browned loaves. With a start he realized the girl was his daughter Sarah. When had she begun to look like a woman in miniature? With obvious care she walked slowly across the grass toward the table. A pair of boys raced past her, one chasing the other, and she raised the platter above her head while voicing a sharp reprimand. The boys obediently slowed for a few paces, and then, once out of reach, took off again at a run. Shaking her head, she continued to the table.

It was such an adult gesture, that shaking of the head. Not yet ten years old, Sarah conscientiously performed many of the tasks that should have been learned at her mother's side. Amos lifted his face to the sun, blinking. He did his best to do right by his children, laboring on his farm to keep food in their mouths. They worked hard at their chores, even Celia and little Karl, as was proper for an Amish family. His children would learn the discipline of hard work and the satisfaction of a task completed. But they would not learn a mother's devotion. That was one thing he could not provide for them.

Nor could he provide for himself the thing he wanted with deep and desperate longing: a wife with whom to share his life. For a while he had entertained the hope that one of Jonas's daughters might be willing to fill the role. Alas, God intended otherwise. Emma married an *Englischman,* and Rebecca did not return his interest.

A call came from below, and another long board was lifted up. Amos grabbed the end and fed the length of it down the line until the men were able to station it firmly above the other. When he applied his hammer, he spared a thought for the man beside him. If his thoughts were troubled today, Jonas's must be doubly so. It had been eight days since Rebecca ran off. Amos had heard she'd left in the night, leaving a brief letter to explain her actions. Had they further word of her? He wanted to ask, but a glance at Jonas's expressionless face stilled the question. Some things a man must suffer alone.

A bell rang, drawing him from his thoughts. The tables below were full to overflowing with food, and the women gathered about, shooing flies and children away with their hands.

"Come, Amos." Jonas hooked the head of

his hammer over the edge of the board they had just secured. "The meal is ready and in good time. Hard work leaves a man *hoongerich*."

Amos dismissed his thoughts and slapped Jonas on the back. "A bountiful meal we enjoy today, my friend."

They climbed down the posts they had erected early in the morning and soon were surrounded by hungry men near one end of a long table. Bishop Miller waited until the last worker had joined them, and when the entire assembly had gathered, he bowed his head. Amos did the same, the German words of a familiar prayer of blessing rising from his mind heavenward on silent wings. The silence of prayer, and the awe of knowing that the Almighty bent His ear close to hear the humble words of a lowly man, had sustained him through many a hard time. Prayer had been Amos's only safeguard against the devastating grief of loss when his wife died, and against wrenching loneliness in the years since.

The sound of shuffling feet alerted him to the end of the prayer. He looked up to find those men nearest the table beginning to fill their plates from the endless line of steaming bowls. The women stood along the opposite side, hovering over the food. Their happy chatter filled the air and settled a feeling of community on the meal. A glance to the far end told him that Sarah had taken charge of her sister and brother. He caught his daughter's eye and rewarded her with a smile and a nod.

An approaching horse halted the meal. Hooves pounded the well-worn path that led to the Hostetler farm. Amos turned to see an *Englisch* rider approach. He slowed his mount as he passed the row of identical black buggies lining the wheat field beyond the house and came to a stop nearby.

His dark eyes scanned the table, and he spoke to the assembled without dismounting.

"I'm looking for a man by the name of Jonas Switzer. Can someone direct me to his place?"

Heads turned, Amos's included, and gazes fixed on Jonas. Had he not been standing right next to the man, Amos would have missed the almost imperceptible intake of air. Within a second or two, the worry he'd seen flash in Jonas's eyes evaporated, and he stepped toward the rider speaking in a calm voice.

"I am Jonas Switzer."

A slim figure elbowed her way through the group of women on the far side of the table and stood wringing her hands, watching. Marta Switzer was not as adept as her son at masking her worry. The lines around her pursed mouth deepened to crevasses.

The *Englischman* dismounted and untied a strap on a bag hanging beside his saddle. "Got a letter for you. Came on the train last night. Charlie down at the post office asked me to bring it to you."

He extracted an envelope from the bag and handed it to Jonas, who took it with a hesitant though steady hand. Mrs. Switzer hurried to stand at his side, her gaze fixed on the object her son was holding.

"That is not our Rebecca's handwriting." Dread weighed down her words. Whispers buzzed among the watching women.

Bishop Miller stepped in front of the rider. "Friend, we are about to enjoy a meal together. Will you be our guest?"

The man's eyes lit up, his gaze fixing hungrily on the table. "That would be mighty welcome. Thank you."

The bishop raised a hand and gestured toward a group of men standing nearby. "Make welcome our guest. Fill your plates. Enjoy the bounty God has placed before us."

Not a man, woman, or child missed the unspoken meaning. Some moved away, eyes averted, to afford Jonas and Mrs. Switzer privacy.

Amos lagged behind the others while keeping a concerned eye on Jonas. Did this letter concern Rebecca? His pulse thrummed. He respected the Switzers and Jonas as he did few others in Apple Grove. No matter the trouble that befell a family in their Amish community, Jonas was among the first to lend aid. More than once he had arrived at Amos's farm at first light during harvesttime, ready to help. His silent, everconstant composure had served as a model for Amos more than once, though Amos devoutly hoped he would not be called upon to emulate the man's widower status forever. Jonas felt no need to remarry; Amos longed for a companion. Someone to lie with at night, to talk about the day, and share concerns.

If anything had happened to Rebecca, Jonas would no doubt respond with the strength of his faith unshaken, but Amos sincerely hoped his friend would not have to suffer through such a trial. Every so often a young person left the safety of the Amish community, only to find they were unprepared for the ways of the *Englisch*. A prayer formed in his mind. *Let no evil have befallen young Rebecca.*

At the end of the line, Amos stepped closer to the table as the men in front of him moved down the row of food. To his right, Jonas broke the seal on the letter. Beside him, Mrs. Switzer craned her neck to read.

"She is safe."

Jonas's soft voice, though barely louder than a whisper, carried to those gathered in a huddle. Relief filled Amos when a chorus of *"Gott aber sei Dank!"* met the news.

Indeed, thanks be to God, he echoed silently.

In the next moment, Mrs. Switzer screeched, "Jail?"

She clamped a hand to her chest with more than her usual amount of drama and wavered on her feet.

Amos quickly stepped to her side in time to catch her in his arms when she collapsed.

Jail?

Their Rebecca was in jail?

"Aren't you finished with that yet?"

Rebecca stabbed her needle with force into the ruffle, ignoring Colin's question. The point sank through the fabric and into her already sore finger, and she hissed at the pain. She cast a resentful glance through the bars to the place where he leaned

206

against the edge of his desk, arms crossed, watching her. His worrisome habit of staring at her with that scowl gathered on his handsome forehead had begun to grate on her nerves. He seemed to take pleasure in prodding her patience.

"Why do you ask? Are you eager for Sassy's next fitting?"

She had the satisfaction of seeing a spot of color rise high on his neck, and she hid a smile as she repositioned her needle.

"I'm eager to have this dress business over and done with, and to get my jail back to normal." His frown deepened. "Did you talk to the ladies?"

"Regarding what?" *Why do I test him? I know what he's asking about.*

She had not spoken to the women about delaying the temperance protest until after he had left town, nor did she plan to do so. Keeping harmony in Lawrence was his job. Hers was to languish in jail for eighty-three more days. The needle paused. Why was he so eager to leave town?

"You are not being truthful, Miss Switzer. I thought your kind always tells the truth. The whole town knows Annie Diggs and her followers are raising money to cover your fine."

Relief settled over her. He had not, then,

heard rumors of the planned peaceful protest or news of their impending out of town guests.

"I am assured that donations are made daily, though not many have funds to spare."

As of this morning, when Gladys Collins came by for a visit, the balance had risen to seventeen dollars. If Rebecca allowed herself to dwell on the declining frequency of donations, despair would overcome her. Instead, she asked Gladys to spread the word that she would gladly take in any sort of work she could perform during her confinement.

His lazy gaze studied her. "What happens when you get the bail money? Are you heading home — where you should be?"

She bit off a thread. "If my Jesse has not yet come, I shall go to him."

"If he's such a fine man, why hasn't he come to your rescue and paid your fine?"

Now it was her turn to fight a rising flush. Truth was, she had considered writing Jesse and asking for his help, but to write asking for money after a four-year absence would destroy her plans for the touching reunion she envisioned. Her fervent prayer was that her fine would be paid well before he knew of her unfortunate arrest. Dwelling on any other possibility tied her stomach in queasy knots.

"My Jesse is an honorable man. If he knew of my situation, I haven't the slightest doubt he would rush to my aid."

A smile started at the corners of his mouth. "If he knew? I gather he isn't expecting you?"

She tilted her nose in the air. "I do not need to explain my actions to you."

"No need to get touchy." He shoved away from the desk and returned to his chair.

"Why are you so interested in seeing me freed?" She would think that her situation meant little more than a nuisance to him.

"I'm not, but I want this place back to normal before the new sheriff gets here."

Her hands paused. "Mrs. Evans told me you planned to leave. You must be pleased."

"Yes, ma'am. Six more days, and I'll head east."

"You have employment elsewhere?"

"No."

"New town?"

"No. New interest."

"I'm listening."

The silence lengthened, and at first he wouldn't meet her gaze. Finally he said, "I plan to start an orphanage."

She paused in her work to stare at him. "A what?"

"An orphanage. Not large. I'll maybe take

in five, six kids who need a home and a hand up in life. Farm a little. Grow some wheat."

A new respect for him dawned. Not many men would be willing to care for children not their own. Only a loving man with a kind heart.

"Why do you want to do this?"

"Oh, I don't know." He seemed to dismiss her question at first, but then he appeared to change his mind. "Comes from my past, I guess." He lifted a shoulder in a shrug. "When I was a boy, a schoolmate lost both his parents to consumption. I remember hearing my ma tell my pa late one night about how he and his sister had no place to go. Nobody to take them in. My pa said they could come live with us, and they did for a month or so until an uncle from New York showed up to get them."

He fiddled with the inkhorn on his desk, taking the stopper out and putting it back in again.

"I'll never forget how worried those kids were. No kid ought to have to worry about having a bed and food and somebody to watch after them."

Rebecca's own heart twisted. What if something happened to Emma and Luke? Would little Lucas worry about how to feed himself? Of course not, because he had a great-grandmother and grandfather and aunt who would give him a loving home. But not all children were so blessed.

Her thoughts turned to poor Amos Beiler and how he struggled to raise his little brood when his wife passed away at such a young age. Rearing a family was difficult with only one parent.

"But you are a single man," she said. "Caring for children is hard work."

Colin gave another shrug. "I'm single for the present. By the time I settle, I hope to find someone who shares my dream."

She resumed her rocking and stitching as she spoke, much as she had seen *Maummi* do evenings at home.

"I think opening an orphanage is a most commendable goal, Sheriff Maddox."

During the pause that followed, she looked over at him to note his countenance. To her surprise, a flush had risen from his neck into his cheeks. "You don't think I'm crazy?"

"No. I think your dream is most worthy."

He glanced at the door, and she wondered if he was worried that someone might overhear their confession.

"Eventually I might even form a little church."

"An orphanage and a church. It seems you

have given this much thought."

"Some. If the Lord takes me in that direction, I'll follow."

"You seem a peaceful man. What made you choose to become a lawman?"

"The law chose me. I stepped up to take my grandpa's place when he died. The job was supposed to be short term, but it's going on two years now. Sheriffing isn't in my blood — not like it was in Grandpa's. I planned to hang around until Grandma passed, which she did last spring, and then be out of here." He ran a hand through his thick hair. "But what I really want is to follow in my other grandpa's footsteps. He led a church back home in Kentucky. And in six more days, that's what I aim to do."

Understanding dawned, and with it a sense of awe. "You are following the Lord to start a new district?"

He shook his head. "Not a district. A church. And I'll paint the wood white as snow. It'll be small to start out, with a pitched roof and a bell. And on top? A tall wooden cross."

He had surely given the subject much thought, and his words painted Rebecca a well-defined picture. Amish church services were hosted every other week by a family in the district, though she had seen the buildings where the *Englisch* held their services. There were several in Hays City, and she'd even seen a few during her brief walk through the streets of Lawrence.

But the thing that captivated her imagination wasn't his description of the building. It was his keenness for his vision.

"You will preach in this church?" she asked. He did not look in the least like Bishop Miller, who led the Amish back home in worship. Would the Lord allow such a young man, a man who carried a gun strapped to his side, to lead others in the holy rites?

"Oh, yes. I make no claim to be as sharp of tongue as your friend Annie, but when it comes to preaching, I can hold my own." Though he answered her question, he seemed almost not to notice her, his gaze fixed on a faraway image that reflected in his eyes with a light that shone. "But that won't be what keeps folks coming to my church. It'll be the others, the families, the caring for each other and helping each other when the need arises. Just like my grandpa's church back in Kentucky. And there'll be the kids, the orphans. They'll have a decent life, with good values and good examples all around them."

A wave of homesickness washed over Rebecca. "Your dream will be a place like Apple Grove."

Only not like Apple Grove. She had seen the stoic expressions on the faces of the men as the lots were drawn during church services back home. She watched Papa's jaw, set resolute and firm, and could almost hear his prayer that the lot pass him by. To be chosen for a life of service in an Amish district meant a commitment of time and a burden of responsibility that few relished. To see Colin's eyes alight with enthusiasm stirred a passion inside her. Imagine, hearing the call of the Almighty and answering that call with wholehearted devotion.

She realized he was watching her, his expectant gaze resting heavy on her. Then the door burst open, and Hal Lawson appeared.

"Trouble's brewing." The deputy's words set Rebecca's heart to pounding. "I just spotted Cyrus Hughes and Elijah Calhoun coming out of the Horseshoe Saloon."

Though the names meant nothing to Rebecca, the grim expression on Colin's face told her everything she needed to know.

As much as this man wanted to serve the Lord more than the law, it looked as though the good sheriff might not get his wish for six more peaceful days.

FIFTEEN

"Yeah, they were in here all right." The man behind the bar wasn't as big or as burly as Ed, but he had a reputation for being every bit as tough. He'd have to be. Tucked onto a less affluent street on the northeastern edge of town, the Horseshoe Saloon didn't attract a prosperous lot. A handful of tables, little more than wide planks on pole legs, crowded the room, and the bar was splintered and stained. Few of the bottles on the shelf bore labels.

"You're sure it was Hughes and Calhoun?"

Colin laid wanted posters on the bar so the man could examine them more closely. Though not as notorious as Cleon Benton, these two had been pinpointed as accomplices in a series of stagecoach holdups down in Colorado a few months back. Grandpa Maddox had arrested them twice and told them the next time they rode into town he would haul their sorry hides to the jail and throw away the key.

"I'm sure it was them. Came in around two o'clock and sat at that table right there." The man pointed to a table situated between the door and an ancient-looking potbelly stove.

"Did they happen to mention what they were doing here?"

The men would have to be brazen or half nuts to go against Bull Maddox's warning to "get out and stay out" of Lawrence.

The bartender shook his head. "They didn't say much of anything, Sheriff, even to each other. Downed three shots of whiskey each and then left. Looked trail weary, both of them, like they'd been rode hard and put away wet. I had the feeling they were just passing through."

Colin frowned. "What makes you say that?"

"I watched them leave." He jerked his head toward the window that took up half of the front wall. "Their horses were packed heavy and their saddlebags were full. They mounted up and took off that way." He pointed east, where the town of Lawrence ended at the shores of the Kansas River.

"Let's hope you're right." Colin snatched the wanted posters off the bar and walked out of the saloon. Hal waited on the weather-beaten porch, watching the street.

"They left town," he told him as he mounted Gus.

"That's where I spotted them, headed toward the river. Couldn't have been more than ten, fifteen minutes ago."

Colin set his jaw with frustration. Because he'd assigned himself jail duty this afternoon, Gus was at the stable. When Hal ran in with his big news, precious minutes had been lost going to the livery and saddling up. He nudged his horse with his knees and urged him into a gallop, Hal following behind.

The few buildings to the east of the Horseshoe were spaced wide apart and small. One horse stood hitched in front of the auction house, and a small shanty beyond that looked to be deserted. There was no sign of movement either place. The road they followed became a trail that curved along the river and disappeared to the north behind a tree-covered bend.

"I'll ride north. You take the east. Find John and the others and tell them who we're looking for, but be quiet about it, Hal. We don't want to start a panic. If we're lucky, they've ridden on through and this is just an irritation."

"What do we do if we find them?"

"Bring them in. I want to talk to them. There's some reason they're in the area, and it's big enough to make them careless."

"Sure thing, Colin." Hal turned his horse and rode off like the wind.

The sheriff urged Gus into a gallop again. If the two men had ridden this direction, then Lawrence had not been their aim. Passing through or not, that made three wanted outlaws in his town in the past seven days, all of them gone before he'd even realized they were there.

His stomach churned as a river-scented breeze met his nose. Something was about to go down. Something big and ugly.

He rounded the bend, eyes scanning the landscape in front of him. The river continued north, cutting a swatch through a series of swells in the land. The trail rose, dipped, and then disappeared behind a thick tangle of river birch and white oak trees that ran all the way down to the bank. Not a single rider was in sight.

Colin slowed the horse's pace. If Calhoun and Hughes had headed this way, then they were up ahead of him, heading east or north. In that case, they posed no threat to Lawrence. If they did, he'd be after them quicker than a spring jackrabbit.

With one last scan of the horizon, he

turned around. Call it a hunch, but he'd bet good money that a search for these two men would prove as frustratingly useless as the one for Benton.

When the jailhouse door opened, Rebecca set her sewing aside. Judging by Colin's expression, she knew without asking that he had not caught the outlaws. She watched as he hung the posters back on the wall, pounding the tacks a little harder than necessary. The stern set of his jaw gave his mouth a hard, unbending appearance that made her glad he had never turned that particular look on her. She much preferred the smiling sheriff, even when that smile held a touch of a smirk.

He had barely sat down when the door opened and a man entered. Though she had not seen him in the week since her trial, she recognized Mayor Bowerstock. A stout man who barely stood taller than Rebecca, the mayor nevertheless projected a commanding presence, enhanced by an immaculate black jacket with wide lapels, a crisp white shirt, and a mustache whose ends swooped nearly to his ears.

Disbelief dawned on his face as he gazed at her cell.

"What in tarnation happened to the jail?"

219

He eased forward, his eyes moving to take in the furnishings, bedding, and curtains.

"Don't ask," Colin said.

The mayor caught sight of Rebecca in her rocking chair, and he started as though he hadn't known she was there. He planted a hand on the top of his hat and lifted it a couple of inches off his head as he ducked a nod in greeting.

"Afternoon, Miss Switzer."

Rebecca inclined her head but didn't speak. According to Mrs. Evans, the mayor was partially responsible for the lawless sale of liquor in Lawrence. She reached into the basket for the collar she intended to sew onto Sassy's dress, and bent her attention on her project.

The mayor recovered himself with a shake and rounded on Colin.

"I heard a couple of desperados are in town."

"You heard wrong. They were in town. As far as we can tell, they rode in this afternoon, bought supplies down at Sumpter's Mercantile, had a few drinks at the Horseshoe, and then left. If Hal hadn't spotted them leaving the saloon, we would never even have known they were here."

"Well." Bowerstock's deep scowl faded. "That's a relief."

"Is it? I can't shake the feeling that something's going on — something more than a couple of thugs riding through town." His gaze slid toward Rebecca, who was bent diligently over her task.

The mayor clasped his hands behind his back and thrust his rotund belly out in front. "Doesn't matter, as long as it doesn't happen in Lawrence."

Colin pushed on one end of an ink blotter and watched it rock on its rounded bottom. That he did not agree with the mayor was evident in the troubled lines etched on his forehead.

Though Rebecca wouldn't wish vicious criminals on the town, she couldn't help thinking that at least if the sheriff was busy chasing after the men on those posters, he was not snooping for details of the movement's peaceful protest.

"Glad to see you have everything under control, Maddox." Bowerstock's glance slid toward Rebecca again. "Though what Mulhaney will say when he sees this . . ." He left the jail shaking his head.

Colin didn't look up when the mayor left. His finger continued to tap the blotter, his stare distant. The expression disturbed her. While he'd been out searching for the outlaws, she had thought about their earlier conversation and the fire of passion that had been in his eyes when he spoke of the church he would build. She much preferred that to the brooding scowl he now wore.

She interrupted the silence. "Who is Mulhaney?"

Her question pulled him out of his moody reverie. "Who?"

She gestured toward the closed door. "The mayor mentioned someone named Mulhaney."

"He's the new sheriff. He's coming in from Chicago next week."

Rebecca did the math. Today was the eighteenth of May, the seventh day of her stay in jail. That meant the new sheriff, this Mulhaney, would arrive on —

Her head jerked up. "He arrives on the twenty-fourth of May?"

"That's right. Train's due in around noon."

The noon train on May twenty-fourth. Thoughts raced through her mind. That was the day of the peaceful protest, the day the important leaders of the movement would arrive. They would be on the same train as the new sheriff.

Does Mrs. Diggs know? I must get word to her.

Rebecca glanced around her cell. She had

paper and ink, thanks to Mrs. Evans, but if she asked Colin to deliver a note to Annie Diggs, his suspicions were sure to be aroused. No, she would have to wait until her next woman visitor. Or, at the latest, when Mrs. Evans arrived at bedtime, as she did every night.

"Are you worried?"

She looked up quickly. "Pardon me?"

"About the new sheriff?" Colin's gesture indicated the contents of her cell. "You may have to clean house."

Rebecca forced her taut muscles to relax, lest he become suspicious. "I hope to be released before that day arrives."

Mrs. Diggs kept assuring her that the movement would not leave her in jail a minute longer than necessary, and she intended to make an appeal to the eastern members. Rebecca held more hope in Mrs. Evans' calm assurance, though she would not share the details of her plan.

"And I hope to be reunited with my Jesse before then," she added.

"Ah. The great Jesse."

At least his face remained impassive. Lately he had taken to scowling when Rebecca mentioned her love. She suspected he did it in order to irritate her, but today he let it pass. She much preferred his mocking smile to this moodiness.

"Will you stay in Lawrence for a while after this Mulhaney arrives?"

He shook his head. "Only long enough to show him the jail and introduce him to his deputies. If I'm lucky, Gus and I will be out of Lawrence by suppertime."

"And then you will go west and find a place to start your orphanage and build your church." She bent toward the basket beside her to retrieve a new reel of cotton thread. "When you preach, what will you say?"

"I don't know. I'll probably give some sermons that have meant something to me." He opened the middle drawer of his desk and took out a Bible.

Even from this distance, Rebecca could see the worn pages and scribbles that filled the wafer-thin paper.

"All I need to know is found in this book."

"That is *Die Bibel?*"

He nodded. "This one belonged to my grandpa." He ran a hand over the cover. "Many a fine sermon he preached out of these pages. I'd sit on the front row of his church, close enough to see the sweat glisten on his forehead when he got to going. And his eyes." A faraway smile curved his lips. "When he read from the Psalms, it looked like the sun was shining out of his eyes."

Rebecca watched Colin's face, fascinated. Gone was the dark brooding scowl. At the moment it looked as though the sun were shining out of *his* eyes. What would it be like to hear a man with Colin's integrity preach on church Sundays? Certainly her mind would not wander as it did when Bishop Miller or the other men spoke.

Rebecca rocked for a moment. Though she had never been to an *Englisch* church, Emma once described it for her. The songs they sang did not come from the *Ausbund,* as did all the songs in an Amish service. And the preacher spoke in English, not German. Imagine hearing someone speak of *Gott* and read from *Die Bibel* in English. The idea was oddly fascinating, though faintly scandalous.

"I would like to hear you preach. Will you?"

Startled, he jerked toward her, alarm painted on his features. "Here? Now?"

Her chair halted. Perhaps he considered speaking of *Gott* in a jail disrespectful. "I am sorry. I did not mean to offend."

"You didn't offend me." He would not meet her eye. "I'm just not prepared to speak."

Suspicion dawned. "You have never

225

preached."

"I have!" His head jerked up. "Just not to people."

"If not to people, then to whom?"

"Cows. Okay? I've preached to cows."

She blinked. "You preach to cows?"

A sheepish, though highly appealing, grin softened his lips. "When I was a boy they were my main congregation. I'd leave church with Grandpa's message burning in my mind and write down everything he said. Then I'd head out behind the barn where Pa kept a couple of milk cows, and I'd preach Grandpa's sermon to them at the top of my lungs. Eventually I branched out and grew my flock. I had three or four friends who would listen to me preach Sunday afternoons. We'd go down to the river, and I would preach and baptize. Then one or two of them caught the fire, and they would speak and the rest of us would go forth and ask to be baptized." He looked up. "I must have been dunked at least a hundred times during those years."

"Dunked?"

"You know. In the river."

She looked blank.

"Don't Amish people get baptized?"

Ah, baptism. "Yes, after the classes. We kneel before the bishop, and he pours water

226

over us in front of the community."

"Well, in my grandpa's church we got dunked." His hand swept up and then down. "The whole body under the water."

A picture rose in Rebecca's mind of a dark-haired boy going under the moving surface of a river every week. She covered a giggle with her hand. "Quite an unusual congregation you had — cows and young boys."

A chuckle lightened his voice. "I had to tie them up with a rope so they wouldn't wander off in the middle of my preaching."

"The cows?" She snickered.

"The boys."

Her laughter broke free, and after a moment he joined in. It felt good to laugh with him, and Rebecca gave herself over to her mirth. When the laughter faded, they were left smiling at each other.

"I would like to hear you preach, Colin Maddox." She waved a hand around the cell. "Even without a rope I will not wander off."

"You would likely be a more receptive audience than a couple of bulls."

Rebecca found her gaze drawn to his. She had not noticed the color of his eyes until this moment. Even from the distance between her cell and his desk, she could see they were blue, as blue as the sky on a sunny morning. Not like Jesse's eyes at all, which were as dark as her own.

With a pang of guilt, she tore her gaze from Colin's. *Jesse's eyes are much nicer.*

Though just then she was having difficulty remembering their exact shade.

Colin slid the Bible back in the drawer.

The moment broken, Rebecca reached once again for her sewing. The sooner Mr. Diggs arrived with Jesse, the better.

Amos stood on one side of the Hostetlers' living room and kept an eye on Mrs. Switzer lest she swoon again. If she would but sit instead of pacing around the room, he could slip out of the house and return to work. He felt like an intruder witnessing the turmoil of this family whose daughter had brought shame on the Switzer name.

Compassion stirred in him at the sight of Jonas's slumped shoulders. His friend sat in a straight-backed chair with his hands folded in his lap and his gaze fixed on the floor.

"It is the way of some young people on *rumspringa*." Bishop Miller stood beside Jonas, his normally impassive face full of compassion. "To try the ways of the world and fall victim to the trying. Our Rebecca has ever been a willful girl."

Mrs. Switzer turned to glower in the bishop's direction, something Amos affected not to notice. The bishop but spoke the truth. Always one to fidget in church was Rebecca. A bold gaze she had, her eyes rarely downcast with modesty like the other girls. Amos had heard the talk of those who said that Jonas Switzer allowed his younger daughter too much freedom, and even her grandmother did not teach her self-control as she ought. Mrs. Keim had once used the example of Rebecca Switzer to caution him against overindulgence with his girls.

But Amos saw nothing wrong in a woman with spirit, so long as she was properly pious and obeyed the *Ordnung.* In recent years, ever since Rebecca had bloomed into a lovely young woman, he had considered the idea of courtship. Though thirteen years her senior, he had much to offer a wife. A good farm. A sturdy house. A peaceful life without want of any basic need. And Rebecca would be an admirable role model for his girls, no matter what Mrs. Keim said.

"We must leave at once, Jonas." Mrs. Switzer's skirts swirled around her feet when she turned to cross the room. "I have money laid aside. We will rescue our Rebecca from jail."

Jonas looked up, sadness heavy on his features. "This Mrs. Evans says the cost is one hundred dollars." He shook his head. "Between the two of us we do not have that. Perhaps after the harvest."

"Months from now is the harvest." The old woman's eyes flashed. "My granddaughter cannot stay in jail until harvesttime."

Amos spoke up. "I also have some coin put aside. Though not close to that amount, you are welcome to use it to buy Rebecca's freedom."

Jonas cast a grateful glance his way.

A heavy sigh sounded from the bishop. "The cost is not at issue. Rebecca's behavior is." He turned an unbendable gaze on Mrs. Switzer. "You must not go after her."

Outrage flashed in her eyes. "Leave her in an *Englisch* jail? Never!"

Bishop Miller's mouth hardened. Amos averted his eyes. To defy the bishop was to defy the church. And to defy the church was to risk the ban. Mrs. Switzer must have realized her error, for her lips snapped shut.

The bishop directed a softer gaze toward Jonas. "Nor you, Jonas. Her family may not interfere with her *rumspringa*. Harsh though the consequences may be, perhaps she will learn from them. A hard heart must be softened before the seeds of peace may be sown."

Jonas nodded. "Yet acts of kindness are the plowshare of our faith. What better way to learn kindness than to receive it from those who share our way of life?"

Bishop Miller did not reply. His hand rose to stroke his long beard beneath eyes that narrowed in consideration of Jonas's question. Mrs. Switzer's pacing came to a stop. Amos's breath caught in his chest as he awaited the bishop's answer.

Finally, he nodded. "The point you have made is sound. But assistance must come from the community, not only from her family, lest she mistake the kindness for indulgence."

Amos took a forward step. "I will go. I will represent Apple Grove and ensure she knows the reason for our assistance."

The look Jonas turned on him was so full of gratitude that a blush threatened to rise into his face.

"But someone must tend my children while I am away," he added.

"I will." Mrs. Switzer nodded.

"And I will take care of your farm," added Jonas.

A smile appeared on Bishop Miller's face. *"Einer trage des andern last, so werdet ihr das gesetz Christi erfullen.*"

Amos nodded at the familiar Scripture that expressed everything he loved about his Amish brothers and sisters. *Bear ye one another's burdens, and so fulfill the law of Christ.*

And perhaps Rebecca would look favorably upon the one who delivered her from the harsh environment of an *Englisch* jail.

And marry him.

Sixteen

"It's perfect!"

Sassy's enthusiasm in the dress was all Rebecca could have hoped for. She had bitten off the last thread on the final stitch late the previous night, while Mrs. Evans snored softly in the next bunk. Now, watching Sassy twist and turn in the center of her cell, her skirts dancing around her feet, Rebecca couldn't help feeling pride in her handiwork. The ruffles she had removed from the shortened train formed a layered collar that started at the girl's neck and ended in a lacy edging that lay across her bosom. Bows taken from the simplified hem puffed atop each shoulder. If *Maummi* were here, she would scowl at the collar and call it prideful frippery, but at least it provided a decent covering for the bare expanse of Sassy's chest.

From her seat at the small table, Mrs. Evans nodded approval.

233

"Tasteful but stylish. And modest enough that even Annie would have trouble finding fault."

"Oh, her." Sassy's pretty face pulled into a scowl. "I don't give two figs for her opinion. She'd find fault just because of me wearin' it." She turned to Rebecca. "She don't like me on account of she don't approve of singing."

Rebecca's loyalties warred within her. Though she owed Annie Diggs much, Sassy had provided a welcome distraction to the tedious hours spent in her cell the past few days. She had also grown fond of the cheerful blonde, far beyond the fact that Sassy had promised to contribute toward her fine in addition to the seamstress fee.

"Perhaps it is not singing she disapproves of," Rebecca said, twitching at a seam in Sassy's skirt so it fell in a straighter line.

"She's right, my dear," Mrs. Evans agreed. "You do work in a questionable establishment."

Blond curls bounced at a toss of the girl's head. "I'm making an honest living, that's all." With a quick motion, she slid open the curtain that had protected her modesty while she donned the garment. "Sheriff, do you have a mirror around here? I want to see how the dress hangs in the back."

The strained look Colin turned on her brought a grin to Rebecca's face.

"No mirror in the jail. You want to see yourself, go home."

In reply, Sassy pulled a face that made Rebecca laugh.

Mrs. Evans stood and reached for the bag containing her nightdress.

"I must go too. The glass for the new window has finally arrived, and the carpenters come today to install it."

Rebecca gathered Sassy's skirt and blouse and handed them to the girl. Sassy reached into a deep pocket in the skirt. Coins jingled when she scooped them up in her hand.

"Here." She thrust the money at Rebecca. "You done a fine job."

Rebecca looked down at the coins and did a quick tally. Ten dollars. She shook her head and held out her hand toward Sassy.

"There is too much here. The price for this dress is four dollars, as we agreed."

With a grin, the girl folded Rebecca's fingers around the coins. "It's yours. I might not be one of those women who run after Mrs. Diggs, but I can make a donation to help my friend if I want, can't I?"

Touched, Rebecca looked gratefully up at the girl. Her friend. Yes, in a few short days Sassy had become a friend.

Maummi would be scandalized.

On impulse, she stepped closer and wrapped Sassy in an embrace. Unaccustomed to physical demonstrations though she was, it felt good to wrap her arms around her new friend.

Mrs. Evans lingered after Sassy swept out of the jail with a toss of her hair and a flounce of her skirts. The elderly woman paused in the doorway of the cell, her expression disturbed.

"Child, I've done something." She tossed a quick glance over her shoulder toward Colin, whose attention was focused on a newspaper spread across his desk. "I hope you won't mind."

"What have you done?"

Creases deepened on her brow while watery eyes held her gaze. She stepped back into the cell and whispered. "I'm working to gain your release. You know I want only what is best for you, don't you?"

Warmth for the woman standing before her washed through Rebecca. Mrs. Evans had done nothing but help her since the moment Rebecca arrived in Lawrence. For the second time in as many minutes, she embraced a new friend. She pressed her cheek against the soft one that smelled faintly of lavender.

"I am grateful for all your efforts on my behalf."

"Oh, I hope you —"

The door opened and a man stuck his head into the room. "They said I'd find someone from the millinery here? My men are ready to install a window."

"Oh!" Mrs. Evans turned and bustled away. "Thank goodness. We'll talk more later, my dear." A hand waved above her head as she hurried after the carpenter. "Don't worry about a thing!"

When she had gone, Rebecca stood at the cell bars for a moment to watch Colin. Engrossed in his newspaper, he didn't look up. She pulled her cell door closed and returned to her rocking chair. The time passed so much more quickly in conversation, but he was not so inclined today.

With a sigh, she picked up the next piece of stitching.

Amos sat on the train bench with his satchel in his lap, his hands clutching the handle. His back protested hours of inactivity, accustomed as he was to working on his farm, plowing and planting and milking and feeding the livestock. This hard bench's continual swaying with the train's motion was far worse than a buggy on an uneven path, and the good food Mrs. Switzer packed for his lunch had gone uneaten for fear his stomach might revolt.

He shifted his weight to ease the numbness in his limbs. The train had made several stops since leaving Hays City, but he had remained in his seat rather than risk missing the whistle. Now that he had set out to fetch Rebecca Switzer, he was eager to have the task complete and return home, where they both belonged.

At least he'd had a bench to himself for the whole trip. The passengers behind him in the half-full train car had kept up a nearly continuous chatter that Amos was happy to be left out of. He did not feel comfortable talking with strangers. Or, in truth, with anyone. Silence had served him well his entire thirty years, and he enjoyed the peace of his own thoughts.

His glance slid to the *Englischman* across the aisle and one row ahead. When the man selected that bench during the last stop, he had turned in his seat to glare around the train car, and his gaze had settled on Amos. His eyes had narrowed to slits as he noted the traditional Amish garb in which Amos had dressed his entire life. The round hat, the black trousers held up by braces over a white shirt, the collarless coat — in Apple

Grove these garments symbolized the bond he enjoyed with his Amish brothers. All the same, with no signs of rank or privilege. Here, in the *Englisch* world, they made him conspicuous and uneasy. A sneer had curled the nose of the fellow traveler, and he had spat upon the floor in an obviously offensive gesture. Amos could not fail to notice the pair of guns hanging from the man's belt, and his pulse had sped up to a trot. He managed, he hoped, to maintain a properly peaceful countenance, drawing on the familiar words of the Confession, "According to the example, life, and doctrine of Christ, we are not to do wrong or cause offense or vexation to anyone." When the scowling man turned to face forward, Amos had closed his eyes and offered up a prayer of thanksgiving.

The train lurched. Thrown sideways, he clutched at the bag while maintaining his seat. He could not afford to release his grip even for a moment. If the angry *Englischman* knew he carried money in this bag, he would most likely be robbed. His community back home would find no fault when he responded with peaceful nonresistance, but the failure in his mission would burn in him. He would buy Rebecca's freedom and take her home to her family and community, where she belonged. And maybe even to a new family, if she were grateful enough to accept his offer.

The train's whistle blew, and the speed of the landscape rushing past the windows slowed. Behind him, his fellow passengers began gathering their belongings. The train must be approaching Lawrence. Relief washed through him. Though grateful that the train had reduced the time of his journey, he nevertheless would be glad to be quit of it, at least until the return trip, when Rebecca would be by his side.

As the car drifted to a stop, Amos studied the town outside his window. His heart pounded with increased speed at the sight of all the buildings, rows of them, lined up for a long way to the south of the train. Some of those buildings were houses, no doubt, where the townspeople lived practically on top of one another. With longing he thought of the solitude of his farm as he had seen it last night, the sun setting over the neat rows of corn in the western field.

The train ceased to move, and shortly afterward the door in the front opened. A tall *Englischman* wearing a uniform and an odd little hat came into view. The conductor, he had called himself when Amos boarded back in Hays City.

"Lawrence," he announced as he pulled a watch from a pocket in his vest and inspected it. "Five thirty-five. Five minutes early."

The passengers moved toward the exit but stopped when the man with the guns rose from his bench. He half turned and aimed his scowl around the car again. Before Amos could do more than acknowledge the nerves that threatened to destroy his peaceful countenance, the man stepped into the center aisle. An audible sigh rose from the other passengers as he left the car. Only when he was out of sight did they continue disembarking.

Amos stood politely in place, his bag clutched in both hands, and waited for the last of them to file by. Then, when he was the last passenger left on the train, he followed them.

The conductor, standing on the platform, raised a hand toward him.

"I'll hold that while you climb down, sir."

"*Danki,* no."

Amos gripped the bag's handle with his left hand and used his right to grasp a bar beside the door to steady himself as he moved down the steps from the train car. When he stood with both feet on firm soil, he paused for a minute to offer a prayer of

241

gratitude for a safe arrival. Then he took a look around him. The area was alive with activity. Men were unloading cargo, hauling crates out of the cars toward the back of the train, and piling them on wagons. Others stood nearby, waiting to load yet more crates and boxes onto the train. Men astride horses passed by, intent on their errands, and in the distance, a carriage turned a corner and disappeared from view. The passengers who had shared the car with him were heading for the buildings in pairs and small groups. Within moments the town would swallow them up. The man wearing the guns was nowhere in sight. Amos released a relieved breath.

"Have a good evening, sir." The conductor started to step away, heading toward the cargo cars.

Amos held up a hand quickly to stop him. "You will direct me, please?"

"Sure. You need a place to stay? The Eldridge is the best hotel in town. Not the cheapest, mind you. There are boardinghouses, and some of them are even clean."

A hotel or even a boardinghouse was not his immediate concern.

"Where is the jail?"

The man's eyebrows arched. "The jail?"

Though curiosity fairly danced across the

man's features, Amos offered no explanation but merely waited patiently for directions.

Finally, the conductor lifted an arm and pointed toward the far end of town.

"It's about halfway down Massachusetts Street. It'll be on your right, just past the feed store and livery."

"Danki."

Amos bobbed his head in thanks, tightened his grip on his bag, and turned in the direction the man's finger pointed. He was aware that the conductor stood watching him for a long moment before he returned to his duties.

Rebecca stood on the chair and thrust her face toward the metal bars in the window. The sounds of a busy afternoon drifted to her from outside — the clop of a horse's hooves, the rumble of a wagon, a woman's voice calling to a child. She could see little beyond the building behind the jail, which she had discovered housed a laundry business. The sight of clothes dangling from the lines strung between the buildings stirred nostalgic feelings inside her, though no Amish clothesline ever held such a variety of colors. When the clothes had been newly laundered, she could smell the soap as the breeze stirred the fabric. But this late in the day, the lines were empty and the odors were different. Somewhere not far away livestock was housed. That was also a familiar scent, though not nearly so pleasant.

Noise drew her attention from the window. She turned, still standing on the chair, and scanned the jail. Colin sat with his head bent over a piece of paper, working with industry on something. The scratch of his pen had continued all afternoon.

The noise came again, a quiet rapping, though so timid she might have missed it if there had been any other sound in the room. Colin, intent on his writing, didn't raise his head.

"Someone is knocking, I think."

He glanced up at her. "Knocking? Nobody knocks on a jailhouse door."

Setting his pen aside, he rose and crossed the floor. Rebecca watched as he cracked the door open to peek outside. Then he turned to look her way.

"I believe you have a visitor."

Another of the ladies of the movement most likely, though it was late in the day for them. No matter. She was grateful to all who spent a few moments talking with her. Anything to relieve the boredom of long, tedious hours with nothing to occupy her time except more sewing.

When Colin swung the door open, Rebecca's mind at first did not register the identity of the person standing in the entryway. In a glance she took in the familiar Amish clothing, the untrimmed beard. When she looked into the man's face, recognition struck her a blow so sharp she nearly fell off her chair. The round face, the slightly cross-eyed stare.

"Amos? Amos Beiler?"

His eyes moved as he inspected her cell. His thoughts of the furnishings he kept hidden behind an impassive mask, though Rebecca had no doubt her shock at his unexpected appearance was quite visible on her face.

"We don't stand on ceremony around here." With a sweeping hand, Colin invited him inside. "If you're here to visit the prisoner, come on in."

Amos nodded. "I am here to speak with Rebecca."

Rebecca shot Colin a hurt look. Must he mention the fact that she was a prisoner and be sarcastic to poor Amos? It was true that the jailhouse door swung open as frequently as the Lucky Dollar these days, but folks were only being kind.

As she climbed off of her chair, questions

swirled in Rebecca's mind like dust devils on the open range. The appearance of someone from Apple Grove was unexpected and unwelcome, but it should not be surprising. She had written to let Papa know of her safe arrival in Lawrence, though she certainly did not expect him to come after her. And he had not. But Amos?

With a nervous gesture, she smoothed a wrinkle from her skirt before facing him, the cell bars a comforting barrier between them.

"Why are you here?"

Amos did not approach the cell but came to a halt in the center of the room. Behind him, Colin closed the door and returned to the desk.

"I am sent by Bishop Miller to represent Apple Grove."

The bishop knew of her whereabouts? She hid a cringe.

"How?" She had worded her letter so carefully. "How did you know to find me here?" She waved to indicate the cell.

"Jonas received a letter." He stooped to place the black bag he carried on the floor at his feet. From inside he withdrew a piece of paper, which he extended toward her. "You have a *gut* friend. She wrote your papa to alert him to your need."

She covered a groan with her hands. So this was what Mrs. Evans was referring to this morning. She had taken it upon herself to write to Papa to ask for money to pay the fine. Amos's presence told her Papa had responded, but why did he not come himself? Was his disappointment in his daughter for breaking the law too much for him to tolerate?

"I will not take Papa's money. He has little to spare." She turned away. "Take it back to him."

"The money did not come from Jonas." Out of the corner of her eye she watched him bend over the bag again. This time he pulled out a pouch. "Everyone helped. Together we collected one hundred and twenty dollars. Enough to pay the fine and for your train ride home."

Her head spinning, Rebecca wavered on her feet. "Everyone?"

"Ja." The round hat bobbed up and down. "The whole community."

Humiliation burned in her face. Everyone in Apple Grove knew she was in jail?

"Well, now. That should make you proud." Colin stood up. "You can pay your fine. I'll get my jail back. Miz Evans can start sleeping in her own bed again, and you can go home with — Amos, was it?"

Amos nodded, and Colin crossed the room and slapped him on the back.

"Everything can go back to normal."

He seemed eager, almost giddy, to be rid of her. Tears pricked behind her eyes. Not, she assured herself, that it mattered what he thought of her. But after spending the past week together, and after confiding his plans to build his orphanage and church, she might have expected him to at least miss her. A little. Maybe frown. Once.

Stiffening her back, she turned and walked to the rear of her cell. Through the tiny window she could see the blue sky above the rooftop of the laundry. Oh, how she longed to walk beneath that sky. It had been nine days since she felt the sun's warmth on her face.

But to take money from the families of Apple Grove? Why did Papa not come, or *Maummi?* Were they so ashamed of her that they did not wish to see her? Perhaps they were angry with her. If so, would they be reluctant to accept Jesse when she returned with him?

Jesse. He would be here within a few days, according to Mrs. Diggs. She'd had word from Mr. Diggs that he was wrapping up his business and nearly ready to head to Cider Gulch, and then home to Lawrence.

No. She would not take their help. She would solve her own problems and return to Apple Grove on her own. No one would determine the end of her *rumspringa* except her.

Blinking back threatening tears, she raised her chin and faced Amos and Colin. She lowered herself into her rocking chair.

"I will not go," she announced.

Colin's jaw dropped, and she had the satisfaction of seeing Amos's crossed eyes bulge.

The sheriff recovered first. He took a step forward. "That's crazy talk, Rebecca. Take the money and go home. It's time —"

Whatever he further intended to say was interrupted by the heavy pounding of boots against wooden boards of the front porch. The door opened and Deputy Callahan, eyes wild, grabbed Colin by the arm.

"We got a live one, Colin." His eyes gestured to the door. "Marvin Kaspar just came in on the train not twenty minutes ago, big as sin."

It took Rebecca only a moment to identify the name. For the past nine days she'd had little else to read but the wanted posters pinned to the jailhouse wall.

Colin reached for a Winchester hanging on the wall. He stopped long enough to repeat, "Rebecca, take the money and go home." His gaze locked with hers in a silent plea.

She crossed her arms. "I will not take money from those who cannot afford to spend, nor will I leave."

The bars of her cell rattled with the force of the door slamming behind him.

SEVENTEEN

Colin grabbed his horse's lead from the post in front of the jail and sprinted into the saddle.

"I was watching the train, just like you said." John mounted up. "He was first off, and headed straight down Louisiana Street. I thought he looked familiar, but it took me a minute to place him. I'm almost sure it was Kaspar."

Colin sent him a sharp look. "Almost?"

"Well, I didn't go up and ask his name, if that's what you mean." The deputy returned a defensive stare. "Mean-looking fella. Has a scowl that'll set your innards to shivering. I was afraid to let him out of my sight on account of the others disappearing so quick-like. I followed him all the way up to Pa Parker's."

Pa Parker's restaurant sat on the river end of Ohio Street, one street over from Louisiana at the northern boundary of town.

"Let's hope he's still there," Colin said.

The last thing he needed was another wanted man strolling into Lawrence and back out again without a word.

Rebecca.

Her name flashed through his mind. She should take the money and leave. Why did he find the idea worrisome? He thrust thoughts of his pretty little prisoner from his mind. No time for that right now.

"I peeked in the front window," John told him. "Made sure he'd taken a seat and ordered a steak before I came after you."

"Good work, John." Nervous tension raced through Colin's veins as he galloped toward Ohio Street. Maybe now he would finally get some answers.

The suppertime crowd at Pa's place bore testimony to the quality of the food. Or maybe it was the prices, which were among the cheapest in town. A half dozen horses waited at the post out front, and a couple of carriages lined the street beside them. Colin reined up. A crowd like this was a bad place for a confrontation with an outlaw. If there was any way to empty the building without alerting Kaspar . . .

No ideas came to mind. Best clear the street, though, in case the man bolted.

He dismounted in front of the building

next door, well away from the restaurant's front window, and waved to an approaching trio of men.

"Stay clear," he called in a loud whisper, and pointed toward a couple sauntering down the other side of the street. "Get those folks out of here."

Excitement dawned on the men's faces. "Something going on, Sheriff?"

One of the men cast a wide-eyed stare at Pa Parker's. "You gonna have a shoot-out?"

"I hope not." Colin motioned for them to move in the opposite direction. "Clear the street."

The men ran, looking back over their shoulders. Momentarily they paused and engaged in a hurried conversation with the man and woman, who, instead of leaving, turned expectant gazes his way. He made a shooing motion in their direction and then focused his attention on the restaurant.

John had his back pressed against the building on the far side, watching for the sign to move in.

Stomach muscles tight, Colin unstrapped his holster strap and lifted his weapon a little to ensure a quick draw, should that become necessary.

Lord, if this can be done peacefully, I sure would appreciate it.

He glanced back at the people across the street and saw that their number had swelled to almost a dozen. Groaning, he added a postscript to his prayer.

And don't let anybody get hurt.

With a jerk of his head toward the rear, he silently instructed John to cover the back entrance. The deputy nodded and disappeared. Colin headed for the porch. When his boot touched the bottom step, the door opened. He ducked, his hand grasping his pistol grip.

A man and woman exited the building. Relieved, he released his hand and the pistol slid back into place in its holster.

" 'Evening, Miz Thompson, Mr. Thompson." He brushed his hat brim in greeting as the woman placed her hand on her husband's arm.

"Going in for a bite to eat, Maddox?" the man asked as they approached the stairs.

Colin stepped aside to let them pass. "I might just do that."

"Enjoy your supper."

He started up the stairs again when Helen Thompson's loud voice called after him. "Goodnight, Sheriff."

Wincing, he continued onto the porch. So much for a surprise entrance. He didn't bother to walk softly across the wood. With his hand hovering near his weapon, he caught the door before it closed and entered the restaurant. The smell of frying onions and bacon filled the room. He scanned the customers. Two women were at a table near the front door and five, no, six men gathered around the others.

At a table in the far corner, the one closest to the rear entrance, a man sat with his back against the wall. John had described him as mean looking, and at the moment he had a scowl fixed on Colin that would boil ice. His hat sat low on his forehead, and the tails of his long coat swept the floor on either side of his chair. His gaze pierced, holding Colin's with a rigid grip, most likely hoping to mask the fact that his right hand was heading slowly toward his side. The muscles in Colin's hand twitched.

"Hold it right there, Kaspar. Put your hands on the table where I can see them."

All sound in the room ceased as Kaspar lifted his arms slowly and spread his palms on either side of a metal plate holding a half-eaten slab of meat.

"My name ain't Kaspar. It's Lewis. Gerald Lewis."

Colin moved calmly across the room, his eyes never leaving Kaspar's face. The resemblance to the poster hanging on the jailhouse wall was unmistakable. "I say you're Marvin Kaspar, and you're wanted for cattle rustling, horse thieving, and killing a man in cold blood in Waco."

Chairs scraped the wooden floor as customers rose from their tables and headed for the exit. Colin heard the door close behind him, and then an eerie silence. The only sound was the sizzle of a griddle from beyond the doorway that led to the kitchen on Kaspar's right. Colin's approach took him almost to the outlaw's table, and he saw the man's eyes flicker sideways, toward the open doorway.

"Don't try it," Colin said. "Let's do this peacefully."

John stepped into view from the kitchen, his pistol in his hand. At the sight of the deputy's gun pointed in his direction, Kaspar's tense muscles relaxed. He leaned his head back against the wall, his glittering gaze fixed on Colin.

"Like I said, you got the wrong man."

"I have a poster on my wall that says differently. Stand up."

Kaspar shoved his chair back and stood up.

"Now, drop your gun belt. Slowly."

When the weapons hit the floor, Colin gestured for John to get them. With his gun trained on the outlaw, the deputy extended the toe of his boot and scooted the belt out of reach.

Now that Kaspar was unarmed, Colin's hand relaxed. He nodded toward the chair.

"Sit down. Finish your steak."

Though Kaspar lowered himself back into the chair, he made no move toward his plate. Colin pulled a chair from the next table over, turned it around, and straddled it, facing the man.

"Now, suppose you tell me what brings you to Lawrence."

The man's lips didn't so much move as harden. "Just passing through. Thought I'd get some supper."

A distinct whistle sounded from not far off, the signal that the train was about to pull out.

"I think you just missed your train." Colin glanced at the half-eaten slab of meat. A man who intended to continue his journey by train wouldn't cut it this close. " 'Course, doesn't look to me like you were planning to get back on it anyway." When the comment brought no reaction, he took a different tack. "Where are you headed?"

"East."

The contempt in the outlaw's beady eyes was starting to test Colin's patience.

"Meeting up with friends back there, were you? Planning a little reunion?"

A muscle in Kaspar's cheek twitched, and Colin hid a triumphant smile. The man knew something about the appearance of desperados in town lately, and he would get it out of him if it took all night.

"Come on. On your feet." He rose and slid the chair back beneath the table.

"Where we going?"

"To jail." He put a hand beneath Kaspar's arm and hauled him up.

"But I ain't done nothing! You can't throw me in jail for having supper."

"We'll send a message to the Texas marshals and see what they have to say about you."

Colin nudged him toward the door. A row of eager faces outside lined the window to peer in. No doubt word of the evening's entertainment would spread. He'd better send a message over to the mayor and Tank to let them know he had located trouble.

When he opened the door, the man's chilly calm evaporated, and Kaspar began to struggle. Colin tightened the grip on his arm. A string of foul threats filled the night air as the man tried unsuccessfully to jerk away. From somewhere off to the side, a woman gasped at the offensive words that spewed from his mouth.

From behind, John gave Kaspar's back a shove. "Watch your language! Ladies are present."

There were those, all right, and not only here at the restaurant. An image rose in his mind. Rebecca, stubbornly lowering herself into her rocking chair and announcing her intention to refuse the money her Amish friend brought.

We'll see about that.

Whatever it took, he would have his jail back tonight.

Colin shoved Kaspar inside the jailhouse, with John coming in behind them.

The Amish man in his funny round hat, baggy black trousers, and pocketless coat stood in the center of the floor, exactly in the position he had been in when the sheriff left.

Inside her cell, Rebecca sat unmoving in her chair, the rockers still, staring through the bars at her visitor, her feet primly peeking out from beneath her shapeless black dress. Both wore bland expressions.

They look like a matched set.

The thought, for some reason, disturbed him. What was their relationship that this man, this Amos Beiler, would come after her? Had she jilted him by running off to chase another man?

"Wouldja look at that?" Kaspar slowed to gawk at the brightly decorated cell and its occupant. He threw back his head, and biting, harsh laughter filled the room. "This here ain't a jail! Why, it's prettier than a fancy hotel."

Colin propelled the man forward. "That's right, and I saved the best room in the house for you." He shoved him into the empty cell farthest from Rebecca's and slammed the door.

Kaspar's glare circled the bare room. "Hey, don't I get a pretty blanket and a rocking chair too?" His snide taunt ended in a snicker.

"The minute you put on a skirt and start riding sidesaddle." Behind him, John guffawed at his own lame humor.

Colin sent a disapproving frown in his deputy's direction and then pointed a finger at Kaspar.

"Sit down and shut up. I'll get to you in a minute." He strode to stand in front of Rebecca's cell. "I thought I told you to leave."

She raised innocent eyes to his face. "Where else would I be? I am your prisoner."

He shook his head. "You're not my prisoner. You're the town's prisoner, and you aren't even that anymore. Your friend's offering to pay your fine, and I'm taking the offer."

The Amish man stepped to his side, pulling banknotes from a thick leather wallet. "Here. It is enough to buy her freedom."

Rebecca jumped to her feet, eyes blazing. "I will not take it!"

Colin raised an eyebrow in her direction. "You don't have to. I will." He plucked the money from Amos's willing hands.

"No!" She stomped one foot, both hands balled into fists at her side. "I do not allow it."

He crossed to his desk and dropped the money in a drawer. First thing in the morning, he would deliver it to Judge Tankersley. The keys dangled from the lock in her cell, and he headed there to open it. If he had to go in there and shoo her out like a chicken, he would do it. But before he could reach the door, she dashed forward and thrust a hand through the bars. She snatched the keys and then retreated to the far corner of her cell, glaring defiance at him and clutching the key ring to her chest.

Anger flared to life. Stubborn female! That expression was the same one that got her locked up to begin with. "You bring me those keys."

Her chin jutted into the air. "I will not."

From the far cell Kaspar's raspy laugh met his ears, and even John was snickering. The sound inflamed Colin.

"Rebecca Switzer." Amos's quiet voice managed to be soft and disapproving at the same time. "Have you been absent from home so long that you have forgotten our teachings? This behavior is most unbecoming a woman of our faith."

A flicker of remorse dampened some of the defiance on her face, and her tight grip on the key ring lessened.

Then the door opened, and Colin swung around. When he caught sight of Mrs. Evans, a tray balanced against her hip, he paused.

"Helllooo. I've brought your supper, child," the old lady said as she entered. When she spied the outlaw, she gasped. "Oh, my."

"I'm glad you're here." Colin didn't intend to shout, but frustration gave his voice volume. "Talk sense into this . . . this mule-headed woman."

Rebecca's lips pursed in a return of defiance, but when her gaze slid to Mrs. Evans, hurt darkened her eyes and she turned away.

"What's happened?" Mrs. Evans noticed Amos then, and her eyes widened. "Has Rebecca's fine been met?"

"She's free to go," Colin said. "And she refuses."

"I do not want help." Rebecca spoke to the wall. "I will pay my fine with funds I have earned or I shall serve my sentence."

Kaspar's laugh became a guffaw. "I ain't never been in a jail where the prisoners fight to stay." He threw himself down on the bunk, stretched his legs out and folded his hands behind his head. "I think I'm going to like it here."

The outlaw's needling fell on deaf ears. Colin turned to Mrs. Evans.

"Please talk to her. Make her understand that she needs to go home to her family."

With an affirmative nod, Mrs. Evans approached the cell. "He's right, Rebecca. Go home to your folks. We can handle things here. Poor mite. You got caught up in something not of your doing. I should have realized that sooner."

When Rebecca didn't answer, Colin stomped across the room to his desk. The force with which he jerked on the bottom drawer pulled it all the way off its runners, and it crashed to the floor. He snatched something out of it and left it where it lay as he returned to Rebecca's cell.

"You don't think there's only one set of keys, do you?"

Her pout deepened when he held the spare key ring up for her inspection. A second later, he'd unlocked the door and stormed inside. She didn't budge, though he stood right next to her, towering over her and glaring down at the white *kapp* that covered her hair.

"You are the most confounding, irritating, infuriating woman I've ever met, and that temper of yours has gotten you into trouble more than once. You've plagued me for over a week, and turned my jail into a laughing-stock. Well, it's over, do you hear?"

The tension left Rebecca's muscles, and her shoulders sagged. When she looked up, she focused on Colin, her eyes watery with tears.

The sight doused the heat of his fury. He hadn't meant to hurt her with hasty words, but he couldn't have a woman in jail when two doors down was a murdering outlaw, could he? It wasn't decent.

Turning away from her corner, she stooped to pick up her sewing basket and then left the cell.

"Rebecca." Colin snagged her arm gently. "Look. The past week has been slow and

I've coddled you, but things are changing. My days in Lawrence are short, and I won't leave you here in this town. You belong in Apple Grove, with family. Let Amos take you home." His eyes softened. "Put away childish thoughts. If your Jesse is the man God intends for you, he'll find you."

She met his gaze, her eyes alight with emotion behind the tears, and then turned away.

Mrs. Evans gathered her close. "Come along, dear. I'll help you prepare for the trip home."

Rebecca allowed herself to be steered out of the jailhouse. When the door closed, Colin turned, aware of Amos's gaze fixed on him.

"You can leave now, Mr. Beiler. You can take Rebecca home."

"I have no bed tonight." The cross-eyed gaze lowered to the empty bunk in the cell Rebecca had vacated, and his eyebrows rose with a question.

"There's a hotel down the street. Or you might try Miz Sawyer's over on Lancaster Street. The jail is not an Amish boarding-house."

"I'm heading toward Lancaster Street now," John said kindly. "I'll show you where it is, if you like."

Amos nodded, picked up his bag, and followed the deputy out. Colin stepped to his desk to slide the drawer back in place. Loneliness settled over him as tear-filled eyes haunted his thoughts. What kind of man made a girl cry? He'd never been good with women, and tonight proved that he hadn't gotten any better at it.

"Hey."

He glanced up to see Kaspar standing at the cell door, his arms dangling through the bars.

"What do you want?"

"Since the little gal left, can I have her supper, seeing how I didn't finish mine?"

EIGHTEEN

"There, there, child." Mrs. Evans set a tea tray on the table in her cozy sitting room. "A bite to eat will soothe your nerves."

Rebecca stared at the tray laden with a bowl of round, plump fruit, yellow cheese, and thick slices of cake with a sugary glaze, all intended to tempt her appetite. The thought of eating turned her stomach. Colin's words rang in her ears. *Go home.* Tears threatened, but she sniffed and blinked until the prickle stopped.

Mrs. Evans hovered, her hands clasping each other. "At least have a cup of tea. You can't go to bed on an empty stomach."

Nothing would help tonight, but she nodded to make her hostess happy. Her *rumspringa* was nine days old, and what had she accomplished? She had stolen Papa's horse, lost Emma and Luke's money, shouted at a judge, been thrown in jail, and shamed her family in front of the entire district. Her goal of reuniting with Jesse was no closer than when she started out. And now it appeared that the tentative friendship she'd begun with Colin was not what she'd thought it was. She had been nothing but an irritant to him, a — what had he called her? A plague.

What if Jesse thinks I am a plague too?

Therein lay the source of her misery. What if the man she loved turned her away, as Colin had? As, apparently, her own papa had, since he hadn't come himself.

Lord, please let Jesse love me. I cannot bear it if he doesn't.

Mrs. Evans handed her a steaming teacup, and she held it in both hands to warm fingers that had gone cold with the gloom of her thoughts.

"Rebecca." The soft tone pulled her attention to the elderly face. Sorrow had carved the lines deeper. "I am truly sorry for writing to your family. The donations from the movement weren't coming in as they should, and I don't have the strength of conviction Annie does. To her and the others, a peaceful protest in your honor would have the same effect whether you marched with us or not. I heard whispers among the ladies that if you were still in jail when Frances Willard and Anna Howard Shaw arrive, then our statement would be even stronger."

The words fell on her like yet another blow. She lowered the cup from her lips. "But Mrs. Diggs promised to work for my release."

Mrs. Evans slid onto the cushion beside her and placed an arm around her shoulders.

"And she has. Annie Diggs is a woman of honor. But not all the ladies in Lawrence share her strength of character, as evidenced by the lack of their donations. I hadn't the money to give, or I would have." She squeezed. "I did the only thing I could think to do. I knew a sweet child like you must come from a family who cares."

Yes, she thought miserably. *They did care, until I shamed them.*

The arm was removed, and Mrs. Evans clasped her hands in her lap.

"Will you forgive a meddling old fool who only had your interests at heart?"

Forgiveness in such a circumstance was easy. How could she fault the woman who had been her friend and loyal companion through the most difficult days of her life? She'd had plenty of time to think while she sewed, and she knew the blame of the last nine days lay with her. If she had not lost her temper with the judge, none of this would have happened.

If she had not sneaked off in the middle of the night, she would be at home now, with her loved ones. Growing up was harder than she imagined.

She managed a genuine smile. "I bear you only gratitude, Mrs. Evans. You have been a true friend." The smile slipped. "It seems my only one."

"Oh, I don't know. That young man who came for you seems quite taken."

The idea brought a laugh from her. "Amos Beiler is here at the direction of the bishop. If he is interested in me, it is only because he seeks a mother to raise his children."

"He is a widower?" Mrs. Evans' gaze flew to the picture of her and her late husband, her expression tragic. "Oh, the poor man."

Seeing the pain play across the woman's face, Rebecca experienced a stab of remorse. She had never considered that poor Amos might be lonely. He always seemed so composed and emotionless.

Mrs. Evans leaned forward and slid a slice of cake onto a small plate. "Mr. Beiler isn't the only one who is taken with you, you know."

Rebecca watched her cut a bite-sized piece with her fork. "What do you mean?"

The fork paused in front of Mrs. Evans' mouth. "Why, the sheriff, of course. One had only to watch his eyes and hear his words to see that."

The idea was so ludicrous she couldn't stop a laugh. "He does not like me, and I have" — she swallowed — "plagued him. Like grasshoppers and locusts, if you are to believe him."

A twinkle winked in the old lady's eye. "Oh, my dear, you can't tell what a man thinks by words spoken in haste. No, you must look for the reason behind the words." She placed the cake between smiling lips. "You really should try this. It's quite good."

A hot, uncomfortable dampness gathered beneath Rebecca's collar. Could Mrs. Evans be right? Did the cause for Colin's rejection lie in his feelings?

She shook her head, unwilling to let the thought lodge there. No. The enforced time together had resulted in what she thought was a budding friendship, but nothing else. Besides, she loved Jesse and had never made a secret of that.

But she couldn't deny the fact that Colin's words no longer stung the way they had a moment before. Beside her, Mrs. Evans watched her with a shrewd eye. With an effort, Rebecca schooled her expression. To cover the smile that threatened, she leaned toward the tea tray and picked up the second plate.

"I will have cake, thank you."

Morning brought a resurgence of hope that Rebecca would not have thought possible the night before. She had spent the first hours of the night reexamining her plans. True, she had accomplished nothing thus far with her *rumspringa* except to humiliate herself and possibly alienate her family. Also true, she had not yet found Jesse. And Colin . . . well, she was not sure what to think of Colin. The more she considered Mrs. Evans' suggestion, the less credence she gave it, but she could not deny the fact that when he spoke of his desire to build his orphanage and church, the passion she glimpsed in him stirred something similar in her. It made her even more determined to achieve her goal.

And that goal was marriage to Jesse and embarking on a peaceful life. A Plain life. Colin had said, "Put away childish things." What she felt for Jesse was anything but childish — but then, her thoughts of Colin were starting to become confusing.

She cupped her hands and splashed water from the basin on her face. Her path to accomplishing her goal had been altered, but she would not return to Apple Grove. Not yet. She had given her word to participate in the peaceful protest, and she would do so. If Annie Diggs was known as a woman of honor, so would Rebecca Switzer be. The protest would occur on the twenty-fourth, four days from now. In the meantime, she would finish Sassy's dress and take on more sewing. Four days might not be long enough to earn the money she owed Luke and Emma and now the people of Apple Grove, but it would be a start. Somehow she would repay her debts and earn Papa's approval again, no matter how long it took.

Her face clean, she straightened. From the burnished glass above the dressing table her reflection stared at her. She raised a hand to her hair, unbound and tousled from the night. Not the gleaming gold of Sassy's curls, but the sunlight streaming through the window reflected off her chestnut locks and gave them a lovely color all their own. She twisted a strand around her finger. What if she didn't wear her *kapp* today? She was on *rumspringa,* wasn't she?

Five minutes later she descended the narrow staircase to find Mrs. Evans stirring a steaming pot on the surface of the iron stove. She tapped the long-handled spoon on the edge.

"There you are, child. I fixed porridge — oh!" Her eyes grew wide when she caught sight of Rebecca, and she turned. "Don't you look lovely this morning?"

Self-consciously, Rebecca ran a hand over the thick mass of hair that hung past her waist while the woman walked in a circle around her.

"Yes, quite lovely." A merry gleam appeared in her eyes when she turned back to the stove and began to spoon porridge into bowls. "After breakfast, I'd like to ask a favor."

Rebecca cradled a warm bowl in both hands and carried it to a small table that had already been set for breakfast.

"I will help you however I can."

"If you'll just go across to the jail and bring my things back, I would appreciate that ever so much."

The bowl slipped from Rebecca's startled fingers and fell with a clatter onto the table. The jail?

Mrs. Evans ignored the racket and set the second bowl down gently in front of her chair. "I must open the shop, you know."

"But . . ." Face Colin again? So soon? The sting of his words still lay heavy on her heart. Her appetite gone, she sank into the chair. "Perhaps I could open the store and you could go with Amos to get your things?"

"No, I have an early customer. You must see him sometime, dear." Mrs. Evans picked up her spoon and took a dainty mouthful. "Afterward, you can take my wagon and drive to the dairy, if you don't mind. I think the cream has gone sour, and I only purchased it yesterday."

Rebecca stared at the rapidly cooling porridge. Though she would give much to avoid seeing Colin this morning, perhaps Mrs. Evans was right. The sooner they got past the awkwardness of yesterday, the easier she would feel.

Only by facing him could she put behind her any lingering doubt about his feelings.

Amos sat on the rigid boards in front of the milliner's shop, his shoes resting on the dusty road. Although the sun peeked above the buildings that lined the wide street, the town was almost deserted.

Unlike farmers, town folk kept odd hours.

Sleep had eluded him long into the night, put off by the sounds of revelry and activity outside the window of his boardinghouse. The three men who shared his lodging had stumbled in and fallen onto their cots long after nightfall, their breath filling the air with the reek of alcohol. When Amos rose before sunup, their snores were still echoing off the rough-cut timber walls. Even Mrs. Sawyer, the woman who had taken his money and showed him to his meager cot last night, had not yet risen when he slipped out of the boardinghouse into the predawn stillness of Lawrence.

Back home he would already have eaten breakfast, milked the cows, and started spreading manure in the east field. A breath filled his lungs and seeped out in a sigh. Jonas had promised to care for his animals, but no doubt the task of fertilizing would have to wait until he returned. And how were his children faring with Mrs. Switzer? He missed their sleepy yawns when he roused them to do their morning chores.

For a moment he battled resentment. Rebecca Switzer had disrupted his family and his life, and she had not greeted his arrival with proper gratitude. She had ever been headstrong, and last night proved that recent events had failed to teach her the meekness of an Amish woman.

A noise alerted him to the opening of the door behind him. Amos stood and turned to look into the astonished face of the object of his thoughts. How young and lovely she looked, but with increasing disapproval he noted her unbound hair and the absence of her *kapp.*

"Amos." She sounded surprised, even shocked, to see him. As well she should, to appear in the light of day in such an immodest fashion.

"Rebecca." With an effort he schooled the emotion from his voice and expression. It would not do to offend her when he wished her cooperation. "I have purchased seats on the train to Hays City. We leave at noon."

The stubborn set to her jaw was not what Amos expected from a woman who had so recently been the recipient of grace from her community. She folded her arms, her manner most unrepentant.

"My business here is not finished."

With dawning disbelief, he realized the meaning of her words.

"But I paid for your freedom."

Her eyes snapped. "Am I to be bought like a cow or a goat?" Then she softened her tone. "Amos, I am grateful. Truly I am. But I have given my word, and Amish do not give their word and then take it back—"

"There you are, Becca!"

A female voice echoed down the street. Amos turned to see a woman coming. Golden hair circled her head like an unkempt halo, and her full figure was set off rather than hidden by an abundance of ruffles and lace. Flames erupted in his cheeks at the sight of her.

"Some of the boys were talking last night and said you'd paid your fine." She brushed past Amos. "Excuse me, sweetie." She gathered Rebecca in an embrace. "Good for you. I was hoping you'd be here. This hem don't fall right in the back. You think you could fix it for me?" She twisted her hind-quarters around to face Rebecca and twitched her billowing skirt.

His face burning, Amos tore his gaze away. Had he thought Rebecca immodest a moment before? Surely Jezebel had stepped straight from the pages of *Die Bibel.*

The woman's gaze fell on him and swept him from head to foot. An amused grin pierced dimples in her plump cheeks.

"Well, wouldja look at you? Ain't you the cutest little thing in that squirrely hat and scruffy beard?"

Amos drew himself up to stand straight under her scrutiny. A thousand responses tore through his mind, but none made their way to his tongue, so he simply returned her gaze.

A woman appeared behind Rebecca. The elderly lady he recognized from the previous night awarded them all with a delighted smile.

"Sassy, so good to see you. I was just about to invite Mr. Beiler in for breakfast. Would you care to join us?"

With a deepening of the dimple the saloon girl turned his way, tossed her head, and grinned. "Don't mind if I do."

A fog descended on Amos's thoughts, throwing them into chaos. Rebecca, who looked nearly as bemused as he felt, beckoned him into the widow's house.

"Come eat some breakfast before you start for home."

Sometime in the past few minutes, control had been wrested from him. Feeling slightly sick, he removed his hat and trailed the ladies inside.

Colin ran a comb through his hair and then placed it on the dresser. Had he ever spent a more restless night than the one just past? Not in his recollection. Kaspar's questioning had proved a waste of time, with the sour-faced outlaw repeating his denial of everything and anything. He was "just passing through town." And all the while Colin had been haunted with images of a sweet-faced Amish girl and tear-flooded brown eyes.

He put on his leather vest and paused for a moment to finger the shiny tin star pinned there. Four more days and he would hand over that star to his successor.

Can't come a minute too soon.

But with the thought came a flood of emotions. In all conscience, how could he leave Mulhaney with so many unanswered questions? Outlaws popping in and out of town. Women whispering behind his back.

And one little Amish girl who haunted his thoughts.

She's not my problem. I need to leave her to Amos, or better yet, to the elusive Jesse she speaks so highly of.

Even though he'd reached the conclusion when his head hit the pillow, sleep had hovered out of reach the whole night, his restless thoughts refusing to settle. Why hadn't he taken longer to explain his order to leave? He couldn't abandon her here in Lawrence, alone and unprotected. Mulhaney most likely wouldn't be as patient with her as he had been. And exactly why had he been so patient? Because he knew she was young and followed foolish dreams. Jesse. Who knew where the man was and what he'd become? If he loved her, he would have sought her out years ago.

"Hey, lawman. Where's the coffee?"

Kaspar's growly shout from the cell beyond his small room jarred his nerves. The man's snores had raised the roof. With a final tug to settle his vest over his shoulders, Colin walked into the office at the same time the door opened. Time was when the jail was pretty quiet. When a familiar figure slipped through, he smiled. Rebecca. He figured she would be so angry with him that she would leave town as quickly as she'd come. Her striking, fresh-faced appearance this morning stopped him. Her beautiful hair hung freely down her back instead of being caught up in the severe knot he'd grown accustomed to.

Or maybe it wasn't her hair that looked different. The tentative smile she turned his way stopped him short. Desire thickened his tongue.

"We have come to clean my cell . . . I mean, your cell."

He noticed that Amos had filed in quietly behind her. Nodding, he said, "That would be nice. Thank you."

Her quizzical gaze searched his face. "I . . ."

"Things got heated last night. I'm sorry."

A smile softened her lips. "I too am sorry. You have been most kind to me — more often than not."

From the cell behind him came the sound of slow applause.

"Now, ain't that tear-jerkin'?" Kaspar's voice dripped sarcasm. "You two want to kiss and make up?"

Still holding her gaze, Colin said, "Pipe down, Kaspar."

Amos stepped between them, a troubled frown gathered on his brow. "We will begin. There is much to carry."

Two trips across the street emptied the cell of lace, frills, and womanly stuff. Amos carried the rocking chair while Colin loaded the table and chairs into Mrs. Evans' small wagon to be returned to Abigail Lawson. Rebecca watched as he set them in place.

"So you're a free woman. I'm happy for you, Rebecca. Guess you'll be leaving with Amos on the noon train?"

"No. I will remain in Lawrence."

He laid a chair down so it wouldn't fall during the bumpy journey across town and turned to her. "I thought we'd settled this last night. You need to go home."

"I need to be a woman of my word, and Mrs. Diggs expects me to be here when Mr. Diggs returns with Jesse."

Conflicting emotions rose as he set the other chair in place. He couldn't see her with Amos. A woman with her spirit would suffocate with an emotionless man like him. But Jesse was a wild card.

Lord, I hope he's as fine a man as she says he is. She deserves a good life.

He straightened when Amos returned from Mrs. Evans'. "Well, I wish you God-speed, Miss Switzer."

"And His to you also, Sheriff Maddox."

He nodded. "You're a good woman, Rebecca — and I'm praying that Jesse knows what a lucky man he is."

Standing there in the sunlight, her head tilted back to look up at him and her hair spilling down her back, she made a lovely picture.

A smile escaped her. "It would give me great pleasure to hear you preach, Colin."

With an effort, he returned her smile. "I'm getting a little rusty. I haven't been around many cows lately."

She gently grasped his hands. "But some-day?"

He nodded. "Someday."

Though in his heart he knew that day would never come.

NINETEEN

Rebecca sat on the bench of the small wagon beside Amos, studying the buildings they passed. Though ten days had gone by since her arrival in Lawrence, this was her first real look at the town. On Massachusetts Street the buildings were nearly all businesses, set close together. The streets farther away were narrower, and the buildings had more room between them and boasted more homes. Fascinated, she stared at the neat little yards and whitewashed porches decorated with pots of flowers. In a few windows she glimpsed lace curtains, an indulgence not seen in Amish households.

Amos slowed the wagon to execute a turn, following Colin's directions to the Lawson home. He handled the horse with ease, and Rebecca noticed he looked more at home here, on a wagon bench, than sitting at Mrs. Evans' breakfast table, trying not to stare at Sassy with a sort of fascinated horror he could not completely mask by his normally impassive expression. She hid a grin.

Sassy had eaten porridge and bread like a lumberjack while detailing the escapades of a heated poker game in the saloon the night before. She seemed to take an inordinate amount of pleasure in watching a flush rise on Amos's face, and Rebecca suspected she exaggerated her tale with flamboyant gestures simply to watch the color deepen.

Mrs. Evans' words from last night returned, and Rebecca's conscience prickled. Was Amos lonely? He had been a widower for five years, and the desperation of his desire to find a new wife had become a joke among the young women of Apple Grove. If talk turned to marriage, someone would inevitably remark, "There's always Amos Beiler," and everyone would chuckle.

How unkind of us, she realized as she watched his profile. *I hope he never heard.*

"Thank you for helping," she told him. "The cell is as it should be now. Bare."

He replied with a nod and did not turn from his study of the street ahead. The horse's hooves fell upon the packed dirt with a rhythmic *thud-thud-thud.*

With a stab of guilt, she realized she hadn't said anything about his errand. He would have had to arrange for someone to care for his children and farm. Not easy tasks, to be sure.

"And thank you for coming to my rescue. What trouble you have gone to for me."

"Not only I. All the families of our district."

Rebecca sank a little lower on the bench and tried to filter the hurt out of her voice. "All but my own."

His head turned, and he gazed at her through his small, dark eyes. For the first time she realized he wasn't really cross-eyed. His eyes were merely set so close together they appeared to cross if one didn't look closely. The query in them faded when realization dawned.

"Jonas would have come." The words were pitched softly. "Also Mrs. Switzer. Bishop Miller refused them. He thought it best if help came not from an indulgent family, but from the district."

Rebecca's spirits lifted. Papa had not washed his hands of her. He had merely obeyed the bishop. Perhaps, then, he was not angry with her after all.

Before she could fully react to the news, Amos continued. "I had yet another purpose to come." He wet thin lips above his bushy beard and stared ahead. "Perhaps if you felt gratitude, you would look kindly on me."

Rebecca looked quickly away. Was that a declaration of love? No, she didn't believe so. His voice quivered with emotion, but she did not think it was love. More likely need, thank goodness. Tenderness welled up from somewhere deep inside her, and she swallowed against a tight throat.

"Amos, you are not in love with me," she said softly.

"No, but perhaps I could come to love you." He flashed a sideways glance at her but failed to hold her gaze. "In time you might return my affection."

"I'm afraid not." She laid a hand on his arm. "I'm sorry, but my heart belongs to another. You deserve more than me."

His shoulders slumped, and he gave a slow nod. "It is the sheriff."

Now it was her turn to flush. What a thing to say.

"No," she hurried to reply. "My true love is on his way to me. He will arrive soon. This is why I cannot leave Lawrence yet."

Silence fell between them while the wagon slowed and then stopped before a square house of unpainted wood. He secured the rope.

"I cannot leave either, then." The statement came out as an announcement. "I will stay and return when you do."

"But you have commitments, a family," she protested.

"My family is cared for." The look he turned on her held a stubborn determination that left no room for argument. "I gave my word to bring you home. A man is only as good as his word."

Her chin lifted. "And I've given my word to remain here and wait for Jesse."

At that interesting moment, the door to the house opened and a woman appeared.

"The news is true then!" Abigail Lawson hurried to the porch, a chubby baby propped on her hip. "I heard you were out of jail, Rebecca."

With a last look at Amos that warned him they had not finished the conversation, Rebecca climbed down from the wagon in time to be swept into a quick embrace. Surprised by the sudden squeeze, the baby let out a squeal and Abigail stepped back, laughing. Rebecca admired the child, noting a strong resemblance to Hal, with whom she had spent hours while he was on duty in the jail.

Amos also climbed from the wagon to begin lifting the small table and chairs down.

"Just put them anywhere inside." Abigail waved toward the door. "We'll move them later." She turned back to Rebecca. "Gladys

Collins told me last night that a friend came from home and paid your whole fine. I guess that's him." Without waiting for an answer, she rushed on, full of news that couldn't wait to spill out. "You know what else she said? Annie had a letter from back East."

Rebecca cast a quick glance over her shoulder to be sure Amos could not over-hear.

"About the peaceful protest?"

"No, not that." Abigail bounced the baby on her hip and lowered her voice. "It's about the new sheriff. She wrote to a friend and asked them to do some checking, and turns out he's known for wild living and drinking whiskey!"

Amos appeared from inside the house, and the ladies fell silent while he made another trip to the back of the wagon. They waited until he picked up a chair in each hand and headed for the house again.

Abigail continued in a rushed whisper. "Annie about had a conniption when she heard! Says it's a plot by the mayor and judge to get away with selling more liquor than ever, and our protest is timely because it'll bring national attention to Lawrence, and she's fixing to write a whole series of newspaper articles about it." She raised her eyebrows. "With pictures too."

"Oooh." Rebecca widened her eyes appreciatively. What would Colin think about his replacement now?

Amos reappeared, empty-handed.

Abigail bobbed a quick curtsey, her arms wrapped around the baby. "Thank you kindly, sir. Do the pair of you want to come in for a visit? I could put on the kettle."

"No, thank you, Abigail. We have errands yet to run. More deliveries and a trip to the dairy."

Amos assisted Rebecca to her place on the bench and then climbed up on the other side. The wagon wheels began to turn when Abigail called out, "Oh, Rebecca!"

She twisted on the bench to look at her friend.

"Will I see you in church tomorrow?"

Church? With a start, Rebecca realized today was Saturday. Tomorrow the faithful of Apple Grove would gather in someone's home to worship together, and she would miss it. But to attend an *Englisch* church? Well, why not? She would like to see the kind of church Colin would one day build.

"Yes," she answered. "Yes, perhaps you will."

"Good. And wear your hair that way. You look mighty fetching."

Smiling, Rebecca lifted a hand in farewell. When she faced forward again, she saw that Amos's lips formed a disapproving line. Whether because of her unbound hair or the idea of going to an *Englisch* church, she didn't know.

After a silent ride back to Massachusetts Street, Amos guided the wagon slowly toward Mrs. Evans' milliner's shop, mindful of the heavier traffic. Try though she might, Rebecca couldn't help staring at the jail, hoping for a glimpse of Colin, but the door remained closed and the chair on the wooden boards out front empty.

A few buildings away from the milliner's, they passed the Lucky Dollar Saloon, where the trouble had all started. The doors stood open, though no music drifted from inside. As they drew alongside, Rebecca strained her eyes to see the interior. What did a saloon look like?

A noise from above drew her attention to the building's second floor, where one of a row of windows was thrown open with a bang. In the next instant, a bright scarlet garment flew through and dropped toward them. She barely had time to open her mouth to warn Amos when the fabric landed on his head.

"That's what I think of your fancy dresses!" A shout that was more like a shriek sounded from inside.

Rebecca quickly grabbed the reins as Amos's hands batted frantically at the silky dress that covered his head. *"Ach! Ach!"* came his muffled voice.

As Rebecca pulled the fabric off of him, another dress flew through the window along with an exclamation of, "And this one too!" This time she recognized Sassy's shrill tone.

With an alarmed look upward, Amos took back the reins and flicked them. The horse lurched forward, and the ornate garment fell to the dirt behind their wagon as a man's voice bellowed from the upper floor of the saloon.

Passersby stopped to stare, and a small crowd gathered as Rebecca leaped from the slowing wagon and ran to stand beneath — and safely to one side of — the window.

"I don't care a fig at Christmas what's good for your business," came Sassy's voice. "I ain't doing it!"

Another item sailed through the air, this time an object of more substance. The crowd below sidestepped, and a hairbrush struck the ground with a puff of dirt. An ornamental comb followed.

"What's going on out here?"

At the familiar voice, Rebecca turned to find Colin push his way through the crowd. He caught sight of her and flashed a grin. "Are you causing a ruckus again?"

Rebecca planted her hands on her hips and faced him. "I am not. Apparently, Sassy is upset."

Another dress flew through the window, immediately followed by a water basin. The crowd skipped back when it shattered on impact.

The man shouted, "I'm taking that out of your pay!"

Sassy answered, "Yeah? Well, add this to my tab." A pitcher arced through the air.

Amos came to stand beside them, his eyes fixed on the window. "I believe she is angry."

Colin sighed. "You think so?"

A shriek pierced the air, followed by Sassy's outraged cry of, "Take your hands offa me, you big ox. Don't touch me!"

The crowd drew in a collective gasp.

"That's enough." Colin strode forward quickly and entered the building.

Rebecca stood watching the half doors swinging behind him, torn. Was her friend in trouble? Should she follow him? Beside her, Amos fixed on the window through eyes as round as wagon wheels.

Mrs. Evans bustled up to Rebecca. "I heard a commotion out here." She stooped to retrieve the hairbrush from the street. "What's happening?"

A woman standing behind them said, "The saloon girl is pitching a fit about something."

"Oh, dear."

They heard voices, the words unclear, but Rebecca recognized Colin's firm tone. Then a muscular arm shut the window with a slam. Moments later, the doors swung open, and Sassy stormed through. Her blond curls seemed alive as she whipped her head back and forth, taking in the watching crowd. Then she spied Rebecca and marched over to her.

"I ain't never been so mad in my whole life! If that man knows what's good for him, he'll stay out of my way."

"What happened, dear?" Mrs. Evans asked.

The townspeople drew near to hear her answer.

"He don't like my new dress!" Outrage filled the girl's voice.

Someone snickered, and Rebecca bit down on her bottom lip to hide a smile. Colin had accused *her* of having a temper?

Amos wore an expression of complete bemusement.

"For this you throw out your clothing?"

"Oh, those aren't mine. Those are the ones Ed told me I have to wear if I want to work at the Dollar anymore. He said the one Rebecca fixed up for me makes me look like a schoolmarm, and the customers ain't coming in to see a schoolmarm."

Her head turned as she searched the items littering the ground. Spying the scarlet dress, she marched over to it and jerked it up. She held it up for the crowd to see.

"This is what he wants me to wear, and he said if I didn't I couldn't work there anymore. So I quit."

Besides being a most flamboyant color, the neckline plunged to a more daring level than even the one Rebecca had altered. It took no imagination at all to see that Sassy's full figure would create quite a distraction in that garment.

"Oh, my," muttered Mrs. Evans.

Amos turned abruptly away, his face approaching the color of the dress.

The saloon doors swung open again, and Colin exited. He raised his voice to address the crowd.

"All right, folks, the show's over. You can go on about your business."

As the people started to disperse, some

reluctantly, he approached Sassy.

"If I were you, I'd stay away from Ed for a while. He's a bit riled up."

She tossed her head. "Good for him. So am I."

He gestured to the dresses and shards of pottery strewn across the street. "Take care of this mess."

His gaze flickered to Rebecca. Was it her imagination, or did his eyes soften in the moment before he turned to go?

Without a word, Amos began the task of cleaning up the street.

"My mama would have risen up outta her grave to whip my backside if I put that dress on and pranced around in front of a bunch of men full of whiskey." She glanced toward the saloon, and sniffled. "That job wasn't all that good after all, but it was the best I could find."

Mrs. Evans patted her arm. "You did the right thing, honey."

Rebecca agreed. "What will you do now?"

"I guess I'll head to New York City soon." The hard line of her mouth softened, and her voice became thoughtful. "But it'll take me a day or two to get the funds together. No sense in being in an all-fired hurry."

Rebecca followed her gaze down the street, but she saw nothing that would cause such serious regard.

Only Amos, stooping to gather broken pottery.

TWENTY

The church Mrs. Evans led Rebecca, Amos, and Sassy to on Sunday morning was an impressive building. Rebecca admired the shining white walls and doors of polished wood that shone in the morning sunlight. Atop the pitched roof a steeple reached high into the sky, crowned with a cross that was all the more impressive for its simplicity. Just two pieces of timber, rough and unfinished, lashed together. On just such a cross the Lord might have hung. The thought lent a spirit of reverence as Rebecca approached.

The people gathered on the lawn in front of the church steps chattered away as they would at any Amish church service. Rebecca glanced backward at Amos, who trudged along behind with a face even longer than usual. That he had agreed to come at all had surprised her because he clearly lacked any desire to attend an *Englisch* church. She felt a stab of sympathy. Poor Amos. Having failed in his task of escorting her back to Apple Grove, he seemed to have assigned himself the task of trailing her around Lawrence.

Sassy pranced along with her head high, an eager smile on her lips. Mrs. Evans had generously offered the girl a bed. She had lost her room along with her job at the saloon.

"I haven't been to church since I left Texas," she'd admitted to Rebecca as they readied themselves for the service. "Ed insisted I work late Saturday night, so I never could get outta bed early enough the next day."

"There's Annie." Mrs. Evans pointed to a cluster of women standing near the doors. "I want to introduce you properly, dear." She looped an arm through Sassy's and tugged her away.

Rebecca started after them, but she was stopped when Abigail Lawson's waving hand caught her attention. Smiling, she veered in that direction, delighted to see several of the women who had visited her in jail.

After a few moments of friendly chatter, she caught sight of another familiar face. Her heart gave a curious skip to see Colin coming up the walk. She watched him nod and smile at one couple, tip his hat to another, and stop to exchange a word with a gentleman in a black suit. When he turned away, his gaze strayed toward her. A smile lit his face, and warmth flooded Rebecca at the sight of it.

He approached across the grassy yard, sidestepping a pair of children who raced in front of him.

"I wondered if you would be here this morning," he said when he neared. He extended a hand toward Amos. "Glad to have you visiting, Mr. Beiler."

His eyes were the same color as the sky above them, she noticed. Rebecca tore her gaze from his face, disturbed at the fluttering in her stomach. She stared instead at the slightly lopsided tie beneath his chin and fought an urge to reach up and straighten the loops of fabric.

"I did not realize you attend this church," she managed.

"Whenever the job allows." A grin drew lines at the corners of his mouth. "I like taking notes on the sermons."

The comment contained a private message between the two of them, which caused another delightful tickle. She was spared answering by the ringing of a bell. The doors of the church opened, and the people began to move toward the building. She caught sight of a bright blond head across the crowd and saw Sassy's gesture for her to join them. Colin fell in beside her, and they entered the building side by side, with Amos following close behind.

The press lessened as people filed into rows and took their seats. As she made her way toward the place where Sassy and Mrs. Evans had settled, Rebecca glanced back at Amos. His eyes darted everywhere, his face registering surprise. She knew why. Unlike an Amish service, men and women sat interspersed. No doubt he was thoroughly scandalized, even though he did recover himself enough to surge in front of Colin and follow Rebecca when she reached the place Mrs. Evans had saved for them. He took his seat beside her. Colin eyed him with a slight frown before sitting beside him.

The seating was only the first of many differences. The service began when a man with a pleasant smile welcomed them and invited them to sing.

Colin leaned forward and whispered to her over Amos. "That's the preacher."

Amos's stare became wooden, while Rebecca studied the man with interest. Bishop Miller was a kind and friendly man, but when he led services his countenance became solemn, his manner reverent. This man looked neither solemn nor reverent, and his smile beamed as his gaze swept his flock. She could easily envision Colin in his place. Though when he led them in a song that was definitely too lively to come from the *Ausbund,* even Rebecca had to battle an unsettled feeling when she pictured what her Apple Grove community's reaction might be. Sassy sang with gusto in a lovely voice that drew appreciative looks from several seated around them.

But when the preacher picked up a large book from a table in the front and began to read, Amos gave a start.

"Das ist nicht Deutsch!" he rasped, scandalized.

"No," Rebecca whispered back. "It is not German. They have *Die Bibel* in English."

Mrs. Evans glanced sternly at them and then pointedly directed her attention on the preacher. Beyond Amos, Rebecca saw Colin smile.

Whether Amos heard the sermon or not, Rebecca didn't know. She listened with rapt attention. The man did not speak with eloquence, as did Bishop Miller when the message rolled from his tongue in the language every Amish person learned from infancy. Nevertheless, the preacher's passion shone, carried to his listeners on the wings of plain, everyday words.

Near the end of the sermon, Rebecca glanced at Colin, who listened with rapt attention. Was he memorizing the preacher's message so he could sit at his desk later and write it down? His gaze slid sideways to meet hers. The smile he awarded her was private and full of meaning for her alone. She looked quickly down at her folded hands, disturbed by the jolt of happiness that smile delivered. Her thoughts turned guiltily to Jesse, who might even now be on his way to her.

When Jesse arrives, she promised herself, *everything will be good. And clear.*

She forced her mind to conjure up Jesse's image and her dream of their happy life together. She had no difficulty picturing Jesse in Amish trousers and braces, and the image helped to settle her fears.

Colin would never look right with an untrimmed beard covering his chin.

Amos sat on the front step of the milliner's shop long after the sun had gone. Music came from the Lucky Dollar Saloon, and the glow from lanterns inside created rings of light that spilled onto the street. Behind him Mrs. Evans' shop was dark. The women had kindly invited him to share their supper, and then they had bid him goodnight. Why return now to the uncomfortable cot in Mrs. Sawyer's boardinghouse when he would only lay tormented by his troubled thoughts?

Two days he had been in this town, and he wanted to be quit from it with a longing that reached to the very depths of his soul. He yearned to stand in the middle of his fields and breathe the scent of growing plants. To watch the wind ripple across the hay field. To catch a glimpse of Karl as he carried the egg basket from the coop toward the house.

He heaved a heavy sigh. If only Rebecca would put her *kapp* back on and return home with him. A few more days, she promised. By the end of the week, surely the man she professed to love would be here and she might see the error of her ways.

Amos shifted on the step, but he could not get comfortable, either with his position on the hard wood or with his thoughts. If he could be sure that this man, this Jesse, would treat her well, he would leave her here. But what would he say to Jonas? That he had left his daughter in the hands of an *Englisch* cowboy she had not seen in four years? And if this man did not return her

304

affections, as Amos devoutly prayed he would not, then perhaps Rebecca might look more kindly on him if he had proved his loyalty by staying at her side.

The door behind him opened, and a soft voice exclaimed, "Why, what are you doing out here, sweetie?"

He turned in time to see Sassy pull the door closed behind her. She crossed the porch and dropped to the stair close beside him. Too close. Uncomfortably close. As unobtrusively as he could, he scooted sideways.

She noticed. "You act like I'm a desert rattler or something. You're not afraid of me, are you?"

"No," he said hurriedly, glad that the darkness hid his blush.

"Hmm. So you didn't answer my question. What are you doing out here?"

"Waiting."

"For Becca?" When he didn't answer, she went on. "I hate to break it to you, sweetie, but she's aiming her gun at another man."

As usual, her choice of words was unfamiliar, but he understood their meaning. "This I know." He was embarrassed at the glum tone in his words.

"Aw, it'll be okay." She leaned sideways and gave him a shove. "You'll find a gal someday."

He shifted over a little more. Whether he was more uncomfortable at her words or the touch of her shoulder on his, he didn't know. To cover his embarrassment, he rushed to ask a question. "And you? Why are you here and not inside with the women?"

"They're sewing." She planted her elbows on her knees and dropped her chin into her hands. "I don't sew or knit or any of that stuff. Besides, I have some serious thinking to do."

Amos eyed her sideways. She looked nearly as sad as he felt. "About what?"

"I don't rightly know what I'm goin' to do. I planned to go to New York City and be a famous actress, but . . ." Her gaze flickered toward him. "Don't tell anybody, but I don't actually know how to act."

Because she sounded as though she was relaying a great confidence, Amos responded with a nod and said, "I see."

"I mean, I might be good at it. Everybody always said I was pretty enough to be an actress, and I sing like a lark, but lately I've started to realize being pretty and singing don't always get you what you want."

"And what is it that you want?"

"I want to be rich. I want fine clothes and

jewelry and a fancy house. I'll give fabulous parties, and everybody will want to come to my parties because they will all like me."

For a moment, Amos could see her in that life, surrounded by fine things and laughing people. But when he looked closer into her face, he caught a glimpse of longing in her eyes, a longing for something he himself understood very well.

"Possessions do not satisfy the soul." He pitched his voice softly. "They do not turn a house into a home. Only love can do that. The love of *Gott* and family."

Moonlight glittered in suddenly wet eyes. "I wouldn't know about that. I never had anybody but my mama, and she was a saloon worker too."

Compassion stirred in him with a strength that surprised him. How fortunate he was to have been surrounded by friends who shared his burdens. Yes, his days — and especially his nights — were lonely. But *Gott* had provided a home for him and his children. This woman knew nothing of the things in life that were worth having.

"Perhaps now is a time to reconsider your plans," he said. "Perhaps being an actress is not the life *Gott* has called you to."

Head tilted, she gave a nearly impercep-tible nod. "Maybe." Then she glared down the street toward the saloon. "One thing I do know is that I'm going to stick around this town long enough to march with those women. That'll show Ed and the others."

"March?" Amos shook his head. The word he understood. But its meaning?

She gave a start and then a quick smile. "Sorry. Don't mind me, sweetie. I'm just chewing the fat and spitting it out before I think, as usual." She straightened and turned toward him. "What about you? What will you do when you leave here?"

"Go home to my children," he said simply.

"Children?" Moonlight gleamed on her smooth skin. "I didn't know you had children." A crease marred the expanse between her eyes. "I guess I figured since you'd set your cap on Becca that you didn't have family."

Amos stared at his folded hands and let the long-familiar sadness wash over him. "My wife died giving life to my son."

A soft hand slid over his. "I'm sorry. I can't imagine how hard that was. You must get real lonely."

She spoke as one who understood, and he could only nod in answer.

"How old are they?"

"Karl is five, Celia seven, and Sarah is nine."

"Sarah?" A delighted grin displayed a row of white teeth. "That's my name. Sassy is a nickname my mama gave me on account of I used to sass her every so often. I figured that sounded more like an actress's name than Sarah, so when I left Texas, that's what I used."

Amos studied her face. Her eyes were hidden in pools of shadow, but the soft light reflected off of high, finely shaped cheekbones and soft pink lips. Since meeting her, he'd been too shocked by her flamboyance to really see her. Tonight she looked more vulnerable than he would have ever thought for such a strong-willed woman.

"I do not know what an actress name is," he told her, "but I will call you Sarah."

A smile curved her lips. "I'd like that real well . . . Amos."

With a shock, he realized her warm hand still covered his. Such personal gestures had never been comfortable for him, and he thought of pulling away. But then, with an even greater shock, he realized he didn't want to.

TWENTY-ONE

Gus's reins were loose in Colin's hand as they plodded down the street on their afternoon rounds. It felt good to be back to a normal routine, calling a word of greeting to familiar faces, returning a wave here and a nod there. This would be the last time he executed this particular duty in Lawrence, because by this time tomorrow Patrick Mulhaney would have the sheriff's badge pinned to his vest.

Tomorrow. It seemed like only yesterday he'd read the letter that told him he would soon be free to pursue his dream, his calling. And yet the time had been nearly three weeks ago, and much had happened since then. He hadn't met Rebecca three weeks ago.

Thoughts of her put a melancholy damper on his mood. Sitting on the same pew at church on Sunday had been a curious form of torture. After an initial flash of irritation, he'd been thankful for Amos's glowering presence between them. Otherwise he might have been tempted to drape an arm casually across the pew behind her and to scoot as close to her as decorum allowed.

In other words, to make a fool of himself.

The days since she'd been released from jail had dragged long and dull. Kaspar wasn't an engaging conversationalist, and he spent his time bellowing, not sewing. The only highlight in the past four days had been the few times he saw Rebecca, and then he'd had to steel himself against her presence.

When had he fallen for her? Was it when she defied him and locked herself in her cell? Or when he told her of his dreams and she asked to hear him preach?

Or was it when he saw her black-clad figure standing firm and rigid before Judge Tankersley, fire in her eyes and determination evident in the stubborn tilt of her chin?

He pressed his heels into Gus's sides. What difference did timing make? He'd fallen for a woman who loved another man. Who, in fact, took advantage of every opportunity to flaunt that man's name in his face.

Jesse Montgomery, you'd better be good to her, or I'll . . .

A laugh arrested the thought. Or he'd what? He had no need to pursue a woman whose heart belonged to another man. An Amish woman. Their lives and beliefs were worlds apart.

When he reached the bridge that spanned the Kansas River at the end of Massachusetts Street, he pointed Gus northward, intending to progress through each of the town's streets. But before he could turn onto Vermont, something caught his eye. Up ahead, a lone rider headed north along the river trail, a spare horse keeping pace beside him. Two horses, one rider. Normally such a sight wouldn't spark a second thought, but in light of recent events, Colin studied the rider. From this distance he could see nothing more than a straight back and a hat. Packs bulged on the back of the riderless horse. Supplies for a long journey, perhaps? A man traveling with a spare horse was nothing new, unless . . .

An outlaw languished in Colin's jail. He'd arrived in town on the train and had not hired a horse. Like Benton, who arrived on the same train as Rebecca. What if Kaspar had arranged a meeting, one he had failed to keep?

Hesitation caused Colin to slow Gus to a walk. In one more day he would turn his badge and his responsibilities over to Mulhaney. What use was there in following a traveler who had done nothing more than pass through Lawrence and replenish his supplies for a long journey? None. He did not intend to waste his last night chasing suspicions that would more than likely lead nowhere — or, worst case, somewhere. He was almost home free.

Still . . .

The man had seemed to turn from Louisiana Street and head north. Sumpter's Mercantile lay halfway down that street. No harm in checking, was there? He urged Gus to a faster pace.

The mercantile supported a brisk business for a Tuesday afternoon. Colin tethered the horse alongside a wagon, where a hired hand was loading several bags of feed while a gentleman stood watching. Inside he found Aaron Sumpter busy behind the counter, weighing dried apples while a customer watched the scale with a sharp eye. He ducked his head at the woman before fixing his eye on the store owner.

"Have you seen a stranger through here this afternoon, Aaron? Would have been buying supplies for the trail."

Sumpter glanced up from the scale. "Had a man come through not ten minutes past.

Never seen him before. Bought beans and jerked beef and such. That the one?"

"Might have been. Did you notice if he was packing two horses or one?"

The man considered and then shook his head. "I've been too busy to see who loads what, Sheriff. But I do remember what he asked me."

"Yeah? What's that?"

"He asked about news in town. If there had been any shootings or killings. I told him no, but we did have a famous outlaw over at the jail." His head cocked sideways. "He seemed mighty interested in that."

A grim sense of satisfaction took hold of Colin. The stranger had been poking around, trying to discover what had happened to Kaspar.

"Thanks," he said as he left the store.

Let it go. I'll tell Mulhaney about it when he gets in tomorrow. It's not my business anymore.

But even as the thought occurred to him, he knew he couldn't let the matter lie. The safety of the people of Lawrence was still his responsibility, at least for another day. He mounted Gus and headed swiftly toward the north river trail.

Rebecca turned Mrs. Evans' little wagon

314

onto the river road in time to see Colin disappear around the bend at the north end of town. Though she'd unobtrusively watched for him all day yesterday, she'd seen him only once, and that had been from a distance. They'd had no opportunity to talk since leaving church on Sunday.

And they likely wouldn't again. She had come from an errand for Mrs. Evans without Amos following along for once, and she had stopped by Annie Diggs' home to ask news of her husband. Mrs. Diggs had received word yesterday that his business was concluded and he would return by way of Cider Gulch on Wednesday, the day the ladies from the movement were scheduled to arrive for the peaceful protest.

Jesse will be here tomorrow.

The news had stirred up an excited flutter in her belly. Tomorrow she would finally see the man who held her heart — or did he? Confusion had begun to cloud her thoughts, and she didn't want it. She had to press on with her goal, and she knew exactly how their meeting would go. He would insist on finding her the minute he arrived in town. Mrs. Diggs knew of her whereabouts and would direct him to Mrs. Evans' shop. The door would open, and she would see his frame filling the doorway. He would scan the room, and when he caught sight of her, amazement at the changes four years had wrought in her would light up his face. She would go to him, deliver her well-rehearsed speech, and they would fall into each other's arms. And then . . .

And then I will never see Colin again.

The thought brought an accompanying sadness. Their friendship would end tomorrow. She would return to Apple Grove with Jesse, and Colin would disappear into the west, where he would care for orphans, build his church, preach his sermons, and take a wife who shared his faith.

The idea was depressing.

Not that I mind him taking a wife. The man has a right to true love, just as I do. But I do wish I could hear him preach once before we part ways.

No sooner had the idea occurred in her mind than she put it into action. She flicked the reins, and Mrs. Evans' horse broke into a trot. The wagon bounced along the road that edged the river. When she passed the town's last street, she barely glanced down it but urged the horse onto the rough trail that led into the surrounding countryside.

She rounded a bend and left the town behind. Thick trees grew all along the river, and far to her left lay the plain she had seen from the train window when she arrived in town. Closer up and ahead, the ground swelled in a series of irregularly spaced ridges, high and sporadically covered with thick stands of trees. Cattle dotted the hillsides and wandered in and out of the trees. Colin was nowhere in sight. Had he followed the river that curved to the right, or had he veered away toward the hills? After a moment's indecision, she decided to follow the river a ways. The trail looked more defined in that direction.

The sound of rushing water created a peaceful cushion for her thoughts. She hadn't realized how accustomed to the noise of the town she'd become. When had she last heard birdsong or the wind rustling the leaves? She would not be sorry to leave the city behind when she returned home, but she would miss many things about life in a town, such as being surrounded by friends like Sassy and Mrs. Evans and Abigail. Of course, now she would have Jesse.

A movement in the trees to her left jerked her from her thoughts. She peered through the leaves, a chill creeping across the back of her neck. Was it an animal? If so, it was a large one. The size of a man. Perhaps following Colin away from town had not been a good idea after all. If she were to be attacked by a bear or a cougar or — she swallowed against a dry mouth — a man, no one would hear her scream for help. Her grip on the reins tightened. Should she try to outrun whatever it was? No, a horse pulling a wagon could never outrun an unencumbered animal intent on its prey. The hair on her arms rose inside her sleeves.

She saw the movement again, this time closer and headed her way. Definitely a man. A terrified scream caught in her throat. And then a familiar figure stepped out from behind a tree.

"What are you doing out here?" Colin strode onto the trail.

Relief wilted her tense muscles, and she sagged on the bench as she brought the wagon to a halt. "I saw you ride this way."

A frown gathered on his face. "Don't you know it isn't safe to wander around out here alone?"

Rebecca's temper flared in response to his testy reprimand. "I can take care of myself."

He opened his mouth to argue, but then he snapped it shut. "I hope Jesse Montgomery has the patience of a saint. He's going to need it."

She tossed her head, the way she'd seen Sassy do. "He is the most patient man in the world."

"I'm sure he is." His eyes closed and his chest inflated with a deep breath. When he spoke again, his tone was calmer. "Did you have a reason for following me?"

"I . . ." The reason now sounded hollow. She averted her eyes. "After tomorrow we will not see each other again."

He went still, and she felt his gaze on her. "No, we won't," he said in a voice soft as a caress.

A heavy silence hung between them. An uncomfortable feeling grew in her chest and threatened to rob her of breath. The danger of a moment ago was past, but this new one was far more alarming.

She cleared her throat. "You promised to preach for me. If not today, I do not know when we will find time."

"What, here?"

"Better here than in jail." A grin took possession of her lips. "I saw some cows not far away. I could lasso them for you in no time."

The offer produced a laugh. "That I'd like to see. You with a lariat."

She straightened. "I can lasso. I have not practiced in several years, but I knew how once."

The smile she gave him was returned, and she relaxed. The ease of their friendship was restored.

"Gus is waiting. Let me go get him, and I'll escort you back to town." He started to turn away and then stopped. "Why don't you come with me? It's not safe for you to be here alone."

A glance at the thick woods surrounding them brought back her original fright. No, she definitely preferred to stay with Colin. They secured the horse and wagon and then took off on foot through the trees.

"What are you doing here?" she asked as he helped her climb over a fallen log.

"I was following a man, but I lost him."

"An outlaw?"

His expression grew troubled. "I wish I knew. Something's going on, but Kaspar won't tell me anything." He gave her a sideways glance. "And I know Annie Diggs is planning something too. She rented rooms at the Eldridge Hotel for tomorrow night."

She averted her face on the pretense of ducking beneath a low-hanging branch.

"I hope whatever you ladies have planned isn't going to interfere with my leaving."

A flush crept toward her face. The peaceful protest would cause no trouble. But the ladies' discovery that the new sheriff would be lenient toward liquor sales in town might make his reception uncomfortable for him and the town council. She realized Colin was watching her for a reaction, and she gave him what she hoped was an innocent smile.

A flash of white up ahead proved to be Gus, whose reins had been looped around a low branch near the outer tree line. A half dozen of the cattle she had seen earlier grazed nearby, two of them within a few feet of the horse. He tossed his head and stamped a hoof when he caught sight of Colin and Rebecca.

Colin ran a soothing hand over the horse's neck and untied the reins.

"I was hoping to follow that man back to a camp, but he disappeared." His gaze strayed over the nearby hills. "I thought he might be hiding in the woods, but my guess is he went that way. I did find something interesting, though. A still."

Rebecca shook her head at the unfamiliar word. "What is a still?"

"It brews liquor." He grinned. "Want to see? It's nearby."

She trailed him around the edge of the tree line, Gus following along. Cattle grazed all around the area. They hadn't walked far when Colin pointed ahead. "There it is."

A clearing contained the strangest-looking contraption Rebecca had ever seen. A huge metal barrel sat up on three legs over the ashes of a recent fire. A blackened pipe ran from the top to a second metal container, this one not quite as big, and a spiraled tube connected that to a third. Barrels and bottles littered the ground around the tubs. A rough plank fence formed a circle around the area.

Colin looped Gus's reins over a dilapidated rail and led Rebecca through a narrow opening in the fence.

"They use corn mash in that one." He pointed to the biggest of the containers. "Then they light a fire under it, and if they keep the temperature just right, the alcohol steams up through that pipe over to that one."

"Who makes this whiskey?"

His face contorted with a grimace. "I don't know, but this still has been recently used. Those ashes are fresh."

Rebecca's gaze searched the area. Annie Diggs and the other ladies would be outraged.

"It's illegal to make whiskey in the state of Kansas." A thoughtful expression came over his face. "Something needs to be done, don't you think?"

He sounded so much like Mrs. Diggs that Rebecca turned a startled look on him.

"Did you not say that saloons were to be left up to politicians?"

"That's what I've been told." He traced a finger along the curling tube. "Never sat well with me, to be honest."

She stepped up beside him, close enough to the still that her hem trailed in the ashes. "The new sheriff will do nothing to stop this, will he." It was a statement, not a question.

He gave a soft snort. "Not a thing. But I am still the sheriff, at least for today." A sudden grin came over his face. "You want to be my deputy for a few minutes?"

For a moment she simply stared at him, uncomprehending. Then his meaning stole over her. "You intend to tear the still down?"

In answer, he grasped the tube and jerked. The top of the second container came off. With a look of intense satisfaction, he twisted and pulled until he had separated the pieces into two, and then he dropped the lid on the ground and stomped it with his boot. The smile he turned her way took on a note of triumph.

Rebecca drew in a breath. She had never been purposefully destructive. It was not the Amish way. And yet there was something exhilarating in his actions against wrong. According to Mrs. Diggs, an abundance of liquor destroyed men's lives, and as Colin said, operating this device was against the law in Kansas.

Heart pounding with excitement, she leaned forward and placed her hands on the biggest of the containers and shoved. It rocked on its legs but did not fall.

"Allow me to assist you, ma'am."

Colin placed his hands beside hers and together they shoved. The barrel tipped and crashed to the ground. A laugh escaped her as she lifted the heavy pipe and beat it on the ground while Colin picked up a log and pounded dents into the barrel. What Bishop Miller would say she didn't know, and at the moment she didn't care. Finally, she had done something worthwhile with her *rumspringa.*

In short order the still lay in mangled pieces around them. Surveying their handiwork, Colin heaved in a deep, satisfied breath. "That felt good."

Rebecca smoothed a lock of hair away from her face. It *had* felt good, and more because they had done it together. She sensed that the act had been cleansing for him, and he had shared it with her. Somehow, smashing the still had confirmed their friendship. Words tumbled from her lips before she could stop them.

"I will miss you when I am gone."

He took in another deep breath, and his features softened. "I'll miss you more."

The gentle tone sent her pulse racing, and suddenly she could not look into his face. She averted her eyes.

"I must return Mrs. Evans' wagon to town."

In the pause that followed, her heart pounded so loudly in her ears that she couldn't hear her own thoughts. But when he spoke, she heard resignation in his voice.

"Come on. I'll take you back."

During the walk back to the wagon, she forced herself to focus on one important fact. Jesse would arrive tomorrow.

And not a moment too soon.

TWENTY-TWO

Wednesday arrived. Colin's first waking thought, even before he opened his eyes, was, *Today is the last day I'll see her.* An empty hole gaped in his chest. Maybe, in time, the ache would fade. Maybe when he had built the church and the Lord started gathering a flock for him to care for, he would find solace. But today the thought uppermost in his mind was that Rebecca would be gone.

With Jesse.

Biting back a groan, he rolled off of his narrow cot. The tin star winked at him from atop the chest of drawers that had already been emptied of his few belongings. Two bags in the corner waited to be strapped onto Gus's saddle. When Mulhaney's train arrived at noon, he'd hand over the badge, load up, and stop at the bank for his savings on his way out of town.

When he left his room, he glanced at Kaspar. The man sat on the corner of his bunk with his back against the wall, knees bent and arms draped across them. That was one duty he'd be glad to hand over. Maybe Mulhaney could get something out of the surly outlaw.

Kaspar's greeting this morning was different than his usual demand for coffee. "Today's the day, Maddox."

A note in the man's voice made Colin stop and look into the cell. His grimace held a smugness that Colin hadn't seen before.

"You mean the new sheriff taking over?"

The roughened lips twisted into a smirk. "Yeah. Sure. That's what I mean."

Suspicion niggled Colin's mind. What did Kaspar know?

"I wouldn't be too eager about that, if I were you. From what I hear, Mulhaney doesn't have much use for lawbreakers."

There was no reply, but the smirk didn't leave the man's face. Uneasy, Colin continued toward the small stove in the corner to get the coffee going. Between now and when the train arrived, maybe he'd station his deputies around the outer edges of the town and tell them to keep an eye out for anything unusual. After that, whatever was going on would be Mulhaney's problem.

At eleven thirty, Mrs. Evans locked the front door of her shop. Rebecca had watched the door all morning, her nerves mounting with every passing minute. Jesse had not yet arrived. Mrs. Diggs had assured her that Mr. Diggs wanted to be in town in time to witness the women's march, so she was sure he would have arrived this morning. But now it was time to assemble with the other women at the train station, and still there had been no sight of him. She fell in step beside Sassy and Mrs. Evans. What if he didn't come? As they headed down Massachusetts Street, she cast a quick backward glance toward the jail. She hadn't seen Colin today, either.

Amos stood watching them morosely from the front step of the milliner's shop. For a moment she'd thought he would forbid her to participate, but when Sassy stepped in, his arguments ceased.

"Hello, Imogene," Mrs. Evans called to a woman near her age on the other side of the street.

The woman waved, a wide grin on her broad face. She and her companions were also heading in the direction of the train station.

"This is so exciting!" Sassy's step was bouncy and eager. "I can't wait till we march past the Dollar and Ed sees us with those important women."

Rebecca couldn't help but smile at her enthusiasm. Her eyes sparkled and dimples creased her cheeks. She made a pretty picture today in the dress Rebecca had finished last night. A touch too many frills still, but at least this blue was not as garish as the other.

Rebecca ran a hand self-consciously over her dress. Amos had scowled when she appeared in the buttery yellow fabric instead of her Amish clothing, but she didn't care. After consultation with Sassy and Mrs. Evans, she had decided that this dress would make a more favorable impression when Jesse saw her for the first time in four years. Later, after they returned to Apple Grove, she would don her Plain garb again.

At the end of the street they turned the corner and had their first glimpse of the train station.

Sassy squealed and clapped her hands. "Would you look at that? We're gonna have every woman in town here."

"Not quite," said Mrs. Evans, "but this is

most encouraging."

A crowd of at least two dozen had gathered outside the station office, and more joined their ranks every minute. A stream of billowing skirts traveled in that direction, both behind and in front of Rebecca.

"Look. There's Mrs. Diggs." Sassy pointed out a commanding figure in the midst of them, hands gesturing as she spoke.

But Rebecca's attention was drawn to the person with whom Mrs. Diggs spoke. He stood a head taller than most of the women gathered around him. Her heart lurched at the sight of him, followed by a stab of guilt. What was wrong with her that she could be so happy to see Colin when her one true love was even now riding to meet her?

They followed the stream to the main group.

"Let's get closer," Sassy whispered. She grabbed Rebecca's hand and began weaving her way through the crowd. When they arrived at Mrs. Diggs' side, Colin was shaking his head.

"I've known you were up to something for a while, but this?" He gestured to indicate the crowd. "What are you trying to accomplish here?"

Nearly as much excitement showed on Mrs. Diggs' face as Sassy's. "We will make our statement, Sheriff. We will make our statement."

He focused on Rebecca. "You know what happened the last time you tried to make a statement." He folded his arms. "Don't think I won't throw you in jail again at the least sign of trouble."

A triumphant gleam shone in Sassy's eyes. "You don't have room for all of us."

He bent toward her. "I have plenty of room for the ringleaders."

A whistle sounded in the distance, and an excited titter rose from the ladies.

"The train's comin'." Sassy bounced on her feet, grinning like a child.

The sheriff's gaze returned to Rebecca's and, holding it, he took off his hat.

"By the way, you look mighty fetching today, Miss Switzer."

Mrs. Diggs took advantage of his distraction and started to move away. Tearing her gaze from Colin's, Rebecca started after her and stopped her with a hand on the woman's arm.

"Have you news of Mr. Diggs and my Jesse?"

She replied with a distracted pat on Rebecca's hand. "Not yet, dear, but don't worry. Very soon now."

Not at all comforted, Rebecca turned back

to see Colin striding away. For a moment she considered going after him, but she could think of no valid reason to do so.

Colin left the group of ladies, his emotions roiling. Why did she have to wear that dress today? He recognized it instantly as the one she'd worn the first time he laid eyes on her. Only he didn't remember her looking as lovely as she did today.

She's dressed herself up for Jesse.

The thought churned in his gut like acid. He swiped a hand across his face, trying to dismiss his jealousy. He had plenty of other concerns today. This pack of women was going to ruin his departure. There had to be thirty-five or forty of them. And though no one had identified the people on the train, the excitement whipping through the crowd told him it would be someone important. Whatever plans the women had for today, he'd have to call in a couple of his deputies to keep an eye on them. This crowd might be composed of the fairer sex, but one cross word could transform them into a mob.

My last day, Lord. Couldn't this have held off until tomorrow?

Mulhaney would be here soon to help. Colin brightened at the thought.

Someone poked his shoulder. When he

turned and caught sight of the mayor's scowling face, he groaned. The members of the town council surrounded him, their expressions grave. Come, no doubt, to welcome the new sheriff to town.

"What is the meaning of this?" Bowerstock demanded. "What is that woman up to now?"

"I wish I knew."

"Well, do something about it!" he bellowed, and the other council members murmured agreement.

"They haven't done anything wrong, Mayor."

The train's whistle sounded, much closer this time. Smoke billowed into the sky from an unseen point behind the town's buildings.

"The new sheriff will do something," Bowerstock blustered. "Unless he's so put off by the sight of this lot that he gets right back on the train and leaves."

After a few minutes of uncomfortable silence, the train pulled into view. The ladies' animated voices rose above the sound of the puffing engine. The engine slid past them and, with a screech of metal on metal, came to a stop. They pressed closer as one.

Curious faces appeared in the windows to

stare into the crowd. The conductor climbed down and made his way to the passenger car, glancing nervously at the ladies grouped around the station. Colin saw Annie push her way to the front to stand beside him, her attention fixed on the door. A splash of yellow in the crowd caught his eye, but he couldn't pick out Rebecca in the press.

The conductor placed a set of steps beneath the door before opening it. A woman stepped into view and paused, her gaze sweeping the watchers. A wide smile parted her lips, and she raised a fist high in the air. A cheer rose from the women, and dozens of arms waved in return.

Colin's discomfort grew as he watched the conductor help six women climb from the train to the ground, each one met with a welcoming cheer. He didn't know who they were, but with Annie Diggs as the organizer, no doubt they were temperance supporters. He only hoped their purpose was peaceful. Real peaceful.

When the last woman had descended, Annie led the newcomers away, and the crowd followed. Colin spared a glance after them, noting that they were headed in the direction of the hotel, and then he turned his attention back to the train. With the women out of the way, a handful of men surged forward to begin the task of unloading the cargo cars.

The conductor closed the door of the passenger car and stooped to pick up his steps. The mayor gave Colin a startled glance. A frantic feeling that something was about to go very wrong blossomed inside him.

"Hold on." He ran toward the conductor, who stopped and turned.

"Isn't there another passenger on this train?"

The man shook his head. "No, sir. We ran pretty heavy on cargo this trip. Not so much on the way of passengers."

"Our new sheriff was supposed to be here."

"Oh?" The conductor nodded. "That's right. I took his ticket. He got off at Jefferson City."

Wordless, Colin gazed after the man's retreating back.

Bowerstock was nearly beside himself. With a fist, he pounded the train car.

"It was those females on the train! They scared him off."

A sinking feeling told Colin he might be right. And where did that leave him? He fingered the star on his vest and considered unpinning it and simply handing it to the mayor. But could he saddle up and leave town to a mob of women?

Mostly, could he leave Rebecca?

TWENTY-THREE

The peaceful protest progressed exactly as Mrs. Diggs had planned. Close to fifty women, including many who had never shown public support for the movement before, gathered near the river on the far end of town to hear rousing speeches by both Mrs. Willard and Mrs. Shaw, who urged them to stand firm in their mission to expel the evil influence of liquor from every corner of society.

To Rebecca's extreme embarrassment, Mrs. Diggs spoke last and pointed out the injustice of Rebecca's treatment at the hand of corrupt men who, all the while, were enjoying profits from the illegal sale of whiskey in Lawrence. Rebecca would have ducked behind the crowd but for Sassy, whose zeal far exceeded her own. Her friend kept grabbing her hand and thrusting it into the air with wildly enthusiastic cheers.

When the speeches ended, the ladies

formed lines to march up and down the streets of Lawrence. Many carried signs proclaiming "My Home Is Dry" and "Salvation Through Temperance." At Mrs. Diggs' insistence, Rebecca took her place on the front line, one arm linked with a tall, stern-faced visitor. Mrs. Carrie Nation said little, but fervor for the cause blazed in her eyes. Sassy hugged Rebecca's other arm close, clearly delighted at her position on the front line.

They sang as they marched. The unfamiliar songs told of ruined lives and vowed "Lips that touch liquor shall never touch mine!" People gathered along the streets to stare as they marched. Several times Rebecca glimpsed Colin's face among the watchers, but she could not force herself to meet his eye. Sassy strutted with her head held high, but Rebecca's spirits sank lower than ever. This "peaceful" protest did not feel peaceful. It felt vulgar. What would Papa say if he saw her here? And where was Jesse? Should he not have arrived by now? What if Mr. Diggs had been unable to convince him to come? She should have gone herself and left these ladies to their march on their own.

They reached the bridge and prepared to turn down Massachusetts Street, the place where all of Rebecca's trouble had started. Colin and Hal stood in front of the jail, looking their way. She caught sight of Amos peeking from behind a building. Mrs. Diggs halted, and the ladies all came to a stop.

She turned a smile toward Rebecca. "My dear, I believe your beau has arrived."

Rebecca looked away from Colin and followed the woman's gaze to the bridge. Two horses rode across, heading toward them. The older rider she recognized as Mr. Diggs, and beside him —

Jesse!

She dropped the arms of Sassy and Mrs. Nation and raced to meet them. When they stepped off the bridge, she searched Jesse's face. Yes, it was he. Her Jesse. Slim and as ruggedly handsome as she remembered — but four years had wrought changes in him. He was not only slim, she realized, but thin. Painfully thin. His cheeks had a gaunt, hollow look she didn't remember. His hair hung long, down his collar, and the length had turned the attractive curl into untidy strings. With dismay she noted his stained shirt and trousers, which gave him a generally unkempt appearance.

Of course, he had been on a horse for two days.

When he has time to clean up, he will look better.

Jesse caught sight of her. His eyes narrowed, and his lips curved in the exact smile she remembered. "Do I know you?"

"I'm . . . Rebecca."

"Who?

Her heart thudded. Did he not recognize her? "Rebecca Switzer — Emma's little sister?"

A horrible suspicion crept over her.

"You remember Emma and Luke, don't you?"

Unfocused eyes fixed on her face, and recognition slowly dawned on his features. "Hey, look a'choo all grown up."

The timber of his voice was the same, but the words ran together in a slur. He wavered in the saddle, and dismay stole over her. "Jesse, are you ill?"

"Me? Never better!" He noticed the crowd then, and his face brightened. "Hey, a party! Looks like we're just in time. Somebody pour me a drink."

He raised up on one stirrup and swung his other leg over the horse's back to dismount. But his foot became tangled. In the next moment he hit the ground, rolled over onto his back, and with a guffaw, lay there staring up at her.

"He's not ill," said Mr. Diggs in a dry voice. "He's pie-faced drunk."

Behind her, the ladies gasped. In horror, Rebecca looked down at her one true love, who made no attempt to rise, but chuckled and slurred, "Gettin' clumsy in m'old age."

"Alvin, what is the meaning of this?" demanded Mrs. Diggs, outrage clear in her rigid posture.

Mr. Diggs shook his head, disgust curling his lip as he cast a scornful gaze down at Jesse.

"I said I'd bring him and I did, but it wasn't easy." He glanced at Rebecca. "When I got to Cider Gulch, I had no trouble finding him. He is well known. The first person I asked knew where to find him."

Dread and disappointment clogged her throat, but she managed to ask, "At his ranch?"

The man gave a bitter laugh. "Ranch? He's no rancher, Miss Switzer, though they told me he hires himself out as a cowhand whenever he's sober enough for the work. No, they said I would find him at his home — a town bench. He was drunk as a skunk."

Jesse was the town drunk?

Her sprits fell and Colin's words came home to roost. *Put away childish thoughts . . .*

341

■ ■ ■ ■

Rebecca didn't bother to hide the tears that slid down her cheeks and dripped onto the butter-yellow fabric of her dress as she helped Mr. Diggs and Sassy drag Jesse out of the street. The ladies, with many disapproving stares, marched on. She couldn't meet their gazes as they passed by. What a fool she had been. She staggered beneath Jesse's weight as they neared a bench in front of the Eldridge Hotel. He had not settled down. Fallen down was more like it.

They dropped him onto the bench.

"I found out this morning that his saddlebags had bottles of whiskey." Mr. Diggs straightened and, with a disgusted gesture, brushed dirt off of his coat. "By the time I awoke, he had drained them." His expression softened when he turned toward Rebecca. "I am sorry, my dear. I should have left him there, but I'd given my word."

Rebecca couldn't manage a response. She silently watched him return to the bridge and the horses.

Sassy put an arm around her shoulders and hugged. "Don't worry about it, Becca. I've seen worse than him."

"You have?" She couldn't imagine what

worse looked like.

"Sure." Sassy waved a dismissive hand. "He'll sleep it off. He'll be okay in a few hours." She placed a hand on her hip and cocked her head to examine him. "He's not a bad lookin' fella. With a little soap and water, he ought to clean up nice."

A shout from down the street drew their attention. A small group of men had formed and taken a stand in the center of the street, blocking the ladies' progress.

"Uh-oh. Trouble is a'brewin'." Sassy's eyes glittered and she rubbed her hands together. "Come on. I don't want to miss it."

She grabbed Rebecca's arm and took off. Allowing herself to be pulled down the street, Rebecca cast a look over her shoulder at Jesse. He sprawled across the bench, arms dangling, and a sound like splintering timber rose from his open mouth. A fresh wave of tears blurred her vision. With all her daydreaming and plans for their future, she had never foreseen this.

The peaceful march had come to a stop, and the ladies' lines had broken directly in front of the Lucky Dollar Saloon. They stood in a close group behind Mrs. Diggs and the leaders from the East, who faced a group of perhaps a dozen men. Sassy pulled

Rebecca around the side and right up to the front. With a start, Rebecca realized the man standing in front was none other than Judge Tankersley, with Mayor Bowerstock right beside him.

The judge caught sight of her. "That's the one." He pointed at her, his glare deepening. "She's one of the women who started all the trouble."

Tears forgotten, Rebecca stiffened. She may have acted foolishly in several areas since she left Apple Grove, but starting trouble with the movement was not one of them.

She fearlessly faced the man. "I did nothing wrong."

Sassy stepped up beside her and threw an arm around her in a stand of solidarity. "You're the one who is wrong, treating a lady like a criminal and throwing her in jail. We won't stand for it anymore." She glanced around the group of women, inviting support. "Right?"

Shouts of "That's right!" and "No more!" answered her. Sassy preened, and her eyes took on a zealous gleam.

Not far away, Rebecca saw Amos watching the confrontation from Mrs. Evans' porch. At the sight of his black trousers, his suspenders strapped over his shoulders, his round hat and bushy beard, a longing came over her. He looked so . . . familiar. Oh, how she missed her home. How she longed to put this noisy, dirty town behind her and go home.

Then someone touched her sleeve. She turned, and her heart twisted in her chest when she looked up into Colin's solemn face.

"Sheriff, I demand that you apprehend these rabble-rousers." Judge Tankersley's finger stabbed toward the crowd of women.

Colin wrapped his hand around Rebecca's arm and managed to maneuver her behind him. This confrontation was going to spark in a minute, and he wanted her out of the way when it happened.

"Now, Tank, let's all stay calm." He pitched his voice to be heard. "Ladies, you've had your protest, and made your point. Go on home now."

Annie Diggs raised her voice to be heard over his. "We will not stop until we have marched through every street in Lawrence!"

A chorus of cheers answered her. Sassy's voice rose louder than the others, her face flushed with fervor.

Colin gave her a warning look, which she ignored.

Bowerstock stepped forward from his place at Tank's side, peering into the crowd with a look of disbelief on his face. "Mildred? Is that you? You get out of there!"

Toward the center of the protest group, Colin caught sight of Mrs. Bowerstock's grim expression as she shook her head and raised her sign higher.

Tankersley, who had turned purple with rage, stomped forward and thrust his face into Colin's. "Arrest them, I say! They're a menace."

This was starting to turn out far too similar to the last "peaceful" protest, and Colin didn't intend to get roped into that again.

"As I said earlier, they haven't done anything illegal." He sent a stern stare toward Annie. "Yet."

"Not done anything illegal?" Tank looked ready to explode. "What about destroying private property?"

Colin shook his head. "Whose property?"

"Mine. I had a . . ." He fumbled for a word. "An item on my land, and these fanatics tore it to pieces."

Colin had almost forgotten Rebecca stood behind him until she stepped forward, her gaze on the judge. "The still belonged to you?"

Triumph flashed onto his face. "See? She did it. I knew she was a troublemaker. Arrest her, Maddox!"

A screech sounded. "A still?"

The ladies shuffled to make way for a heavyset woman who had been standing toward the back. Mrs. Tankersley marched forward, a sign proclaiming "Destroy the Devil's Drink" held in her hands.

She marched over to the judge and shouted, "You have a *still?*"

The blood drained from Tank's face, leaving him pasty looking. "Now, Hazel, don't —"

Before Colin could move to stop her, she raised her sign and bashed him over the head.

It was the spark he'd feared. Chaos erupted among the women. They ran forward, signs swinging. Sassy's voice rose above the fray. "Lips that touch liquor shall never touch mine!" Her call was taken up by several others.

Colin grabbed Rebecca's arm and pulled her away from the mob to the other side of the street.

"You stay out of this," he commanded.

Wide eyes fixed on the fracas, she nodded.

He turned and saw the judge on his knees,

his arms thrown over his head to protect himself from continued blows from his wife's sign. He spotted Hal heading that way. On the opposite side of the street, Sassy stood in the doorway of the saloon, shouting toward the inside. She stepped aside as a handful of men, including Ed, raced out and, after a moment's pause, waded into the brawl. With a satisfied grin, she dashed inside. Colin groaned. Whatever she intended in there, it couldn't be good.

He heard someone shout, "Hey, take your hands off my wife!" A man plowed into the crowd. Fists flew and ladies screamed. Men were running to join the tumult from every direction now, and he lost sight of the judge.

With a groan, Colin started for the saloon. Something caught his eye. Down the street, a man waited beside the mercantile, notable because he was the only one on the street not running to or from the riot. He stood with his back pressed against the side of the building, his hat low on his head. As Colin watched, he slowly slipped around the corner and disappeared.

Alarm prickled the hair across the back of Colin's neck. Something about that man wasn't right. Was Benton making a move?

This was supposed to be my last day on the job. Now the whole town's falling apart at once. Lord, this is not fair.

Not fair. And also not a coincidence. Kaspar hadn't been referring to the arrival of the new sheriff with his smug "Today's the day." He knew something was up. If Benton and the others had somehow gotten wind of the ladies' intent to march, what better day to stage a holdup? The lawmen, old and new, would be distracted trying to keep the peace. He glanced at the riot starting to spread out as women moved away from the brawling men. The distraction had proven to be much bigger than Benton could have hoped for.

What could he be planning?

The answer occurred to Colin the same instant as the question. The man he'd just seen was standing by the mercantile. And on the other side of the mercantile was the bank.

Colin took off at a run.

From his vantage point in front of Mrs. Evans' shop, Amos watched the wild *ufrooish* of the *Englischers* with increasing disbelief. Everywhere he looked, violence was being done. Men hitting men. Women hitting men. Shouting and screaming and rolling in the dirt.

The fighting had spread out, and part of

the riot now occurred directly in front of him. Should he do something to stop it? But how? What? At least Rebecca was safe and maintaining a peaceful stance of non-violence. She stood across the street, watching with an expression of helpless bewilderment.

A man ran in Amos's direction. Behind him, a woman chased him with one of the signs held over her head, intending to use it as a weapon. His suit coat flapped in the breeze created by his speed. When it became obvious that the man would run right into him, Amos stepped to one side.

The man ran up the steps onto Mrs. Evans' porch, the woman following closely. When he reached the door, he turned, his arms thrown up to protect his head. But when the woman brought the sign down, he grabbed it out of her hand.

"There," he shouted. "Now, Hazel, let's talk reasonably."

As Amos watched, the man swung his arm wide, intending to toss the sign off the porch. He must have been standing closer to the building than he thought. Amos winced at the loud crash when the sign's sturdy wooden post smashed through the front window of the milliner's shop.

A furious scream rang above the shouts,

and Mrs. Evans ran out from the midst of the crowd.

"Joseph Tankersley, you've broken my new window!"

If Amos had not been familiar with the sweetness of Mrs. Evans' personality, he would have been terrified at the fury on her face as she bore down on Judge Tankersley.

More glass shattered, the sound muffled, and this time from farther away. A large man bellowed like a bear and ran into the saloon.

Amos glanced across the street. Rebecca was not there. He scanned the crowd, desperate for a glimpse of her yellow *Englisch* dress.

The large man reappeared in the saloon's doorway. Blood drained from Amos's head when he saw Sassy struggling in his viselike grip.

"Let go of me, you big ox!"

His angry shout was directed toward the crowd. "She smashed all the liquor!" He lifted her up by the arms, her feet dangling above the street.

Horror bloomed in Amos. Did he intend to hurt a helpless woman?

Sassy kicked, and the man dropped her to double over in pain. When she landed on the ground, she lost her balance and fell headfirst into the brawl.

Before he had time to consider his actions, Amos's feet were swiftly taking him toward the fight.

TWENTY-FOUR

Colin slipped around the side of the restaurant so he could get a clear view of the back of the bank. He'd taken an alley to cross over to Vermont Street so he could approach the bank from the rear. The man he'd seen earlier stood holding the reins of five saddled horses. The back door to the bank was open. A grim frustration took hold of the sheriff. He should have seen this coming. All of his deputies were watching the outskirts of town except Hal, whom he asked to help watch the ladies' march. He had no backup.

Five horses, one man. That means four more are inside.

And he'd bet a month's pay he knew the identity of at least three of them: Benton, Hughes, and Calhoun. No doubt there were supposed to be six in this gang, but Kaspar was locked up in the jail.

This fellow here wasn't familiar, and he

was on the young side. Nervous. His head snapped back and forth in a jerky motion, and as Colin watched, he raised his arm to wipe sweat from his forehead with his sleeve. New to the outlaw business, apparently. Might even be his first job. Wasn't much good at being a lookout. He kept staring into the bank, leaving his backside unguarded. Taking care of him wouldn't be a problem.

The others, though . . .

Colin couldn't go charging into the bank by himself. With four against one, he'd be dead before he got three steps inside. And once the shooting started, they would probably kill anybody else in there as well, such as the bank manager and any customers that happened to be there when the robbery took place.

Colin scanned the area, looking for anything he could make use of. Barrels and empty crates lay scattered behind the mercantile next door. They were close enough to provide cover, though he wouldn't be completely unseen unless he crouched behind a big barrel. And the wood would slow down a bullet, but it wouldn't stop one.

A plan began to take shape. Desperate, to be sure, and he'd better shoot fast, or he would end up dead on what was supposed to be his last day as a lawman.

First, take care of the kid.

Moving slowly, he unstrapped his holster and slid his revolver out. Crouching, he watched the nervous young man look right and then left. When he turned his head to stare through the bank doorway, Colin dashed out from the cover of the restaurant. Running in a crouch, he crossed the dirt to approach at an angle, using the bodies of the horses as cover. By the time the lookout turned back around, he'd gained the position he wanted.

The next time the kid's head turned, Colin stood, raised his pistol, and brought it down butt-first on the back of the young man's skull. He crumpled to the dirt.

The horses skittered sideways, their reins released. Colin slapped the rump of the closest one as he dove toward a barrel. Only when he crouched behind it in relative safety did he dare to look. All five horses were trotting away.

Now to wait for the others to leave the bank.

Rebecca rounded the corner in time to see Colin disappear down a narrow alley beside a restaurant. He'd told her to stay out of the fight and looked as though he intended to try to restore order. But then he'd gone without doing anything at all.

Unlike the street she'd just left, this one was deserted. No doubt everyone had run to join the fracas. The sounds of the crowd were audible from here, one street away. Shouts and shrieks and the shattering of glass.

Peaceful? A bitter taste invaded her mouth. Never had she seen such violence, and the sight sickened her. Worse, the whole mess was her fault. If only she could learn her Papa's ways. What had made her speak up about the judge's still? So much for Mrs. Diggs' grand plans.

And so much for mine.

Sorrow threatened to overwhelm her at the thought of Jesse lying drunk in front of the hotel. The harsh truth stung like a slap across the face. Her dreams for their simple life together lay in ashes. He was not the man she remembered. He may never have been the man she thought him to be.

As she reached the restaurant, five rider-less horses emerged from the alley down which Colin had disappeared. They slowed when they encountered her, and she stepped back as the nearest one tossed its mane. One saddled horse with no rider trotting through town was unusual enough, but five?

Then the horse spied the water trough beside her and walked toward it, the others following.

Rebecca looked down the alley but saw no sign of Colin. Where had he gone? She slipped past the drinking horses and made her way down the side of the building. When she reached the back, she sucked in a breath. A man lay face-down on the ground. Was he hurt? She started toward him at a run.

Before she'd taken two steps, a movement to her left drew her attention. Colin popped up from behind a barrel. With urgent gestures, he waved her back. Rebecca stopped, confused. Then she saw the gun in his hand. Moving quickly, she backed up and pressed her spine against the side of the building.

The sight of Rebecca running out from the alley sent a bolt of fear through Colin's core. What was she doing here? That woman had a knack for walking into trouble wherever she went. Jumping to his feet, he waved her back, trying to convey the danger without making a sound that would alert the men in the bank. He must have succeeded, for she dashed back in the direction she'd come. A frantic prayer formed in his mind.

Get her to safety.

No sooner had her yellow skirts disappeared from view than the sound of boots pounding on floorboards alerted him to the bank robbers' approach. He whirled in that direction, his gun arm swinging in front of him. The first two ran out with drawn weapons, each clutching a bulging canvas bag. Colin gave them no time to react to the absence of their horses but took quick aim. The blast of gunshots ricocheted off the buildings as both men fell, one with a wound in his shoulder, the other in his thigh. The second man toppled to the ground, revealing the third outlaw in the doorway. Colin squeezed off another quick round, and the bullet took him in the knee. Cries of pain and anger filled the air. Satisfied with his aim, Colin lowered his gun. Enough to put them out of commission but not to kill them.

At the very moment he realized that only three outlaws had left the bank, he heard a sound from behind that chilled the blood in his veins.

The click of a gun's hammer being cocked.

"I think you've done enough damage with that gun for one day, Sheriff. Toss it away."

Colin did as directed. The pistol landed

with a quiet thud in the dirt. With both hands raised over his head, palms splayed, he turned slowly to face his attacker and looked into the grinning face of Cleon Benton.

Rebecca smothered a cry with her hands when the gunshots rang out. Colin! Her heart thundered as a third blast followed the first two. She shoved her fist in her mouth and bit down to keep from screaming. If anything happened to him, her heart would tear right in half.

A man spoke. Not Colin. She couldn't make out the words, but the voice was low and gruff. With fear pounding in her temples, she inched down the wall until she was at ground level. On her hands and knees, she edged toward the corner and then, moving with excruciating slowness, tilted her head and peeked around the building.

Colin stood with his hands in the air, a gun barrel pointed at his head. The man holding the gun was the same man she'd seen on the train two weeks ago. The outlaw Cleon Benton. He laughed, and the evil sound sent chills racing across her skin. Slowly she backed away.

Panic battered at her thoughts and

snatched the breath from her lungs. In another minute Benton might shoot Colin.

I have to do something. I have no weapon.

A frantic laugh threatened to burst out. She, an Amish woman, wishing for a weapon? Bishop Miller would be horrified.

Then a truth hit her. She would deal with Bishop Miller later. The man she loved — yes, loved — was about to be killed, and she couldn't stand by and watch, no matter what the Amish Confession of Faith said.

Wait. Had she seen a coil of rope dangling from the saddle of one of those horses? Could it possibly be a cowboy's lariat? Reckless, probably useless, but she grasped onto the idea.

Crawling on her hands and knees until she was sure no sound of movement could be heard, she headed for the front of the building. Two of the horses had disappeared, but the other three drank noisily from the trough. A coiled rope dangled from a loop on the saddle of the animal nearest her.

Please. Please.

She couldn't spend time thinking of the right words to pray, so she sent a frantic plea heavenward as she grabbed the horse's reins with one hand and the rope with the other. She nearly sobbed with relief when she spied the small, reinforced loop amid the coils. It was a lariat.

Thank You. Thank You!

Her fingers fumbled with the loop that held the lariat on the saddle, and precious seconds were lost. Then the clasp popped open and she threw the coiled rope over her arm. She dashed down the alley toward the back of the building. This lariat felt heavier than she remembered. Or had she learned to throw a lighter one?

When she neared the corner, she uncoiled a good length of rope from her arm. Mouth completely dry, she formed the loop the way she remembered. But what if her memory was faulty? It had been years since she handled a lariat.

Benton's voice came from behind the building. When Colin answered, the sound of his voice fell on her ears as softly as a caress. Determination flooded through her. She could do it. She had to.

Her fingers grasped the stiff part of the rope, and she spaced her feet at shoulder length. Raising her arm, she began to whirl the lariat above her head. At first the loop failed to open, and she bit back a sob. To fail meant Colin would die. With a desperate effort, she spun faster.

The loop opened into a circle. A cry of triumph almost escaped her lips, but she managed to remain silent as she poured even more strength into her arm and concentrated on keeping her wrist loose.

When the noose whirling above her head was the proper size, it was time to throw. Nerves clenched her belly like a fist. How could she lasso a target she could not see? She'd be throwing blind. Tears threatened to blur her vision, but she blinked them back. Every second held the threat that she would hear another gunshot. Relying on the memory of her brief glance around the corner, she tried to picture exactly where Cleon Benton and Colin stood.

Please let this work, Lord.

Drawing a deep breath into her lungs, she stepped out from behind the building. The tempo of her arm did not change in the slightest and her gaze fell unerringly on her target. The outlaw's head snapped toward her, and his gun began to swing her way. With a quick step forward, she snapped her wrist and released the lariat.

The loop sailed through the air, losing its circular shape as it flew.

I failed.

It landed poorly. It fell not over Benton's head, as she'd intended, but on his outstretched hand. With a scream that was part triumph, part terror, she grabbed the rope and jerked.

The gun flew out of his hand and landed a few feet away.

At that moment, Colin acted. He lowered his head and charged toward the outlaw, bellowing like a bull. His skull connected with Benton's midsection, and in the next moment they were both on the ground. She watched as Colin scrambled off of the gasping man and dove for the gun. He rolled and grabbed it in a single motion, ending on his feet.

"Don't move, Benton, or I'll shoot you where you lay."

Benton froze in the act of trying to struggle to his knees.

Colin glanced at her, admiration shining in his eyes. Stunned, she looked down at the slack rope in her hand.

Then a wide grin took possession of her lips.

"I told you I could lasso."

TWENTY-FIVE

Colin led Benton around the side of the bank, his arms secured behind him with a piece of the rope Rebecca had used to capture him. She walked beside the sheriff with a pleased swing in her step. He didn't blame her one bit. In fact, he was so proud of her he could bust.

As they emerged onto Massachusetts Street, he realized he could no longer hear the ruckus of the crowd. Hadn't, in fact, for some minutes. He pointed his prisoner toward the jail, and when they turned, he caught sight of the aftermath of the fight.

Many of the women had disappeared, no doubt returned to their homes. Men lay sprawled in the road or slumped against buildings, some of them nursing black eyes or bleeding noses. Annie Diggs stood near the feed store with a dozen or so of the faithful clustered around her. A similar group of men had gathered around Ed near the entrance to the saloon, casting surreptitious glances across the street. On the step in front of Mrs. Evans' shop, Amos and Sassy sat side by side amid a mess of shattered glass. Across the street Judge Tankersley appeared to be pleading with his wife, whose stubborn expression did not bode well for his cause.

When Colin, Rebecca, and Benton came into view, every eye turned their way.

Mrs. Evans broke the tableau by running toward them, her skirts swishing through the dirt.

"Rebecca, thank the Lord you're okay. We heard shots, and when I couldn't find you I feared the worst." She gathered Rebecca into a fierce embrace.

Colin raised his voice and addressed the bedraggled watchers. "Somebody go after Doc Sorensen. Some injured outlaws are tied up out back of the bank."

A young woman dashed off in the direction of the doctor's house, and the mayor broke away from the crowd near the saloon to stride toward him.

"The bank, you say?"

"That's right, but don't worry. They didn't make off with a cent. The bank manager is putting the money back in the vault right now." Colin grinned at Rebecca. "And this little lady apprehended the ringleader." He gave Benton's arm a shake.

Disbelief stole over Bowerstock's face. "Her?"

Rebecca lowered her head modestly, but not before Colin glimpsed a proud twinkle in her eye.

At the sound of hoofs, the mayor turned. Colin looked up to see a horse trotting down the street toward them from the direction of the bridge. A huge man sat astride the animal's back, at least as tall as Ed and with shoulders that rivaled Will the blacksmith. Colin's grip on his prisoner's arm tightened, and he exchanged a worried glance with Rebecca. Could this be yet another outlaw, riding to the aid of the bank robbers?

The man rode down the center of the street, his head turning this way and that as he passed through the wreckage. His gaze fell on Colin, and he guided the horse toward him.

"Sure, and there's a story to be told here," he said as he dismounted.

His eyes roved over Benton, brows arching when he saw the man's hands roped together. Then he spied Colin's badge and removed his hat to reveal a thatch of fiery red hair.

"You'd be Sheriff Maddox?"

With that lilting Irish brogue, this could only be one person. Colin blew a relieved sigh. "Patrick Mulhaney. We were afraid you'd changed your mind."

"Nay, laddie. I but stepped off the train for a bite. When next I looked, the thing was gone, so I had to hire a horse." He slapped the animal's neck affectionately. "A fine beast she is. Carried me here in no more'n a blink."

Bowerstock sprang forward, hand extended. "J.D. Bowerstock. As mayor of this fair town, let me welcome you to Lawrence." He raised his voice and shouted to the onlookers. "Our new sheriff has arrived!"

As the men of the town council hurried forward, Colin snatched the tin star off of his vest with his free hand. He shoved it toward Bowerstock.

"Swear him in, Mayor. He has work to do."

With a glance at Judge Tankersley, who nodded, the mayor took the badge and stepped in front of the big man. "Patrick Mulhaney, do you swear to uphold the law and defend the peace of Lawrence?"

Mulhaney raised a hand. "Aye. I'll be doing my best for ye."

His chest swelled when Bowerstock

pinned the star on his shirt.

"Congratulations, Sheriff." Colin shoved Benton forward. "Here's your first prisoner, and there are more where he came from. This is Cleon Benton, a cold-blooded killer and thief with a price on his head." He smiled proudly at Rebecca. "And this lady right here earned the reward."

Rebecca's eyes widened. "Reward?"

"That's right," Colin told her. "Five hundred dollars, dead or alive."

"Oh, my," murmured Mrs. Evans. She hugged Rebecca. "Well done, child."

Colin thought watching the shock on Rebecca's face fade into a huge grin was almost worth having a gun pointed at his face.

Annie Diggs marched toward them, her entourage in tow. She fixed a disapproving stare on the new sheriff.

"We've heard of you," she told him with a sniff. "A brawler and a drunkard. Know that the women of Lawrence will continue to work to rid our town of the devil's drink."

The ladies gathered behind her responded with polite applause.

" 'Tis true, what ye've heard, ma'am." Mulhaney ducked his head like a chastised child. "I'm not proud of it. But that was before." He looked up straight into her eyes.

"A changed man, that's what I am. Nary a drop in six months, and I've sworn to live sober for the rest of me days. That's why I've moved to Kansas, where liquor is outlawed."

"What?" Judge Tankersley pushed to the front of the group. "Are you saying you're a *teetotaler* just like Maddox?" He turned a glare toward the mayor. "Bowerstock, you lied to us!"

Colin enjoyed watching the mayor sputter.

Mulhaney turned to him. "Maddox, if ye'll be so kind as to point me toward the jail, I've a deposit to make." He closed a ham-sized hand around Benton's arm.

"Right this way, Sheriff."

He turned to offer his arm to Rebecca, to escort her to the jail where she could watch her prisoner being locked away. But the place where she had stood beside Mrs. Evans was empty. He turned in a circle, searching for her yellow dress. When he spotted her, his heart sank toward his boots.

She was heading for the Eldridge Hotel, where a lone man sat with his head in his hands on a bench beside the door.

A weight pressed against his chest, so heavy it was hard to catch his breath. As he watched her go to the man who could only be Jesse, he feared he might have gained his freedom, but at what price?

The desk clerk inside the hotel gave Rebecca a mug of hot coffee. She carried it outside to Jesse. He took it in shaky hands and sipped the steaming liquid.

"Thanks," he mumbled without meeting her eyes.

She sank onto the bench beside him, words whirling in her mind. Her speech, rehearsed so often in the past weeks, would not come to her lips. Her dreams were dull and hollow now, like the eyes of the man sitting beside her.

Coffee spilled out of the mug and fell on the ground. Compassion stirred inside her at the sight of his trembling hands. This was a mere shadow of the man she had known and loved.

"Jesse," she began.

At the same time he said, "Rebecca." They both stopped and flashed an awkward smile at each other.

He cleared his throat, staring at the mug. "Alvin Diggs told me about you. He said a beautiful young woman had sent him to fetch me." His gaze stole upward toward her face for a second before returning to the mug. "He was right about the beautiful part."

Though the compliment shed a shimmer of warmth on the cold that had gripped her, she did not reply to that. Instead, she said, "Luke and Emma asked me to relay their greetings."

His head bobbed in acknowledgement. "I heard they were doing well."

He gulped another swallow of coffee while Rebecca searched for words that would ease the awkward silence that lay between them. What had Mr. Diggs told him? Did he know of her protestations of love? Embarrassment flooded her at the thought. What had she known of love when she set her sights on Jesse? She had been a child, infatuated by a handsome cowboy. But what was to be done now, when faced with the reality that her childhood dreams had been nothing but childish fancy?

"I thought I loved you." Her face burned as the words fell from her lips. "I hoped you would come home with me to Apple Grove. But that was . . ." She swallowed a lump of tears.

His lips twisted in a grimace, and he slanted his head sideways to catch her eye. "Before you saw the man I've become?"

Remorse washed over her, but before she

could protest he raised a hand. "I get it. Even a drunk like me can see the lay of the land."

She couldn't hold back the tears swimming in her eyes. "I'm sorry."

"Hey, it's okay." He turned his head toward her, a shadow of the old smile playing about his lips. "It wouldn't have worked out anyway. To me you'll always be a little girl in a black dress and a funny white hat."

Sudden compassion overcame her, and she grabbed his arm. "You could come home with me as a friend. Papa would welcome you. If you want to change, Apple Grove would help you."

"What, you mean become Amish? Strap on some of those funny-looking suspenders and a pair of baggy trousers?" He threw his head back and barked a harsh laugh. "That'll be the day."

His words might have offended her if she weren't so sad. She looked away, toward where the sun sparkled on the swiftly moving waters of the Kansas River.

"Hey, I'm sorry." He placed a hand, warmed from holding the mug, over hers. "I didn't mean that the way it sounded. But your way is not my way."

Though she had longed for his touch, now it failed to move her. She stared at his hand a long moment and then raised her gaze to his.

"This is no life for you, Jesse. There is more to you than this. I know it."

A slow smile lifted the corners of his lips. "When you say it, I almost believe it's true." Then his gaze grew serious. "But even sober I'm not the man for you, Rebecca. You know that, don't you?"

The air around them grew quiet. The sound of the river fell away as the answer to his question sang in her soul. There was only one man for her, one future that would satisfy all her dreams.

Oh, Papa! An ache tugged at one corner of her soaring heart. How could he bear losing another daughter? And yet she could not stop the joyful song that rang in her ears. Somehow she must make her father understand that she had found her one true love.

Colin tossed one bag in a corner of the horse stall while he secured the other on Gus's saddle. He couldn't wait another hour to put Lawrence behind him. Let Mulhaney deal with Benton and the others. Let Bowerstock and Tankersley deal with their new sheriff. Let Annie Diggs and the ladies of the movement march all over town if they wanted. He wished them well. But none of those things were his affair any longer.

Time to let go of the past and ride into the future.

An image loomed in his mind. He saw laughing children and a white church building with the doors standing open to welcome all. Soon he would see the reality. He cinched tight the strap securing the bag with his savings tucked inside. He'd have to start out small and trust the Lord to provide the rest. But he had no doubt He would come through as He always had.

Except in matters of the heart.

Oh, what a fine parson's wife that fiery little gal would have made.

Melancholy gripped him like a fist.

The stable door creaked. Billy coming to see if he could help him saddle up.

"I have everything under control," he called to the stable keeper as he picked up his second bag.

Hay rustled with a soft footstep. Colin glanced up, and his hands froze in the act of hefting the bag toward the saddle. Rays from the late afternoon sun seeped through the open doorway to light up a buttery-yellow dress. For a moment the light played a trick on his eyes and cast a halo around her head. Then the pools of darkness that hid her face receded as she moved toward him, revealing soft brown eyes that looked into his.

"I feared I missed you." Her voice fell softly, as though cushioned on the hay. "They told me at the jail you had left."

What was she doing here? Come to say goodbye? No. That would be too painful. Why didn't she let him ride out without a scene? And where had she left her beau? "On my way now."

She stepped into the stall. "Where will you go?"

With an effort, he managed to control his fingers long enough to secure the bulging bag. "I don't know. West, until the Lord tells me to stop."

"I am also going west."

He started so that the clip fumbled in his hand. "Back home?"

She inched forward and raised a hand to stroke Gus's nose. "Perhaps. If that is where the Lord tells me to stop."

Wild hope soared in his chest. He left the bag and stepped toward her, seeking confirmation in the eyes that were fixed on him. His hands itched to reach for her, but he held them stiffly at his side in case he was mistaken.

"Do you have an idea where you're

headed?" he asked.

"Someplace where there are orphans without a home, and a church to be built, and a preacher who longs to have both." Though the sun shone through the doorway behind her head, her sudden smile dazzled him. "I intend to be there to hear him preach his first sermon."

And then Colin did what he had longed to do since this stubborn woman had limped into view two weeks before. He gathered her in his arms and kissed her, with all the might and force that had been pent up for weeks.

He didn't know about Jesse. He didn't care.

She was coming with him.

TWENTY-SIX

By the time the train slowed on its approach to the Hays City station, Rebecca's stomach had twisted itself tighter than a coiled rope. Face pressed to the window, she strained for a glimpse of a familiar figure among those gathered near the station house. Would Papa come to meet her? Two days ago, she sent a telegram informing him of her intended return. If he wasn't here now, she would know he wasn't ready to forgive her for running away, no matter what Amos said. And if he was here . . .

With a nervous gesture she fingered the skirt of the dress Mrs. Evans had helped her make. The blue was dark enough to be considered conservative by any standard. Any standard except Amish.

Her hand was captured in a warm one, and her heart fluttered when Colin raised it to his lips and pressed a kiss on her fingertips.

377

"Relax, sweetheart. Everything is going to be fine."

The rumble of his deep voice, and the softness of the look he fixed on her, worked like a tonic on her jittery nerves. When she saw love gleaming in his eyes, she believed him. Everything *would* be fine . . . eventually.

But not immediately. First, she had to face Papa. Her stomach knotted again.

The train's whistle blew, announcing their arrival. She jerked forward in her seat as the brakes were applied. Colin released her hand with a final squeeze and bent to retrieve the bags at their feet.

"Maybe I should have worn my black dress and *kapp*."

She ran fretful fingers over the soft coil of hair Sassy had helped her arrange before they left Lawrence this morning. The memory of her friend running alongside the train to wave an energetic farewell sent a stab of longing through her. Rebecca could use a little of Sassy's audacity right now.

Colin stroked her cheek with a finger. "Delaying the moment your father discovers you're leaving the Amish church won't make it easier." He leaned toward her, and for one breathless moment she thought he might actually kiss her right here, in front of their fellow passengers. Instead, his eyes held hers in an embrace that was nearly as intimate as a kiss. "I'll be right beside you. We'll face this together."

The same way they would face the future. A fraction of the cold dread in her chest warmed, and she found herself able to return his smile.

Now they were close enough to see the faces of those waiting for the train. Rebecca's gaze was drawn to a small cluster of people standing apart from the others, several of them in black Amish garb. Her heart leaped. Papa stood there, his hands clasped behind his back, the familiar round-brimmed hat centered on his head. Her vision blurred, and she blinked away a sudden rush of tears.

Oh, Papa! How I've missed you.

Beside him stood *Maummi,* the sunlight brightening her white *kapp* and apron. A hand shaded her eyes as she inspected the train windows. The other hand held that of a young Amish boy, and beside him were two young girls, also in Amish dresses.

Rebecca turned in her seat, a note of excitement creeping into her voice.

"Amos, your children are here to meet us."

On the bench behind her, the faraway stare that Amos had maintained from the

379

time they pulled away from the Lawrence station faded a fraction, replaced by a glimmer of interest. One corner of his lips twitched upward as he transferred his gaze from the floor of the train car to the welcome party outside.

She looked again and found three other familiar faces.

"There's Emma! Look, Colin, my sister came. And there's Luke too, and he's holding Lucas." Her nephew's sleeping form was draped across his father's shoulder. Another wave of tears filled her eyes. They had all come to welcome her home.

Twisting around in her seat once again, she focused on the figure slumped on the bench in the rear of the train car. Jesse. The man she had professed to love and traveled all the way across Kansas to fetch. His clothes were still rumpled and stained, his hair in need of attention. She hadn't had the heart to wake him to share the biscuits and chicken Mrs. Evans packed for their lunch. At least in sleep he might find relief from the tremors that shook his hands as his body tried to throw off the ravages of liquor.

Colin had been skeptical of her suggestion to bring Jesse with them. Perhaps a tiny bit jealous, even, though she'd assured him there was no reason. She'd told him, "Jesse has no place to go, no one to help him." Then she grinned and said, "He's an orphan, you know." Colin had laughed, then, and agreed to offer him help if he wanted it.

The train's whistle sounded again, and Jesse stirred. Their eyes met, and Rebecca gave him an encouraging smile. Maybe soon he would find the strength he needed to start a new life.

The two dozen or so passengers stood and gathered their belongings as the train finally came to a stop. Another fit of nerves attacked Rebecca, and she clutched at the hand Colin extended to help her to her feet.

"Everything will be fine," he whispered.

A nod was the only reply she could manage.

The door opened, and the line of people filling the center aisle began filing out. When Rebecca's turn to disembark came, she took the hand of the kind-looking conductor and allowed him to help her to the ground. She busied herself settling her skirts until Colin had climbed down as well and stood beside her. Only then did she dare to raise her eyes to the small group clustered off to one side.

Four sets of eyes, round as wagon wheels, fixed on her. *Maummi*'s open-mouthed stare took in her uncovered hair, swept to her dress, and then slid sideways before coming to a halt on Colin. Emma's expression was nearly as stunned as *Maummi*'s. Her hand rested atop her round belly, which looked to Rebecca to have grown in the weeks of her absence. Luke's brows arched high on his forehead nearly to the brim of his cowboy hat. And Papa . . . well, Rebecca couldn't manage to meet Papa's gaze just yet.

A welcome disruption came when Amos's children caught sight of their father.

"Fader!"

The little boy dashed forward, his sisters close behind him. Rebecca turned in time to see Amos kneel and open his arms. A second later they closed, enveloping his children in an unexpected embrace. The sight of Amos's normally emotionless face alight with joy made Rebecca feel like an intruder. She looked away.

When she turned again toward her family, Emma had recovered from her surprise. She came forward and pulled Rebecca into a gentle hug, made awkward by her belly.

"I'm so glad you're home. So much has happened, and I . . ." Tears swam in her eyes. "I needed you."

"What?" Alarm rang through Rebecca.

She looked around the small group. Her whole family was here. "What has happened?"

Shaking her head, Emma bit her lip and then said softly, "Samuel Miller died a few days ago."

The words fell like a boulder, stunning and unbelievable. Samuel Miller was the bishop's son. His wife, Katie, had been Emma's best friend from childhood.

"How? What happened?"

Emma wiped her eyes. "He was turning sod in the field. It was hot . . . his heart should have been strong. He was a young man . . . And now Katie . . ."

"Oh, Emma." Rebecca wrapped her soft-hearted sister in her arms and held her. Words failed her. Only the strength of the embrace uttered her deep sorrow. Now, with her own love so fresh, she could only imagine the anguish that lay thick in Katie's heart. "I'm sorry I wasn't here to help you and Katie. But I am now."

"Thank the Lord." Then Emma straightened and forced a trembling smile. "Besides, when you stayed gone so long, I was worried you would miss the baby's arrival."

"Nothing could keep me from the birth of my new nephew or niece," Rebecca assured her. She turned a soft smile on Lucas's sleeping form, and encountered a wry grin on Luke's face.

"Did you find what you were looking for?"

"Yes." She gave a nod. "Yes, I did."

Her gaze sought Colin, who stood off to one side holding her bag along with his without a trace of discomfort. The sight of him gave her a courage she didn't possess on her own. She went to him and, looping a hand through his arm, pulled him forward.

"This is Colin Maddox. He's a preacher, and he is going to build a church. And a home for orphans."

He whipped off his hat and gave Rebecca's family a pleasant nod. "Pleased to meet you folks."

"Orphans, you say?" *Maummi* studied him through narrowed eyes.

"Yes, ma'am. The sight of a homeless child stirs my heart, and with the Lord's help, I want to offer help to those forgotten little ones."

Maummi's stern expression gave way to grudging approval.

Papa hung back, his silence and rigid posture expressing his disapproval more effectively than any words. Rebecca could not bring herself to look into his face as she cast about for something to say. Should she introduce Colin as the man she intended to marry? Get all the shocks over with at once? On the other hand, maybe it would be best to save that news for another time.

"I don't believe it."

Luke's startled exclamation saved her from speaking, at least for a few moments more. She turned to follow the direction of his stare in time to see the last passenger exit the train.

Jesse.

The stunned expression on Luke and Emma's faces deepened to concern. Rebecca understood. The Jesse who approached could hardly be recognized as the swaggering, cocky cowboy they'd known on the trail. Emma gave her an alarmed glance, full of silent questions. Rebecca answered with a sad shake of her head.

Luke shifted his sleeping son to his other arm and extended a hand. "Jesse. It's been a long time. You look . . ." He appeared to search for a way to finish the sentence.

Jesse nodded. "Yeah, I know." He ducked his head. "The past few years have been rough. You used to say my rowdy ways would catch up with me one day." His lips twisted into a grimace. "They not only caught up, but they trampled me like a stampede of Texas longhorns."

"Colin has asked Jesse to help him build

his church," Rebecca said.

Jesse shrugged. "I need something to do while I'm trying to get my head back on straight. That and I don't have anywhere else to go. I lost track of my friends years ago, and I've got no family."

A look passed between Luke and Emma, one of those unspoken conversations between husbands and wives. Rebecca's hand tightened on Colin's arm. One day they also would grow so close that they could know each other's thoughts without words.

Emma took Jesse's hand. "You have a family," she said gently. "You have us. And a home for as long as you want. It will take everyone's help to run an orphanage."

Luke thumped his friend on the back. "Good to have you back, friend."

Rebecca smiled up at Colin. This was exactly what she had hoped would happen.

A noise from Papa's direction caught her attention. He cleared his throat, an unmistakable request for her attention. The time had come to face him. Drawing a breath, she released Colin's arm and stepped forward, her gaze fixed on the toes of his boots.

"Papa," she said, "I am sorry I left without telling you and that I took your horse. I have the money to repay everyone in Apple Grove, and I will thank each one when I do.

But mostly I —" A lump lodged in her throat, and she had to take a shuddering breath before she could continue. "Mostly I am sorry for the shame I caused you."

She risked an upward glance into his face. What she saw there squeezed the heart in her chest. His gaze flickered behind her for a moment, toward Colin, and then returned to fix on her. Sadness shone in his eyes, and her own eyes stung with tears at the sight. There was no need to tell him of her decision. He knew.

But something else showed in those gray depths, something she feared she might never see again.

Love. Unconditional love.

His arms rose, and to Rebecca's surprise, wrapped around her. For one moment he pulled her into an embrace like he had not done since she was a small girl. His lips pressed close to her ear, and his whispered words seeped deeply into her soul.

"Welcome home, my Rebecca."

She was home, and with her prayers answered in a way she could never have imagined. God had been good to this willful child.

EPILOGUE

Five months later, orange leaves clung to spindly tree branches even as a chilly Kansas wind rustled through limbs. Rebecca left Emma's house and lifted her skirts so her wedding dress would not drag through the grass when she crossed the yard. Behind her, she knew Emma and *Maummi* watched from the kitchen window. She made her way to the place where Papa stood, hands clasped behind his back, looking out over a field of golden wheat.

The past few months had been difficult. Papa loved her, and he loved the Lord and his Amish faith. It was not easy to lose both daughters to the *Englisch,* but he was gradually coming to accept what he could not change.

Her eyes strayed to the field, purchased from Luke and Emma with the reward money she'd received for capturing the outlaws. It was hers and Colin's land now.

She'd paid everyone back all the money they had so generously given for her freedom and still had enough left to start building their home and church.

Papa did not turn when she approached.

"Papa," she said softly. "It is nearly time."

His round black hat moved slowly up and down as he nodded. "Of this I am aware." He gave no sign of moving.

She stood beside him, close but not quite touching. The joy of the day dimmed when she saw the sadness lurking in his eyes. Sadness that had never quite left from the moment she returned from Lawrence.

"Papa, I am sorry. Truly. I know this is not the life that you hoped for me, but our Father knows His plan for us. We cannot set this plan."

For a moment he said nothing, and when he spoke, he did not look at her. "No. It is not the life I would choose for you."

Tears threatened, and squeezed her throat painfully. How she hated to hurt him. "It makes me sad to disappoint you."

He turned his head then, a shadowy smile lurking behind the sorrow. "And yet all my arguments these past months, and Bishop Miller's, have not changed your heart." His voice grew soft. "From the cradle you were a willful child, determined to have your way and none other. It is a trait you share with your mother, and one of the many reasons I loved her. How could I not love the same quality in you?" His look became tender. "My Rebecca, the choices you have made are not the ones I hoped for, but you will *never* be a disappointment."

She would have thrown her arms around him had she not known how uncomfortable the gesture would make him. The embrace he had given her the day she came home from her *rumspringa* might never be repeated, but that was Papa's way. She edged closer to him until her arm touched his and poured her joy into her smile.

A horse and buggy, clearly of Amish design, topped a rise in the road and headed toward them. Rebecca shielded her eyes and strained to see the driver. "Who is that?"

For one breathless moment, she feared it might be Bishop Miller. He had been tireless in his attempts to dissuade her from marriage to an *Englischman.* He seemed to take it as a personal affront that another Switzer daughter had chosen to leave the community.

The buggy drew closer and rolled to a stop in front of them. Peering inside, she recognized the man who held the reins.

"Amos!"

Gathering the skirts of her wedding dress, she raced toward the buggy as he climbed to the ground. Oh, how glad she was to see him. Missing her friends was one of the saddest things about no longer attending Amish church services.

His close-set eyes narrowed with a smile. "Jonas told me of your marriage, and welcomed us to attend."

Rebecca's grin was huge. "I am honored."

But she spoke to his back, for he had turned away to help someone climb down from the buggy. Children tumbled out amid excited chatter. Amos Beiler's little ones were growing like weeds.

He reached for another hand, and a woman stepped out. Rebecca glimpsed the traditional black dress and white apron, and a white *kapp* over tidy blond hair.

When the guest stood on the ground before her, Rebecca looked again. Delicate features, sparkling eyes, and full lips curved into a familiar grin. Delight, mingled with surprise, zipped through her.

"Sassy!"

Her friend stepped forward and, disregarding Amish tradition, gathered her in a fierce embrace, her laughter ringing in Rebecca's ears.

"It's Sarah now. Whoever heard of an

Amish girl named Sassy?"

An Amish girl? Rebecca couldn't stop a giggle at the thought of the talk Sassy would cause among the women of Apple Grove. She would keep the district on its toes, that much was sure.

Rebecca shook her head. "When did you get here? How?"

"Amos fetched me two weeks ago." A blush colored her rosy cheeks. "He's been writing letters to me, hundreds of 'em, and I'm telling you, this fellow can compose some mighty pretty poems."

Amos flushed scarlet.

The thought of Amos Beiler writing love poems was almost impossible to accept.

"But what of New York City and becoming an actress?"

Sassy, or Sarah — it would take some time to become accustomed to her friend's new name — cocked her head toward Amos and gave a saucy wink. "I found me something a whole lot better."

Then Amos extended his hand again to help a second woman from the buggy. Another wedding guest! This was turning out to be a real community wedding after all. Rebecca caught sight of the woman.

"Katie! Katie Miller!" She rushed forward to grab her hand.

"I've been staying with Katie," Sarah said, "and she's been teaching me all about being Amish. I want to be a proper wife when the time comes." She cut her eyes toward Amos, whose blush deepened.

Katie pressed Rebecca's hand. "A beautiful day God has given you for your wedding."

A lingering sadness lurked among the smiles that wreathed her face. How hard, to celebrate another's wedding without her dear Samuel.

"Having you here makes the day even brighter," Rebecca assured her.

Sarah caught sight of something behind Rebecca. "Oh, my. Sheriff Maddox cleans up real nice, don't he?"

Rebecca turned. Love swelled in her chest at the sight of Colin striding across the grass toward them. His gaze held hers as he closed the distance between them, as intimate as if there were no one else in the world but the two of them. Pausing in front of her, he grinned.

"Are you ready to become my bride, Miss Switzer? For the rest of our lives?"

"For eternity," she said. "And that won't be near long enough, Colin Maddox."

The wedding party stood in the open field,

inside a rope stretched between four posts. Though the church they would build together had no walls yet, theirs would be the first wedding performed there. A short distance away lay a pile of freshly cut lumber, delivered from Hays City only yesterday. Within the week they would begin, and before winter set in, the white church of their dreams would become a reality. And then the Lord would send them children to love. Orphans — and maybe a boy or girl of their own as well. Papa and *Maummi* would be living not so far away, but far enough that she would miss their smiles, their caring, and most of all their wisdom.

Rebecca glanced at the small group gathered with them inside the rope. Beaming, Emma held two-month-old Rachel in her arms. Beside her, Luke kept a firm grip on Lucas's hand. *Maummi's* slightly scandalized gaze kept straying toward Sarah, her eyebrows high enough to be buried in her hairline. This was quite a unique community forming. Different beliefs, varying customs, but all acknowledged a higher source. One had only to look at the brilliant blue sky to see evidence of His presence. White clouds floated so high they looked like individual fields of cotton.

Papa stood beside Amos, a private warmth for her in his placid countenance. She caught Jesse's eye and smiled. These past months had worked wonders in his life. His face wasn't so hollow these days. No whiskey and lots of Emma's good cooking had worked wonders for him.

She turned to Colin, who stood tall and proud beside her, love shining in his eyes. How had she ever thought her heart could belong to anyone else? *Maummi* once said, "Thank the good Lord for unanswered prayer." Today Rebecca finally understood her meaning. She had prayed long and hard that Jesse would be her one true love, but the Lord had other plans.

The parson, who had come from Hays City to perform the ceremony, cleared his throat.

"Are we ready to begin?"

Colin's hand reached for hers. "We're ready."

Her heart in her throat, Rebecca nodded. "I am ready to marry my one true love."

The parson's voice rang out over the Kansas plain. "Dearly beloved . . ."

DISCUSION QUESTIONS

1. When the book opens, Rebecca is dissatisfied with her Plain life on her papa's farm. What is the reason for her discontent? How does that reflect the upbringing she has received in her Amish family and community?

2. Rebellion seems to strike the youth of every generation and every lifestyle. How is Rebecca's rebellion similar to today's youth? How is it different?

3. Colin's deep desire is to start an orphanage. Discuss the elements of his past that have fed this dream.

4. As Rebecca sets out on her *rumspringa,* she embraces every new experience with enthusiasm and awe. Name some of those new encounters, and discuss how a shel-

tered Amish girl would react to those in today's society.

5. How does Colin's past help form his goals for the future?

6. Did the town's perception of Colin contribute to his actions in regard to arresting and imprisoning Rebecca?

7. Sassy is introduced as a scandalous character. How did your perception of her change throughout the story?

8. What is Amos's goal? How is that goal met during the course of the story?

9. After she left Apple Grove, Rebecca longed for the wise council of *Maummi* and Emma. Where did she find replacements for advice and emotional outlets?

10. Rebecca thought Papa had rejected her, but Amos told her that Jonas had not forgotten his daughter. How did Rebecca react? How important is a father's approval to a young woman today, as opposed to 1885?

11. Did the women of Lawrence let Rebecca

down when they failed to meet her bail? Why or why not?

12. Which character in *A Plain and Simple Heart* do you most identify with? Discuss why.

13. Throughout the book Rebecca longed for a reunion with Jesse, yet when that reunion occurred, she was disappointed. Were her expectations for a romantic reunion unrealistic?

14. Though this book was entirely fictional, threads of reality were portrayed in the temperance movement of that time period. How has that temperance movement impacted our society today?

15. What did the act of destroying the still symbolize for Colin? For Rebecca?

AUTHORS' NOTE

We hope you enjoyed *A Plain and Simple Heart,* Book 2 in the Amish of Apple Grove series. Whenever an author undertakes to write a sequel, it's with a touch of apprehension. We wanted to tell Rebecca's story in a way that would delight the many readers who wrote to tell us how much they loved Emma's story in *The Heart's Frontier.* We shouldn't have worried. Rebecca marched onto page 1 and took control, and we quickly fell in love with her. It is our hope that you had as much fun reading this book as much as we did writing it.

Though the story is entirely fictional, the setting is real. Lawrence, Kansas, is a town with a rich Western history. The Kansas Woman's Christian Temperance Union was established near Lawrence in 1878. The members of KWCTU joined a national women's movement to outlaw the sale of alcohol and to promote women's rights. In 1881, Kansas became the first state to outlaw alcohol. Saloon owners by and large ignored the law and continued to run their businesses openly. Lawmen at that time were responsible for protecting the town's citizens and keeping peace but not for enforcing prohibition laws.

Most of the characters in *A Plain and Simple Heart* are fictional as well, though we pulled a few from the pages of history. The real Annie LePort Diggs moved to Lawrence in 1873 and married Alvin not long after. The couple published a newspaper called the *Kansas Liberal,* and Annie was recognized as a powerful writer and a moving speaker. In the 1890s she toured the nation to promote women's voting rights and other issues about which she was passionate.

We have taken liberties with our fictional portrayal of Annie Diggs and given her a few characteristics of another well-known Kansas spokeswoman, Carrie Nation. Mrs. Nation gained notoriety when she embarked upon a series of protests in which she entered saloons armed with a hatchet and smashed the liquor bottles. She was jailed many times for destroying establishments that sold liquor. The timing of Mrs. Nation's *Hatchetations,* as they were known, didn't quite work with Rebecca's story as they began a few years later. So we attributed some of Mrs. Nation's more energetic personality traits to Mrs. Diggs. We got a huge kick out of having Carrie Nation put in a cameo appearance during the ladies' protest march, and of having her witness Sassy's destruction of the liquor bottles in the Lucky Dollar Saloon.

Two other real people make an appearance in this book. Francis Willard and Anna Howard Shaw were both leaders of the temperance movement at a national level.

And now we're on to the next project. As we write this note, we're working on *A Cowboy at Heart,* Book 3 in the Amish of Apple Grove series. You'll encounter some familiar characters and meet some new ones, and you might even learn a thing or two about another facet of the American West in the 1880s. Stay tuned!

We'd love to hear what you thought of *A Plain and Simple Heart.* You can contact us through our website, **www.LoriCopeland andVirginiaSmith.com.**

Lori and Virginia